Slide

T GEPHART

Slide

Cover by Hang Le
      www.byhangle.com
Editing by Perfectly Publishable
      www.perfectlypublishable.com
Formatting by Max Effect
      www.formaxeffect.com

To my family -

the only safety net I need.

My life was perfect.

Okay, so maybe not perfect, but as close to it as I thought I was ever going to get. And I had imagined plenty worse growing up as Melody Williams' daughter.

My mother had been the biggest groupie of the 1980s. No shit, I'm sure if there was a competition she would have actually won that crown. She slept her way through the billboard charts, riding from one coastline to the next on countless tour buses in a big cloud of hairspray and spandex. I'm not even sure she *knows* who my father is. In any case, his name and any support from him have been missing since before I was born. I figured one disappointing parental figure was enough so never bothered to find him—ignorance was most definitely bliss.

So while my DNA pool was seriously lacking, my drive to someday claw my way out of white trash-dom meant I did whatever I could to change my stars. Seriously, it was by the grace of God and my amazing grandparents that I didn't end up working a pole.

Which is where my mother was at this very second.

How I wish I were joking.

While mommy dearest was bumping and grinding, I managed to get a degree through community college and was happily working at a law firm in Manhattan. No, I wasn't a lawyer—something I had to explain to my mother every single time she got picked up for a DUI—I was a paralegal who the firm was promoting very soon. Any day now. I was practically giddy with excitement.

My life checklist was looking pretty damn good.

Shady past left behind. Check.

Steady job with growth prospects. Check.

Amazing boss who also happened to be my boyfriend. Check. Check. Check.

I know what you're thinking about the boss/boyfriend thing, but you would be wrong. Sure, we have to keep it under wraps, but that is only until I get promoted and move departments. Then we will be free to declare our love and show the world what an amazing unstoppable team we are. It would make everything even *more* perfect. Just a few more days—a week tops—and then we can finally stop sneaking around. And, he was totally in love with me as well. Smitten. Completely enchanted. This I knew.

Why, at this very minute he was making his way to the bar I was sitting in so he could ask me to move in with him. Yep, I was going to be happily cohabitating with the man of my dreams. Well, maybe not *the* man of my dreams, but a very good substitute, which was perfect because I wasn't sure the *man of my dreams* was real.

Guiltily, I'll admit there was a guy—not my boyfriend—who made me crazy stupid, and by that I mean he made my insides tingle.

What was even more surprising was that chasing after the hot guy wasn't even in my repertoire, and yet there was something about him that made him impossible to overlook.

He was so gorgeous, my eyes hurt when I looked at him. Not even joking, but to say he was *just* good looking would be an out and out lie. He was more than that with his amazing blond hair and dazzling blue eyes, every inch of him crafted to perfection.

He wasn't just beautiful; he was tall and sexy beyond belief.

Everything about him was super smooth. Even through his clothes I could tell he was rocking a ridiculous body—and his face was flawless. Almost so perfect I wasn't sure he was human; surely he was some mutant model from a fashion show or a genetically engineered robot. All of it combined into one hell of a fantasy, one not even I could ignore.

I'd seen my mystery man a lot. It had started out innocently enough—almost accidental—my eye catching a glimpse of him whenever I was out. The grocery store, the gas station, the movie theatre—every single time he looked more delicious than the last.

No, I hadn't taken up a secret double-life where I hid in bushes and stalked the beautiful man; he just happened to live a block away from my apartment. Which was convenient in that I could enjoy my momentary mental holidays without the risk of a restraining order. I'd made it this far without a mug shot, and I was hoping to keep it that way.

There was something about him, a magnetic draw I was

sure would be dangerous, but like watching fireworks, it was hard to not appreciate the beauty. His sly smile hinted of the trouble he would cause, which is why I never bothered to say hello.

Okay, so maybe that wasn't the *only* reason I'd never said hello, it was possibly because all those times I'd *seen* him he not only never noticed me, but was usually entertaining female company. The kind that had nice breasts and great hair and giggled into their cosmopolitans. He was either gay or a player, my money on the second option.

Not that I would ever cheat on Rob. Never. Not even a chance. He was just a safe fantasy, something I could call on when I needed a little extra kick in the bedroom. Rob didn't always get me there, if you know what I mean. It was okay however, because even though I didn't always get what I needed in the bedroom, he made up for it elsewhere.

Rob Meyers—my guy—had a promising future ahead of him. Graduating in the top ten percent of his class at Harvard Law and aspirations to be a Supreme Court Justice, he was as far away from my questionable upbringing as I could get.

And he saw my potential, which was why he pursued me so passionately. He was a hard man to say no to, so I didn't, and we've been dating for two years and counting—which is why I know he is about to ask me to move in. It's time, and with my promotion all but guaranteed, we have no reason not to.

Sure, maybe I was celebrating a *little* prematurely, but he had been dropping clues all week. Flowers, being especially sweet, and of course the huge giveaway was the *dinner* he wanted us to have late tonight.

We *never* went out to dinner, preferring to eat takeout in

my cozy little apartment. Which meant he was either giving me a key or a ring, the latter freaking me out a little.

I loved Rob, of course I did. He was a good man—a dependable man—and I could totally see a future with him, but marriage? The thought of it made me break out in a rash. Which is why I was nursing the same mojito I'd ordered when I sat down.

Nerves. Excitement. Terror. I was probably going to burst.

"You can't be seriously considering saying yes to him?" Renee sat down beside me uninvited. "Please tell me you're going to turn him down."

While Renee was my best friend, she'd missed the memo where she was supposed to be supportive. And as for my boyfriend, she was not his biggest fan.

"Of course I'm going to say yes. It's been two years; why wouldn't I move in?" I swirled the contents of my glass.

I had no idea why I ordered the cocktail—I very rarely drank. Did I mention my mother was also an alcoholic? I spent more time in AA meetings with her than I did in preschool. I knew the Ten Steps before I knew my alphabet.

"Why you shouldn't move in with him? Because I've seen club sandwiches with more personality than Rob. Seriously, he's like a dial tone. You know when you pick up the receiver of your grandmother's phone? That's him. You want to spend the rest of your life eating dry toast?"

She took the glass from my hand and downed the rest of my drink. "It's supposed to be drank, not held in your hand as an accessory." The glass noisily slammed on the bar.

"He's conservative." Translation: Boring. But he was dependable and that's what I needed; I spun around to face her. "Big deal. He has loads of personality; you should see him in a courtroom. He's brilliant. And he is so smart."

Yep, he was all of those things, which is why I overlooked the fact he rated low on the excitement scale. No one was perfect, and I refused to be like my mother who jumped from one good-looking loser to the next. Call me boring but I had successfully made it through high school *and* college without an unwanted pregnancy. Go me.

"Do you even orgasm during sex?" she said loud enough for the bartender to smirk.

Anyone else's brutal honesty would have probably been offensive, but with Renee I knew she had my best interests at heart. And while I loved her and her swing-by-the-chandeliers inhibition, I wanted something different for myself. The lack of orgasms unfortunately a bi-product of my safety net.

"Renee, there is more to life than sex and orgasms."

"Spoken like a girl who hasn't had one in a while. Please, don't do this. Take a break or something. Screw around for a while. Date other people and *then* if you want to shack up with Mr. *Ambien*, I'll be your biggest supporter."

I was all ready to give my rebuttal. My rote response of "he makes me happy," getting lost on its way from my brain to my mouth. Instead some indescribable, nonsense noise that sounded like I'd recently had oral surgery spilled from my lips. My mouth and my brain completely AWOL as *he* came into view.

"Hello, ladies." His voice purred, sending vibrations through my body.

It was *him*. My beautiful mystery man. The one who I'd seen plenty but never spoken to. He was standing in front of me, *smiling.*

In hindsight, I shouldn't have been so surprised. There weren't many bars in our little neighborhood where you didn't need a Hep C shot before you entered. This particular establishment promised an impressive beer menu without the risk of a communicable disease, so it would stand to reason he would know about it too.

"Hi." Was all I was able to manage, convinced he was probably talking to someone else. Perhaps he meant the Amazonian redhead who was sitting to my left, openly staring—that would make a hell of a lot of more sense. They could probably shoot joint commercials for teeth whitener and make adorable, if not freakishly tall, children together.

"I couldn't help but notice your friend stole your drink. Ordinarily I'd overlook such thievery, but I'd hate for there to be a brawl in my favorite bar. So in the interest of keeping the peace, I'd like to replace it for you." His voice smooth, as was his delivery. I had to remember to breathe.

"She wasn't going to drink it, but you can totally buy her another drink," Renee answered before I'd gotten the chance. Her smile widened as she turned to face me and mouthed the words "he's hot." She needn't have bothered; his hotness was not something that needed to be confirmed.

"That's okay, I'm good." Thankfully words came out of my mouth even if they sounded in no way intelligent.

"Well, glad to hear you're *good*. Nice to meet you, my name is Rusty." He smiled as he moved in closer, his hand signaling the bartender. "What were you drinking?"

In what I can only explain as temporary insanity—probably from the shock of having the beautiful man talking to me—I blurted out, "I have a boyfriend."

I officially wanted to die.

While I did have a boyfriend, and hopefully in a few hours I would be moving into his upscale apartment, there was no reason to announce it so dramatically. Almost as if to prove that I hadn't secretly fantasized about him while in the shower every day this week—which I had. Sweat prickled at my brow.

"Is that some code for you're not thirsty?" Rusty's lips curved in amusement. While the words weren't sexy, the humor in his voice was a definite turn on, a hot button straight to my libido as he stood there grinning at me.

"No, I-I just mean I can't accept . . ." What was the word again? "A drink from you." Yes, that's what I wanted to say. "Or . . . or anyone else. N-not just you." My mouth tried to regain some composure. It really wasn't doing a great job.

"Well, would you look at the time? I have a thing, wouldn't want to be late." Renee tapped her naked wrist—her watch missing in action, as was her tact. "Call me, Ali." She gave me a hug and whispered, "If you don't screw this guy, you're dead to me." And just like that, she evaporated from the room.

Awesome.

"Your friend always bail on you like that, Ali?" Rusty's voice curled seductively around my name as he smiled, moving to the barstool Renee had vacated.

"It's Alison." Ali was just too personal, like him kissing me on the mouth. I totally would *not* have been okay with that. Mostly. "And she has issues with boundaries." And my boyfriend, but I wouldn't be mentioning that.

"Well, Alison, it's a real shame we can't have that drink together, but seeing as I'm sitting here I'm going order a beer.

Feel free to order something too, I won't pay for it but the tip I leave will probably mean the bartender won't charge you. So technically, you're accepting a free drink from the bar."

Here was the thing. It hadn't been *just* Rusty who hadn't noticed me in the past—to most guys I was invisible. I was not the classic beauty. In fact, I was far from it. I was average in every way imaginable. Condemned to mediocrity. The girl you befriended so you could hook up with her hot BFF. Which meant men didn't buy me drinks, not usually, and certainly not ones who looked like him.

"I shouldn't." It was me I was trying to convince more than anyone else. That's right, Ali. You shouldn't. Perfect life, remember?

His smile widened. Please God, don't let me stop breathing. "I like doing things I shouldn't be doing. It's liberating. It's also a hell of a lot more interesting than the stuff I should be doing."

I could hear the words, but all I could do was concentrate on the way his lips moved so beautifully when he spoke. And really, I had no idea what he was *actually* saying, but he sure made a convincing case. Sadly, my situation hadn't changed.

Boyfriend. Mine. Walking in at any minute.

"Thanks, but I'm still going to have to decline." The awkward words tumbled out of my mouth. Much like I was, sitting there with no clue as to why the universe decided to throw him in my path, tonight of all nights.

"Maybe some other time." He gave me a smile that lit a fire inside me that would spontaneously combust any fabric between us. The concern for the disintegration of my panties was real.

"Yeah, sure."

Fate was cruel in that way. I finally had all my shit together and *now* the hot guy noticed me. *Typical.* My fist metaphorically shook in the air. Maybe it was a test? To see if I was ready to settle down? Well, test be damned. I would not be tempted.

"Sooooo I should go. It's been nice." What the hell was I saying? Could I get any more ridiculous? Probably, which is why I should leave.

"No problem. Have a good night." He shot me a wink and then moved away from the bar.

And just like that he was gone. His body disappearing into a crowd of people and I couldn't be sure he hadn't been a mirage. My workload had been pretty intense lately, maybe it actually *didn't* happen.

My phone buzzed from my purse, an incoming message from Renee.

SLEEP WITH HIM.

Well, I guess that confirmed I hadn't totally lost my mind. Just my sanity then. Good to know.

I glanced up in time to notice Rob striding toward me. His beautiful three-piece suit matched his dazzling smile as he made his way through the crowd. He was mine, and that was better than any maybe with a hot guy I didn't know.

"Hey, Ali-cat." He kissed me as he moved in closer. "Let's go somewhere a little quieter."

This was it. He was really going to do it. We were finally going to be an official couple and no longer hide. I couldn't wait to start our next chapter.

Rusty

The chick who'd followed me home wrapped her hand around the doorjamb of my bedroom. She was still naked except for the Foo Fighters T-shirt that was covering all the good bits. Still, not a bad way to wake up. "Hey, do you have any coffee?" She gave me a quick smile as I shuffled up in bed.

"Yeah, in the fridge." Excellent, she was making coffee. This one was definitely getting extra credit.

Hard to believe two years ago my life was so remarkably different. Twenty-four months. That's pretty much all it took for us to be plucked from obscurity, playing shitty bars to playing on a massive tour.

Of course we weren't headlining, no—we were playing second fiddle to Power Station, the big shot rock stars who had more platinum gracing their walls than the Queen of England had in her fancy tower. Our chance of a lifetime had come at the hand of Angie, our front woman, who happened to have once shared a fence line with their drummer. Family friends and all that.

In any case, their regular support act had shit the bed, fucking up hardcore and got tossed off the docket. Enter Black Addiction ready to take up the slack. Their loss was most definitely our gain. And what a fucking gain it was.

Show after show packed to capacity, we played each gig like it might be our last. And realistically, it might very well have been. So we made it count and got some attention from the powers that be. Fancy suits started knocking at our door wanting a piece of the pie and before you knew it, we weren't nobodies anymore.

Of course we didn't just end the tour with a deal and a few more thousand fans. My front woman Angie ended up shacked up with Power Station's keyboard player. They'd gotten hitched and were now expecting a kidlet. It was the ultimate tour souvenir; T-shirts are so redundant these days.

So, we were famous right? Nope, not even close. People knew who we were for sure, and there weren't many nights I spent alone. Girls wanting to be my muse and all that. But as far as fame and fortune went, we were still lacking.

That deal we'd signed, completely shafted us. New York suits trying to make us sound like *5 Seconds of Summer*. I literally want to kick my own ass when I look at our album cover. Sad, sad times.

Luckily for us, while we didn't get the accolades and piles of green rolling in after that bullshit attempt of mainstreaming, we did get our asses pulled from the fire by the one and only Power Station. Seemed liked the guys felt like playing fairy godmothers, because for a second time they'd given us a reprieve. This time in the form of a shiny new contract signed to their new label. The gift of current paperwork giving us total creative control. Gratitude didn't even come close. Although there was that whole procreating with one of my band members, so I guess it all came out in the wash.

"Soooooooooo . . . Should I go?" My lady friend from last night walked back into the bedroom carrying two steaming hot cups of Joe. Her long hair flicked off her shoulder as she sat down beside me on the bed.

"Yeah, I've got a session. Last night was fun though. We should do that again." The cup she had so generously brought to me made its very much-needed journey to my mouth. Mornings were not usually my friend, their existence made better by caffeine and a cigarette. Today I was going to have to settle for just the coffee.

"Last night *was* fun. Do you even remember my name?" She sat smiling as she watched me drink.

"Caroline, and I never forget a name, sweetness." My recall earned me an even bigger smile.

That was my super power, my party trick—and the reason I was able to play a song perfectly after hearing it just one time. Photographic memory. Names, faces, music, dates, phone numbers—all of it stored in the huge vault that was my gray matter. It wasn't even something I had to think about, just boom—it was committed. High school was a walk in the fucking park, I even aced my SATs. And while my folks were creaming their pants over the college offers I was receiving, I turned my back on all of it. The stage was the only place I was going to be spending my days and for better or worse, I made my choice. Which in this case obviously paid off, and I was finally able to give a big fuck you to everyone who thought I'd end up working at 7-11.

"I could call you later? Or we could meet up tonight?" Caroline's hand traveled suggestively up my leg.

"Maybe leave me your number and I'll see where I'm at. I'd hate for you to be waiting around."

The brush off was gentle, but I wanted to be clear nonetheless. We—Caroline and I—were not a thing. We weren't going to be sharing popcorn watching the latest Michael Bay flick nor would we be dating. Not that I had anything against her—she ticked all the boxes—but I wasn't interested in a girlfriend. Hadn't had one in a few years and now that life was throwing me all the pussy I could handle—literally, and I'm talking two hands—I wasn't about to give that up for a ball and chain.

"Okay, well thanks for last night." She leaned in and gave me a kiss on the mouth. It wasn't a sweet kiss, more a calling card to remind me she had sucked my dick so hard last night I wasn't sure I didn't have chafing this morning.

"Sure thing, babe. Let's do it again sometime." And I meant it too; my dick just needed a day or two to recover.

She grabbed a marker that was sitting on my nightstand and scrawled her number on the notebook that was lying beside it. The little love heart added to the end made me second-guess my decision. Maybe a callback wasn't in the cards; the love heart was giving me the heebie jeebies.

Thankfully, she didn't try to convince me further and was dressed and out the door about thirty minutes later. Awesome. Now I could finally get some sleep. My eyes slowly closed as my head hit the pillow.

"Hey, Rus. Are you home, buddy?" The knock at my front door threatened to upset my plans.

While the whole band had made some coin during the Power Station tour, it wasn't enough for us to pack up our shit and head into the city. I still lived in a row house I had inherited from my grandma in the Bronx, with Joey and Max still sharing a place about a block away. Angie was the only one who'd shipped out. With the husband and the bun-in-the-oven, no one was surprised when she'd relocated.

"Rus, open the door. I saw the chick leaving." Joey, my drummer and not too distant neighbor didn't take the hint that I wasn't interested in entertaining this early in the morning.

"Give me a minute."

As much as I wasn't in the mood for company, Joey would probably sit on my front stoop until I opened the door. And being that I didn't want to piss off my neighbors anymore than I already did with my occasional parties and loud music, I figured it was easier to just suck it up and see what he wanted.

I grabbed a pair of sweatpants and made my way to the door as I pulled them on. My debate of whether or not to let him sweat it out a little longer negated by the fact I was already bored with whatever bullshit I knew was going to be coming out of his mouth. Better to just get it over with.

"Fuck, dude. What the hell happened to you?" Dark sunglasses covered Joey's face, and he looked like absolute shit.

"Max's brother is in town. He split up with his wife again and he's crashing on our couch. His snore is like the Texas Chainsaw massacre is going down, I haven't slept all fucking night." He pushed past me and wandered into my living room. "I think she's finally done with his ass, apparently their last showdown was pretty epic. So whatever he's done, I think he's out for the count but there is no fucking way he is staying with us." His ass hit the couch as I followed him back in.

"So what do you want me to do? There's no way he's staying with me." While I was sympathetic to his cause, I wasn't sure exactly where I fit in with this problem. Max's pain-in-the-ass older brother wasn't going to be chilling it in my spare room, if that's what he was looking for.

"I'm not looking for a solution, just fucking refuge. We're recording today and you know I need a solid ten hours or I can't function. You want to be sitting in a booth with me longer than you need to be because I can't keep time?"

Joey was an amazing drummer, which was handy because he wasn't good at much else. He'd skated from crappy dead-end job to crappy dead-end job, and while my choice of not going to college had been my own, poor Joey didn't fair so lucky. Our deal gave the kid a fighting chance at doing something with his life, his future hopefully guaranteed not to include food stamps and unemployment lines.

"Yeah, you can crash in the spare room if you want. Max know you're here?" The words had no sooner left my mouth when there was another knock at my door. It seemed my house was the place to be this morning.

"Speak of the devil." I opened the door to a weary-faced Max who was also rocking a dark pair of shades.

"I'm going to smother him in his sleep." He stormed right in and took a seat beside Joey. "It sounds like a bear is trying to fuck an elephant. There is no way he is staying with us. Whatever he's done can't be that bad. I'll beg Nicole to take him back."

Max was the other half of our rhythm section. Killer bass player and all-around nice guy; we'd been tight since the band's inception. While Angie, our singer, was my best friend, these two guys fell into line directly behind her. Being that she had a full dance card, I was spending more time with these two. I loved Angie, but I drew the line at talking about stretch marks and sore nipples.

"Maybe it's just a phase; she's thrown his ass out before and they always end up back together." I tried to offer a silver lining as I took a seat opposite them in my armchair.

"God, I hope so. He had "Every Rose has its Thorn" by *Poison* on constant repeat until three a.m. I'm not sure whether to put him out of his misery or pay for someone to suck his dick." Max closed his eyes as he leaned his head against the back of the coach.

"Right? It was depressing the hell out of me and I never get depressed." Joey pulled off his shades and rubbed his eyes.

"Okay, so just tell him he needs to find some other place to stay. Tough love his ass." It was simple, Max just needed to man up and tell his brother to take the pity party somewhere else.

"That's easy for you to say, you don't have any brothers or sisters. And while Phil is constantly fucking up, I can't turn my back on him. It's bad enough my parents won't have anything to do with him."

Max was right on two accounts. One, as far as siblings I came up short. The parental units felt they hit perfection when they had me and figured they would quit while they were ahead. Their account is slightly different, citing my lack of sleeping and constant crying which had scarred them for life, but I prefer to think of my earlier infant behavior as character building. Like SEAL training for parents, Mom and Dad can survive anything now. Zombie Apocalypse, they won't even bat an eye. They will thank me later. The second thing he was right on the money was his brother. Phil was a complete and utter fuck-up.

Born eighteen years before Max, Phil had pretty much been disowned by his parents before his younger brother had blown out his first candle. Of course Max didn't have it in him to also shun the dude who shared his DNA, so every time Phil messed up, Max bailed him out. It was an ongoing saga. Never been so glad to be an only child.

"Fine, then at the very least set some ground rules. He's a big boy, he needs to learn to stand on his own two feet." It didn't take a rocket scientist to know this was going to be bad news for us.

With a new album in the works, we were getting ready to get it on the airwaves and take the show on the road. Last thing we needed was family dramas.

"It's cool, I've got it under control." Max didn't convince me he had anything under control.

"Can we stop talking now? I need sleep. Unless you want to tell us about that smoking hot chick who walked out of your door this morning, that would be worth staying up for." Joey leaned back into the couch and threw me a grin. The bastard was predictable if nothing else, constantly looking to me for details. I didn't even want to know what he used them for.

"Nothing I want to share, boys. She left with a smile and that's all that matters."

"I don't know how you do it, Rus. Honestly, all those girls? How do you *not* have an angry pitchfork mob of women on your lawn? You sleep with them and yet they still worship you after you show them the door. It's like your dick has magic powers or something." Joey wasn't giving up.

"Seriously, Joe. If you spent as much time concentrating on your own love life as you did worrying about mine, you'd be a lot happier. Probably getting more action as well." Positives all around. As far as disclosure, they weren't getting jack.

"That's an *avoid* if ever I heard one," Max laughed.

I could have launched on the defensive that the *avoiding* was being done by the two people currently taking up space on my sofa. Considering there was a perfectly good house of their own they could be chilling in. But instead I flipped them off and headed back to my room. I left them to fight over who was getting the spare room and who was getting the couch, the outcome not affecting me either way. What *was* important was that in few hours everyone was going to need to be razor sharp. Studio time was happening, and I wanted to make the new tracks my bitch.

My perfect life was over.

Crushed like a forgotten Oreo at the bottom of the box.

How could I have been so stupid?

As the streetlights slowly peeked through my drapes, so did the realization that everything I'd worked for in the last two years was gone. The man I'd encouraged and loved for two years dumped me without a second thought.

Our *special* dinner did not end up with him giving me a key. Quite the opposite in fact, he sat me down and told me we were over. Done. Finished. Through.

While I had assumed those random acts of sweetness were leading us to the next level, they were nothing other than cowardly sidesteps to showing me the door. He'd been trying to soften the blow. It was over. I was over.

We'd been discovered, or at the very least our fling had been, and the senior partners were not amused. Actually they were the opposite of amused. Talk of unprofessionalism and breaking of contracts was thrown about. Fraternization apparently frowned upon. I really should have read the fine print.

Long story short, they agreed if I left quietly they would give me a letter of recommendation. A message my boyfriend hand delivered with the parting words that although he "cared for me, it was time we both moved on."

When it came down to the crunch, he bailed on me like a bad investment. *Sorry, thanks but no thanks*, my services were no longer required. Even the chance for our relationship to continue now that we no longer had to hide was also shunned. Too much trouble, too many raised eyebrows—the clean break preferred.

Asshole.

So, I was sent packing with four weeks severance pay under a cloud of suspicion. I had been reduced to lunchroom fodder, the gossip ranging wildly from corporate espionage to an unplanned pregnancy. The truth not anywhere near as sensational as the lies, and yet still no one suspected our indiscretion.

"Open up, Ali." Renee hammered at my door.

Her visits over the last week had been a daily occurrence, her stopping by with the excuse of bringing me food. I think it had less to do with the Chinese takeout and more to do with making sure I hadn't hung myself with my shower curtain.

"I'm still alive. Leave the sweet and sour pork by the door and allow me to wallow in peace." I didn't even bother lifting my head from the pillow; I had no intention of moving from my couch.

"I've got sushi and I'm not leaving it on your doorstep. Open the door."

She was persistent; I'd give her that. And probably more caring than I deserved. She'd always known Rob would break my heart and not a single "I told you so" had escaped her lips. Instead she fed me, let me cry and then locked me in the bathroom until I showered. Friends don't let friends smell.

"My life is over and you brought me raw fish?" I opened the door wearing the same stained T-shirt and sweatpants I had been living in for the last two days. There was no need to get fancy; misery didn't have a dress code.

"Your life is not over, this is just a hiccup. And sushi is good for you." She pushed past me and took the five short steps from my door that landed her in my kitchen.

"I'm sorry. I guess I'm a shitty friend as well as shitty girlfriend. Oh, and I'm a shitty paralegal too it seems. Just all-around shitty." I let the door slam as I joined her in the kitchen. As far as wallowing was going, I was still neck deep. It was good to be successful at something, self-pity being my only option currently.

"You aren't a shitty friend." She pulled the bamboo chopsticks from the plastic bag. "Or any of that other stuff." She tactfully added. "But you can't sit in your apartment and hide from the world for the rest of your life."

Reality. Something I didn't want right now, not that my reluctance to deal stopped it from arriving on my doorstep in the form of my best friend and questionable dinner. She was right. Hiding was not the solution. Lord knows I'd been giving it a try, and all it got me was greasy hair and a smelly apartment. My severance pay would soon dry up while my bills would not. And while one of the four weeks was spent wallowing, I literally couldn't afford anymore time off. So while

I wasn't ready to deal with society, I would at the very least have to start dealing with the classifieds. *Who knows, maybe sticking a toe in first by rejoining the human race would prepare me for an interview.* It's not like I had much more to lose. "You're right." My shoulders slumped as I leaned against the wall for support. "I need to get out."

●●●

It would have been easy to get dressed up, get drunk and have sex with some random guy. At least that's what Renee wanted me to do. But every single time we'd walked into a bar, I almost had a full-blown panic attack over the thought of some guy seeing me naked. My confidence—which had always been lacking—was now nonexistent, and even alcohol didn't seem to help.

With Renee as my cheerleader, I persevered for an entire week. Night after night, bar after bar, with only one of us ending up getting lucky—not me. My attempts at flirting bordered on embarrassment next to my cool femme fatale best friend.

Even with my battered bravado and lackluster enthusiasm, I put on my prettiest dress and highest heels in what would be my fourth attempt at trying to get laid. This time without Renee—the pressure of having an audience just making it more difficult. Apparently a one-night stand would cure me, or at least send me into post orgasmic bliss so that I wouldn't care for a while. I wasn't convinced, but I was willing to give it a try.

It was while I was at the bar, sipping a Diet Coke through

one of those ridiculous cocktail straws, that my world went even further into a tailspin.

"Hey, Ali-cat."

The nickname sending chills down my spine despite the bar feeling like a sauna.

"Rob." I twirled around to the direction of the voice, his smiling face greeting me as I made eye contact. Damn it, he still looked good.

"Wow, I thought it was you." His eyes moved over the curves of my body, pausing over my mostly exposed cleavage. "You're looking *well*."

Every night I fantasized about this very moment. The one where Rob would run into me, see me looking fabulous and then declare what an idiot he'd been and beg me to take him back. It was the sweet dream I'd lull myself off to sleep with, concluding with me telling him there'd be a cold day in hell before I'd take him back and crushing him like he'd crushed me. I'd smile as I drifted off into sleepland knowing he'd realized too late that I was the woman of his dreams and I'd leave him crying just as he'd left me.

"Rob." I tried to keep my voice level while my pulse hammered away under my skin. "How lovely to see you."

It wasn't a lie, I was genuinely glad to see him. It might have taken me a couple of weeks but my emotions had moved from sad to mad. And while a few days after my spectacular dumping and firing I might have taken him back, now it was seeing him grovel that would give me the most pleasure.

"You too, Ali-cat." He leaned down and kissed me gently on the cheek. "Seems like you were holding out on me." His brow rose as he eyed my dress again.

"Oh, this?" I giggled shamelessly. "Just a little something I threw on."

Okay, so when it came to sexy and flirty I sucked. The seduction game was as elusive to me as the Loch Ness monster, and me trying to be sexy was probably just as scary as Nessie.

"Well, it obviously agrees with you." He smiled, his hands gently rubbing up my arm. I tried to stop myself from cringing at his touch, or punching him right in the balls, more to see if he still had any.

"Listen, I'm glad I found you. I've been thinking a lot about you the last few days." Rob moved closer, the noise from the bar making it hard to hear him.

"Oh?" I mentally smiled as I prepared to tell him to go take a hike.

There are times in life when you wish there was a pause button. Where the moment just needed to be savored just a little longer than time allowed. Not to gloat, but to validate that good things eventually happen to good people. Karma, payback and all the stuff, would eventually do its duty and the righteous would stand victorious. Sure it was a little conceited, but I figured I'd earned my moment and I wanted it to last just a little longer.

"I'm getting married."

The words had come out of his mouth but just like the night when he told me we were through, it was as if I hadn't heard them correctly.

"What?" My eyes flew open in a shock I had no hope of disguising.

"I know it's sudden but I've known Susan most of my life.

We dated through college and well, we found our way back to each other. Our families are ecstatic. Naturally, our mothers are already naming our children."

I was going to be sick. The room was spinning; the heat that had been mildly uncomfortable before was now suffocating, and my lungs wouldn't expand enough so I could breathe.

"Ali-cat, are you all right?" I felt his hands grip my arms as my body swayed on the barstool I was precariously close to falling off of.

Words failed me as my throat dried up and my mouth refused to function. In my fantasy he begged me to take him back, not tell me he was over me and ready to make some other girl his wife.

How could he have replaced me so quickly?

Had I honestly meant nothing?

Was I so easy to toss aside that he couldn't even give it a few months before I'd have to see his smug-ass face smiling from the engagement announcements of the newspaper?

And just when I felt I was either going to throw up or pass out, a miracle happened and I was able to not only remain upright but conscious too. It would have been asking too much for me to think of something to say, so in the end I didn't try but climbed off that barstool and walked away instead. Just like that—I was gone.

My miracle unfortunately didn't extend much past getting me out of the bar where I stood like a deer in headlights, looking at the street traffic. *Think, Ali, think.* I willed my brain to kick into gear and figure out something that would get me off the sidewalk and away from the nightmare I'd left behind.

Then in a moment of clarity, or further delusion—jury was

still out as to which—I thought of Rusty. Why my mind would go to the sexy, hot and charismatic mystery man when my sanity was swirling down the drain, I had no idea but whatever lifeline I had, I was hanging onto it.

Madness. That had to be the only explanation as I hailed a cab and directed him to the bar where we'd had our first and only real conversation. My pulse raced with every mile we got closer. I literally had no idea if he would be there or what I would even say if he was, but hoped I'd have the chance.

The cab had barely stopped at the curb when I threw myself out of the car and tossed the driver some money. I'm fairly sure that the tip I left was payment enough for my insanity, but in case it wasn't, I mumbled an apology as I made my way from the cab to the door. I was done being safe. At least for tonight.

Channeling my inner Renee, in a move I'm sure she would be proud off, I stalked into the bar with a purpose that even surprised me.

It took me mere moments to locate him, and he was every bit as impressive as the memory. Wearing a pair of faded blue denims and NYFD Tee, he was effortlessly sexy, his smile curling as he lifted his beer to his mouth.

He laughed at some joke I obviously couldn't hear as a posse of women and men surrounded him. The girls vying for his attention as they pawed at him like a puppy. He didn't seem to mind their wandering hands or their constant attention.

It was either bravery or just plain insanity that had me push my shoulders back and walk right to where he was standing. I did my best to ignore the crowd, or at the very least not make eye contact with them. Damn, I wasn't *that* brave.

"Do you remember me?" I almost shouted as every pair of eyes in his makeshift group came to rest on me.

"Sure I do," he said with zero hesitation. "You're Alison." A smile that could impregnate a thousand virgins lit up his face.

Him knowing my name was enough of a sign that I was going to sleep with him.

While some people prayed for weeping Madonna's to show them the way, I contented myself with the beautiful man being able to recall me from the sea of girls he'd no doubt encounter-ed in the last couple weeks. A sign was still a sign, right? And who was I to decide what constituted divine intervention. Hell—a place I was no doubt earning a spot in—I'd been avoiding the whore tag my whole life and it had gotten me nowhere fast. My goal to be everything my mother wasn't hadn't brought me happiness, and if nothing else tonight I would lose myself in that big screaming O that Renee promised would change my perspective. Inner sensible voice be damned, I was having sex with Rusty tonight and it was going to be earth-shattering.

So, in keeping with my new status as the harlot hell-bound vixen, I completely ignored the crowd as I focused on Rusty. His magnetic pull had my eyes locked onto him with anyone else's existence no longer important—at least not in that moment.

The noise, the people, the bar—completely disappeared as I moved forward and pressed my lips to his and kissed him. A real kiss, the kind that sets your whole skin on fire and makes your knees knock together, and thankfully, he didn't push me away or call the cops. Small victories everywhere. Instead, he pulled me closer and kissed me back.

He was much better at this kissing thing than I was. His mouth dominated mine, the kiss surpassing every single one I'd ever experienced in my life.

"That's quite the hello." He grinned when he finally pulled away, our audience looking at us open-mouthed and silent. I'd always wanted to make a grand entrance.

"Do you still want to have a drink with me?" My eyes blinked wildly as I focused on what his mouth had tasted like. It's dizzying effects still rendering me momentarily brave.

"Yes. Even more so now." His eyes stayed glued on mine as I remained unmoving in front of him.

"Good, then let's go."

The chance to change his mind—or my own—wasn't left on the table. Instead I harnessed whatever bravado I had left and gave in to my libido. I'll be honest, I wasn't exactly sure which emotion was currently running the show but my brain wasn't firing on enough cylinders to stop it. And *it* not happening didn't even cross my mind as I grabbed his hand and pulled him closer to me. His body followed mine as I led him away from his group.

"Hey sweetheart, the bar is the other way." He circled his hands around my waist as we got closer to the doorway. They felt nice. His hands on me. Oh God, he was beautiful as another smile lit up his face. "Didn't you want me to buy you a drink?"

Oh, the drink. The request that had served as my ice-breaker—well, after the kiss—wasn't exactly what I was after. Nope, I had something else in mind. Best I clear that up, it's not like embarrassing myself was an issue when I'd just tongued him in front of his friends.

"No, I want you to have sex with me."

Thankfully I didn't stutter. It would have sounded much more desperate if I had to repeat it and as much as I was desperate, I didn't want to advertise it.

"Sure, that works too." He didn't even blink.

Not. Even. A. Little.

Just pulled me closer and kissed me again in a way that could only be described as foreplay. His tongue hinted at the pleasure it was sure to deliver.

Awesome. I was sooooo going to do this.

"Good. Let's go."

Four
Rusty

Recording an album took time. **Even more so when you** wanted to redeem yourself for the watered-down bullshit we'd put out on our first effort. Hours spent in the booth were physically and mental draining. So because of this, and the fact Phil was still camped out on Joey and Max's couch, we headed straight to the bar. Angie with the excuse of a growing fetus in her belly had to take a pass, which meant it was just the three of us.

It'd become a nightly thing, a way for us to hit the re-boot button. Not that we got falling over drunk, but the few beers we enjoyed and some friendly female attention was exactly what we needed. It was a nice way to wind up a day.

The usual routine got an upgrade when my night took a very quick and interesting detour. A chick I'd met a couple of weeks ago came barreling in like a heat-seeking missile and gave me some mouth action. No shit. She didn't even say hi, went straight in for the kiss and that sweet mouth of hers was inviting something *other* than conversation. I was instantly interested in whatever else came after.

The trip back into my memory banks didn't take too long. The recall juicing me up even more because the chick that was on the other side of my lips was the same girl who had turned me down flat the first time we'd crossed paths. She didn't even let me buy her a drink, which was a shame because she had that whole mysterious vibe going on that intrigued me. Turning me down—just fanned the flames.

Seeing her for the first time that night all those weeks ago was like a kick in the balls. There had been something different about her that demanded attention. And it wasn't just that she was beautiful in the most curious way. Sure she was stunning and her body looked pretty happening from what I could see, but it was more than that. It was all so understated, down-played—like she didn't need all the tricks some girls needed to make them look good. She was raw. It got me curious about what was hiding behind those light hazel eyes, and how I'd love to find out. I wasn't shy about saying hello and didn't have to wait too long for my opening. The drink that had been sitting in her hand for longer than it needed to be doing a disappearing act courtesy of her friend. Whatever that was on her mind, drinking hadn't been it.

Girls weren't a problem for me, so usually a no meant I said a goodbye and moved the hell on. Plenty more fish in the sea. But there was something about this one that more than got my interest, which is why when she threw herself at me with her mouth I had zero problem with it. Her wanting to take it to my place, well that was just a bonus prize I didn't think I'd be winning.

"So, I guess the boyfriend thing isn't an issue anymore?"

It hadn't escaped my attention that the first time we'd started this dance, a significant other was the reason she gave me for the turndown.

"No, we're done. You need help with the key?" Her feet shuffled in place like she wasn't convinced that she was cool with what was about to go down, her hands locking together as I opened my door.

"Nope, I've got it."

There was no need to tell me she hadn't done this before, that part was plainly obvious. Her ability to not keep still was the biggest tip off, followed up by the lip biting and her need to get into my house a.s.a.p.

"You okay, you look a little nervous?" Nothing like stating the fucking obvious.

"Yes, I'm fine." She nodded a little too enthusiastically. "Not nervous at all." The laugh that followed told me otherwise. "We're going to do this."

Her words did little to convince me she was on board even as she stepped through the doorway. Her fingers white-knuckled her purse as she moved into the room; her eyes peeling open wide to take in the scenery. "Your place . . . looks nice."

Ironically it wasn't the change in subject that had me suppress the laugh. With the outside security light providing the only illumination, she either had x-ray vision or was attempting small talk. The giggle out of her mouth that followed soon after ruled out the super power.

Assuming anything was going to happen was way premature. I'd say at this point taking her back to the bar was more of a sure thing than getting her naked. We'd still only kissed one time and she was jittery as fuck.

"Alison, you sure you want to do this?" I closed the door behind us and hit the light. "I can take you back to the bar."

"Nope, we're totally going to screw." She turned around to face me. "Each other. A lot. Hard. It's going to happen." Her face determined even if her body didn't seem to be.

"Ok-ay, so *screwing* it is." Not like I could argue with the girl, she made herself clear. Her adorable attempted seduction making it more difficult not to laugh.

"We should probably start." She put down her purse in one of the most awkward displays of settling in. "Um, you should probably do something."

"What is it that you would like me to do?" My grin got wider as I sidled up close to her and moved the hair off her shoulder. Letting her take the lead seemed the smartest decision at the moment. Convinced at any minute she was going to call a time out.

"Maybe you should take off your shirt." Her eyes dipped down to my T-shirt, before coming back to meet mine.

Surely she wasn't a virgin. She'd had a boyfriend; they must have had sex at some point. Unless that's the reason he was no longer in the picture. The dude not able to get it up and seal the deal?

"Alrighty. That better?" The shirt that I'd pulled over my head was tossed to the side, landing on my coffee table.

"Holy shit. How are you even real?" Her eyelids peeled back as they traveled up the length of my chest, every inch of my skin getting her attention. Obviously she liked what she saw and didn't that fucking please the hell out of me. Probably more that it should.

"I work out." My hand reached for hers as I led her closer toward the couch. Her eyes stayed on me as she took the few steps into my living room.

"Yeah, I feel like I should clap or something. Maybe kneel. Last time I saw abs like that they were on a mannequin." If the whole wide-eyed thing was an act, then I was super impressed. Award winning even.

"I'm glad you like what you see. Is there something else you'd like me to show you?"

Usually letting the girl call the shots wasn't my style. I preferred to work things at my own speed i.e. a hell of a lot faster than this. But something about this whole situation had me pull on the brakes and let her set the tone. The night was still young and I still wasn't convinced we were going to be fucking.

"Wow. That tattoo is beautiful. It looks so real." She moved her hand slowly toward my chest, her fingertips just barely touching my inkwork like the thing was going to leap off my skin and bite her.

The show-and-tell wasn't new for me. Girls liked to get an eyeful of my fancy ink before we got down to business—the dragon that slithered up my left side from my hip to my chest, getting the most attention.

"He likes you." I moved my mouth closer to hers as her fingers followed the curve of the dragon's neck. My dick hoping it would be the next thing that got a stroke. *Easy there, buddy. We don't want to scare her off.*

"So, Alison, I'm going to kiss you now." Once again the play-by-play wasn't my usual drill. There was usually no need, and even though my cock was stirring in my pants already, it felt like she could spook at any minute.

"Uh-huh." Her head bobbed up and down as she moved her beautiful hazel eyes back to mine. Seriously, she was fucking stunning.

"We can stop anytime you like." My lips edged closer as my hand wrapped around her waist.

"Yes."

It was the last thing to come out of her lips before I'd sealed them with mine. Her body stiffening in my hands as my tongue tried unsuccessfully to pry her mouth open. And unless you were thirteen with no hair on your balls, what we were doing wasn't even close to kissing.

"Hey." The effort aborted as I moved my mouth from hers. "You are going to have to loosen your lips. If you want it to feel good."

No seriously, was she a virgin? Maybe I should have asked her how old she was? She had to be at least twenty-one, right? We met in a bar. No way they would risk having a minor in there.

"Oh yeah, sorry." She gave me her first smile for the night as she parted her lips. "Here you go," she mumbled with her mouth open as I struggled not to laugh.

I very much wanted to keep kissing her, and get back to the vibe she'd been working when she walked into the bar. What had happened between then and now was a freaking mystery but damn if I didn't want to find out. Rushing it was out of the question. The very notion of doing anything she wasn't a hundred percent cool with made me want to kick my own ass. Nope, I was happy to let it simmer just a little while longer.

My hands stayed on her as my mouth kept its distance.

"Maybe we leave the kissing part for a bit. Did you want a drink?"

"Yes, drinks are good." She breathed a sigh of relief. "I think we need those. Those would definitely help."

Noticing that she hadn't been chilling with a beer the day we'd met, I figured she was more a cocktail kind of girl. Not a problem for me. I had a few bottles of liquor tucked away that would do the trick. Hopefully help her not be so uptight.

She sunk her ass into my couch, watching me as I turned and moved into the kitchen. The grin spread across my lips as I heard her mumble something about my ass when I reached up and grabbed a bottle. The vodka bottle being the closest was the one that I palmed, grabbing a couple of tumblers from the shelf beside it as I turned back to face her.

The plan to grab some ice and possibly a mixer sidelined when I caught sight of her second smile of the night. Maybe it was the drink in my hand or the residual view of my chest, the reason for it not really important other than it was happening. That smile of hers was pretty damn compelling.

"Here we go; I'm assuming you have nothing against vodka." My ass joined hers on the couch as I sat the tumblers down on the coffee table beside us, the bottle tugged from my hand as she pulled it toward her.

"I can mix us up something." I watched as her fingers quickly twisted the lid from the bottle. "I think I might have some juice in the fridge."

"Great, thanks." She brought the bottle to her lips and took a massive swallow.

"Or you can drink it straight, that works too." The OJ obviously not needed. Right. This was turning out to be an interesting evening. Not at all how I'd planned my night, but I couldn't say the latest turn of events was disappointing. The new direction intrigued the hell out of me.

"This is really strong. Wow." She coughed as she moved the bottle away from her mouth, her eyes starting to water.

"Yeah. Straight vodka isn't great. It tastes better if you add it to something." I watched as she once again took another swig.

"Ugh. Yeah this is terrible." She winced, the mouthful of vodka traveling down her throat, her hand clutching at her chest.

"Then why are you still drinking it?" A valid question seeing as she was about to get cozy with the bottle again. I wasn't sure if I should laugh or pull it from her hands.

"I don't know." She shrugged, her smile confirming she had no idea what she was doing.

"Look, why don't you let me make us a drink. It will taste better." And at the very least give the bottle a fighting chance at being appreciated.

"Ok, but don't take too long. I'm not here for the drink. We're supposed to be getting naked. We need to have sex. We need to move to *that* part."

She was so fucking adamant. I think she's said the word *screw* or a variation of it at least ten times since we walked in the door and I wasn't sure which one of us she was trying to convince. I sure as hell didn't need a pep talk.

"I think we should probably hold off on the sex, just for a while." Or at the very least until I was convinced she wasn't going to freak out when we got to the good parts. So far I'd only managed to get my shirt off, give her a half-assed kiss, and she was already looking like she might hyperventilate.

If it had been anyone else, I probably wouldn't have bothered, but there was something about this particular girl that had me perplexed. No way was I not seeing this out. My other concern was if I took her back to the bar and she was still waving the lets-have-sex flag, it might not end well. There'd be a million assholes lining up to help her with that, most of them not giving a rat's ass about her mental health or putting on the brakes if she had a change of heart. Whether I understood the reasons why didn't matter, she was staying with me tonight. Sex completely optional.

"I know what you're thinking." She shook her head as she tried to focus on me, the couple of swigs of vodka already starting to take effect. "This is where I tell you this is a rebound thing because my boyfriend dumped me, and I need to get him out of my head. Where I cry about the fact I was with him for two years and he left me without a second thought. But this isn't a revenge thing, he doesn't even care. He's getting married."

Well, I guess that explained the reason she was no longer part of a couple. The rundown she gave me sounding more like someone was caught up on a whole lot of history rather than just looking for a good time.

"Actually I wasn't thinking that at all." I didn't even try to lie. "What I was thinking was you are really sweet and as much as I'd love to have sex with you, I'm more concerned with making sure that whatever we do, is as good for you as it is for me."

"Are you always so smooth? I've seen you, you know, with girls. How do you do it? They flock to you. You always have a girl." Words just tumbled out her mouth like she didn't have a filter. I liked her this way and hoped I got to see more of it. The revelation that I was so into this girl, someone I barely knew, just as surprising as the situation.

"I don't know, maybe it's the abs." I grinned, hoping we'd broken through whatever wall she had up.

"Bullshit, what do you say to these women?" The wall was definitely gone and in its place some confidence was starting to poke through. I couldn't be sure it wasn't the booze.

"It's not like a party trick, Alison."

"Sure it is. Do whatever you do to them, to me. Seduce me."

Performing that shit on a dime was not happening. It's not like I had an actual routine like a trained monkey or something, I just knew how to talk to women. Knew how to make them feel good about themselves which in turn made them feel good about being with me. It wasn't hard actually; you'd be surprised how by purely being attentive could get you ridiculous amounts of women. And I was all about the finer details.

"Is that what I'm supposed to do? Seduce you? I thought you wanted to *screw*?" She'd been pretty clear about that. Hell the word had gotten more of a work out than I had in the last week, and did anyone even use it in general conversation? Not in relation to sex anyway. Fuck, sex, yes—screw not so much.

"Yes, but I want the line as well." I kid you not, she pouted like I'd taken her candy.

"There aren't any lines. I don't have an act that I perform to get women into bed. I just talk to them." Once again I led with the truth. Lies weren't in my bag of tricks and I wasn't about to start now.

"Just talk. C'mon. Really? What do you do?" She tugged on

my arm as her eyes spelled out their disbelief. "Pretend for a minute I'm not a sure thing."

"Alison, your ex-boyfriend was obviously an asshole and there are clearly some hurt feelings there, but regardless of all that stuff, you are *not* a sure thing."

"But I—" She didn't get a chance to finish.

"You are beautiful. And I think you're really sexy and even though you're acting crazy, I'm almost certain that underneath it all is a sweet girl who isn't a hundred percent sure you're down with this. Any time you change your mind, I'll take you home. There are no assumptions, not on my part."

She didn't talk, just looked at me for a while as my words settled. Not sure what her limp-dick boyfriend was like, but she wasn't going to get bullshit lines from me. Not the way I operated. And if there was one thing I'd learned having a girl as a best friend, it's that there were enough lies in the world without my contribution.

"Wow, now I really want to have sex with you." She moved in closer, her tits heaving up and down as she breathed a little heavier.

"Here's a hint." I tipped her chin so I got a good look into her eyes. "If you want to have sex with me, maybe stop *talking* and let me kiss you."

"Please."

It was more than a word, it was a plea and I was more than ready to take-two on the action she'd started when she'd walked into the bar. My lips moved closer to hers, her mouth parting in anticipation. Her eyes automatically closed as I made contact, her body moving closer to mine. She eased off the brakes a little and moved her mouth giving me better access as I slid in my tongue. Now we were getting some-where. The moan that was trying to jailbreak from her lips, muffled by my mouth. It stayed on hers, hungry for more. She was into it, her hands reaching up and pulling me closer. And being that I like to keep things even, I reciprocated by bringing her head closer to mine, feeling her body against me.

At this point, I had no game plan. I was cutting straight to bootleg play and seeing where the hell it ended up. I wasn't sure that sleeping with her was even a possibility, but I wanted to kiss her and so we were going to do more of that. Who knew, maybe that's all we'd be doing, and I can't say that I'd be pissed-off. Sweet. That's exactly what her mouth was, and I wanted as much of it as she was willing to give me.

"You are so good at this. You should teach a class or some-thing." She mumbled as things started to get more intense.

"Shhh, just let me kiss you some more."

Rusty was an amazing kisser. Ten stars on a five-star rating. Seriously, seriously good. Rob had never kissed me like that, not like he literally wanted to drink me into his soul, which is what it felt Rusty was trying to do.

I wasn't sure if we should be having sex or I should be swearing my allegiance to his lips, he was really that good. It wasn't just his mouth, it was like his whole body was in on it. His hand wrapped my neck bringing my head closer as I laid on top of him, his fingers ever so slightly grazing my skin—it was most definitely a team effort, and I was happy to be their cheerleader.

Any hesitation I'd had slowly faded away. It wasn't even the alcohol, it was him. Something about him made me feel totally at ease. He wasn't rushing me, pushing me to get naked. He was slow.

Deliberate.

Savoring me.

The nerves and uncertainty disappeared as he took his

time, every touch and caress either with his hands or lips, making me feel beautiful and wanted.

Our kissing spectacular—not a lie, he was like Cirque du Soleil with that mouth—had moved from his couch into his bedroom. This was a very welcome development, and while we were still clothed—except for the T-shirt I'd made him lose earlier—we were definitely heading for some adult action. This was it. We were *finally* going to get busy. I was going to have sex with him. *Please Lord, don't let him have a small penis.* Or at the very least, let him know what to do with it.

"Hey." He pulled his mouth from mine; that smile of his dazzling me. He totally must have had braces at some stage, no one's teeth are that perfect.

"Hey." I giggled back wondering if it was too forward to ask him to take off his pants now. He had asked me what else he could show me, and there were things I *really* wanted to see.

"You doing okay?" He brushed the hair out of my eyes.

So. Freaking. Smooth.

"Yes, yes. I am now." The voice that floated out didn't sound like it was mine. No, this voice sounded happier and a hell of a lot relaxed.

"Good." His lips moved back to my neck, they felt nice there, all warm and soft against my skin. It was heaven and I was so blissed out, which is the only reason I could possibly have said the next thing that came out of my mouth.

"In the interest of full disclosure, I've seen you around. The bar wasn't the first time."

"Yeah, I get that quite a bit. It's okay." His grin curled up at the edges. Almost like he'd been expecting it. My mind scrambled with a logical explanation. Oh God, please let him not have been on *America's Most Wanted.*

"Huh? What?"

"I get recognized; the band thing. It doesn't bother me."

"You're in a band?"

Whoa. Band?

We had skipped past the so-what-do-you do conversation that usually happened before you swapped bodily fluids, so I had no idea what he did for a living. Musician wouldn't have been my first guess, but I wasn't sure there was a job that would be suitable to match his talents. His *talents* being that he was unbelievably gorgeous, but as far as I knew people didn't get paid just for being hot. Even models had to strut down a runway or something. Musician? Well, at least he wasn't a criminal; I suppressed the urge to cheer.

"Isn't that where you've seen me?" He eyed me, curiously waiting for an answer.

In retrospect I should have just gone with that. It was so much less creepy than the truth. Yep, the band. That's where I knew him. The big hole in my theory was I had no idea which band and what he even played. The truth seemed like my only option. Well, the only one I could work with in my currently frazzled state.

"Err. No?" It hadn't meant to sound like a question but that's exactly how it squeaked out of my mouth.

"Well now, you have to tell me." His interest looked piqued. It was more conversation than I wanted to be having to be honest. I was more concerned about getting back to the kissing we'd been doing before. I wanted to cry. No, seriously he was just about to touch my ass, and the bulge in his pants felt substantial. He definitely did not have a small penis.

No, we were done talking. We'd talked. Then our lips got busy doing other things, better things than talking. Why did I have to open my big mouth? Who cares about full disclosure, this wasn't a legal contract—it was a one-night stand.

Am I so defective I can't even whore around like a normal person?

I want my orgasm, damn it!

"I don't want to talk." I tried unsuccessfully to flirt. My hands tried to get in on the action, roaming over the large and delectable expanse that was his chest. I wasn't as smooth as he had been but I managed to not look like a complete amateur.

"Yeah, you do." His arms stretched behind his head and anchored themselves. His body relaxed while mine still hovered above him. "So tell me where you've seen me and *then* we'll do other stuff." He wasn't giving in.

"Sex?" I was hopeful, but I really needed to clarify.

"Yes." He rolled his eyes, giving me a grin. "Especially now you're calling it what it is."

"Sorry, habit. Rob called it—" My mouth clamped shut at the mention of the demon's name. Wow. Mood killer.

"It's fine, Alison. You can say his name." He didn't seem the slightest bit annoyed. Not sure I'd have been so cool about the mention of someone else right before we were about to scre— God, damn it. It was like a sickness.

I had successfully not even thought about Rob in over an hour. The hurt and emotions that had been twisting in my gut and head on the way over to the bar had dissolved since being with Rusty. The kissing had most definitely helped too. "But I don't want to talk about him." Sadly, not talking about him did not erase the fact I was now thinking about him. And I didn't want to be. Oh, crap. Talk about rotten timing.

"You know what I think? I think maybe you do. Maybe you're not as over him as you claim to be."

Talking about Rob and how I ended up jobless wasn't how I wanted to be spending my evening. I had grand plans. *One-night stand* and *moving on* kind of plans, which was why I was in bed—granted still fully clothed—with a man I barely knew.

The sigh hadn't meant to come out of my mouth, but much like Rob's name, it spilled out all the same. Uninvited.

"So, tell me." His head settled into the pillow. "First about the dumbass boyfriend, then we can talk about me." Another panty-melting grin. Thank God I was on birth control because I couldn't be sure I wouldn't spontaneously conceive by the glow of his smile.

"So I don't usually go home with men from a bar," I started, my confessional happening whether I wanted to or not.

"Yeah, I kind of guessed." His eyes dipped down to his naked chest. "I usually don't strip on demand before I make out, so I guess we're both trying something new." The smile played on his lips showed no hint of annoyance.

"Well . . . it's made the whole process easier, just so you know. I appreciate it." A smile of my own confirming the sentiment. "Truth is, I suck at relationships. My mother has had more boyfriends than I've had hot dinners and even so, still ended up alone. I didn't want to make the same mistakes, so I didn't date much." I neglected to add guys in general weren't interested in me because . . . well, I was less femme fatale and more plain Jane. "My meager beginnings also didn't give me the best self esteem." I glossed over being teased because I didn't have the right brand of jeans or fancy new shoes. "And we had no cash so the only chance I had was to go to the local college and fight to get a decent job despite not having a degree from a fancy college."

There I was spilling my guts to an almost complete stranger about stuff I'd barely told Renee. I expected to him to run any minute now.

"Fancy or not, you still got a degree. You should be proud of that. What about your dad?" he asked this without judgment.

"Who knows. Any guy in the Tri-State area around the age of forty could be a candidate." I shrugged, no longer concerned about the father who'd been absent my whole life. "He probably doesn't even know I exist."

"Well, that sucks for him, because you're pretty awesome." His finger lazily traced my shoulder.

"You're only saying that to be polite."

"Oh, babe. I'm a lot of things but polite isn't one of them." He laughed, his beautiful toned body shaking below me. "So, go on—loser boyfriend? Let me take a stab in the dark. Acted like prince charming when you first met?"

"No," I scoffed, slightly embarrassed he'd guessed correctly. "Okay, maybe yes. But I didn't just date him straight away; he had to work for it. Things in my life had changed and everything was going so well. I thought maybe it was my time to be happy." The story continued on how my once wonderful life had started to unravel.

God, he was sweet. Listening intently as I retold the whole sordid affair. He didn't even raise a brow when I got to the my-boyfriend-was-also-my boss part.

"So he dumped you and then fired you?" he clarified, the lack of sugar-coating reinforcing what an idiot I'd been.

"Yeah, efficient wasn't he?" The stark realization made me feel even more stupid. How could I have been so naïve?

I expected him to echo my thoughts. To ask how someone who had supposedly been careful most of her life would wind up making such an epic mistake like dating her boss. But it didn't come. No judgmental stares. Nothing. He just waited patiently as I slowly killed any chance I had of sleeping with the fine specimen of man that lay beneath me. Yet another reason to be depressed. Surely my mouth spewing every thought and feeling I'd ever had should have been devastating enough.

"I'm sorry. You didn't deserve that." His hand lightly brushed my cheek. Awesome, now I was pathetic as well. It really *could* get worse.

"No," I almost shouted, my head shaking so hard I wasn't sure my brain wasn't getting scrambled. "You can't be sorry. You're the hot guy, I don't want the hot guy to pity me."

If the floor could have swallowed me whole at that very moment, I would have been eternally grateful. Guess what? It didn't—and I had to live with my mortification some more. Not only had I word vomited my life story to the hot guy, but I'd actually called him *the hot guy*. Never ask if it could get worse, inevitably it will.

"Rusty, my name is Rusty."

He looked amused rather than pissed, his ever-present smile widening. The reminder of his name wasn't necessary; *it* like the rest of him had been permanently burned into my brain.

"God, you are so perfect. How is it that you are so cool about everything? You're like a fantasy."

"I'm the hot guy. It's my job to be the fantasy, isn't it?"

No words. Which is actually why I was staring at him opened mouthed wondering if I hadn't hallucinated the whole experience. It wouldn't have surprised me; it's not like any of this made sense. Me being with him, like this.

"Where did you come from?" My hand gently stroked his face, mesmerized.

"Do you mean evolution or were you looking for a genealogical explanation?"

Oh God, he was smart too. Awesome, so he actually *was* perfect which could only mean bad things. I'd had perfect not so long ago and it all came crashing down around me. Perfect and I did not have a good track record.

"Hey, you zoning out on me? We still haven't talked about me yet." He waved a hand in front of my face; further confirming this was no dream.

There were conversations I never would have had with anyone, yet with him, it seemed like nothing was off limits. I didn't even try to hide the fact that I'd seen him around the neighborhood for over a year and had never worked up the courage to say hello.

The words should have been cringe-worthy, they certainly sounded that way in my head. But as my mouth opened and they spilled from my lips, they weren't. Perhaps it was the alcohol or maybe it was something else, but strangely I felt like I could tell him anything.

"I've seen you around. We tend to go to similar places. Maybe I enjoyed the view a little more than I should."

"Really? Well, there you go."

He didn't even question me further. Just like that. Oh, you've been spying on me through the bread aisle at Whole

Foods? Cool. That's not weird at all. Which is why I guess I decided to make it weird.

"You've never noticed me, huh? I'm pretty good at lurking. I'm not surprised."

See? Making it weird. It's a talent.

"Oh, you didn't tell me you were lurking, now the story is getting more interesting. I hope I made it worth your while." He didn't miss a beat.

Was there anything that would ruffle this guy's feathers? Even just a little bit, so I wouldn't feel like a bumbling idiot near him. Judging by the way the night had progressed so far, I guessed there wasn't.

"Enough of me, let's talk about you. You're in a band?" Great; that was a nice segue. Perhaps I wouldn't totally stumble my way through this conversation.

"I *am* in a band." His face beamed with pride like a little boy showing off his shiny new toy. "I play guitar and sing back up vocals. I help with the song writing as well."

"Like a famous band? Would I know who you are?"

"If you have to ask, then no," he laughed.

We were supposed to have sex, and I was going to feel good about it. That was my plan and the reason I went home with him in the first place. He wasn't supposed to be charming. But charming was exactly what he was—and funny, and intelligent, and witty, and gorgeous. He was all the things. The guy's resume was packed full of so many adjectives I wasn't sure he was human. Perhaps I shouldn't have tossed away my earlier assessment of him being a robot so quickly. He was most definitely one of a kind.

"That explains a lot." I laughed as I positioned myself beside him. "The girls, the self assurance. I should have known you were in a band." My arms wrapped around his body.

"Nah, the band has very little to do with my ego. I was hugged a lot as a kid. My parents believed that I was a genius, and I figured the least I could do was put on a good show. My mouth can usually talk myself in or out of trouble so I had that going for me too, the audience was there long before I had a guitar in my hand. I wasn't shy in welcoming the attention."

"Nice. So that's my problem. I wasn't hugged enough." I elbowed him playfully loving the lighter tone of our conversation.

"Nah, you just need more attention. I highly advocate it. Oh, and to see my band as well. If nothing else to feed my ego a little more. The hot guy wants to graduate to the *famous* hot guy. You wouldn't want to deny me, would you?"

"Okay so I need more attention *and* to see your band. My roadmap for success is assured." I giggled as I threw my head back into the pillow, its warm, cushioned surface not nearly as comfortable as being with Rusty.

"You also need to stay with me tonight. I really like the sound of your laugh, something tells me it's been awhile." His words were so smooth and liquid, I would have agreed to much more than spending the night.

"I'll stay." I agreed with very little resistance. "There's actually no place I'd rather be right now." My mouth volunteered information it didn't need to be spilling.

"I'm glad you feel that way." He hugged me closer, possibly to make up for the ones I'd missed. Either way, I wasn't complaining. "Now let's talk about more about you." His fingers teased at my hips. "We need to compile your list of awesome. Along with your laugh, I feel it's been lacking."

"It will be a very short list."

"Bullshit. It's just hiding under the surface. You've got plenty of awesome."

•••

As my eyes opened to sunlight, I knew at some point I had fallen asleep. That hadn't been part of the plan. I imagined I'd eventually succumb to dreamland but hopefully after more kissing. Possibly hot sex?

Instead, I woke up still wearing the same clothes as yesterday.

In his bed.

Alone.

No, sweet, sweet loving had been had.

Just talking and a lot of laughing.

As he held me the entire night.

I'd never felt more naked in all my life.

Relief should have been the emotion that swept over me, the fact that I was saved from doing something I might have regretted. Or not. Even in the clear light of day, I can't be sure I would have.

Last night would have been the perfect opportunity to do that something reckless, totally justifiable. Your ex-boyfriend —who up until two weeks ago was sharing a bed with you— announcing his engagement was a good reason in my book. The fling totally acceptable, and yet to my utter disappointment, it didn't happen. I wasn't entirely sure why.

For the first time in forever someone had wanted to know

about *me*, and maybe that was more important than sex. I hated that even when I didn't need to be, I was so practical. It wasn't a virtue I was fond of this morning.

Maybe I should have been relieved that he left. Not having to do the morning after dance where I pretend I didn't make a fool of myself and treat him like a therapy session. Yet neither of these levels of relief were what I felt. Instead, I felt—loss.

I was lost.

In addition to my feelings of unparalleled sadness—if I stared at the rumpled sheets any longer I was probably going to cry—I was also not home. Which luckily for me wasn't far. See, there obviously had been a purpose to his proximity of living so close. Sadly, not the purpose I'd hoped.

Ugh! I needed to get out of here and into the safety of my bubble. Possibly to never venture out again. It was too soon to tell.

My shoes weren't far, right where I'd left them when I'd kicked them off beside the bed, which was handy. Meant I could get out and get gone a lot sooner than later. No reason to prolong the inevitable, considering I had no idea where Rusty had gone and when he'd be back. Perhaps that was my superpower—making guys disappear.

Poof! Gone.

My record stood at two for two.

So, with shoes on my feet and my dress straightened, I walked back to the living room—my purse still tossed on the coffee table right beside the shirt I'd been so insistent he remove. Yep, if only I'd stuck to *that*.

It was while I was mentally shaking myself and commiserating my loss that I noticed a note sitting neatly on top of my purse. A small inoffensive square, demanding attention.

> Alison,
> Your boyfriend was an idiot. You're better than that. Had
> to leave and didn't want to wake you. Figured you needed
> the sleep. Lock the door on your way out.
> Rusty
> P.S. Don't rob me. :-)
> P.P.S If you do rob me, please leave the red Stratocaster.
> It's my fave.

Ok so now I definitely wanted to cry. He was even sweet in the rejection. The note notably absent of an I-had-a-great-time or let's-see-each-other-again, I had secretly hoped to see. Not even a phone number and a cheesy *call me* featured. And yet, his brush off had been just as kind as he had been. The memory of his arms around me still fresh in my mind as the empty rattled around my body.

So with my emotions more messy than when I walked into Rusty's apartment, I left, taking with me the note which I reread no less than fifteen times on my short walk home.

P.A.T.H.E.T.I.C.

It was in my apartment that I finally broke down and cried. I mean really cried. So much so that my body was doing a full convulsive heave like my bones had disintegrated under my skin and I was just a body bag of emotions. I know, so attractive. Ugly crying. It was my only agenda. Hard, fully committed tears streamed down my face as I took stock of where I was now.

The job I'd busted my ass for was toast. To have to turn

around and start over somewhere new was soul destroying. Once again, I'd be the new girl, once again having to earn my place, once again having to prove my worth. And I guess that's what it all came down to really. That since my birth I'd had to prove I was better than the life I'd been born into. I had to fight for every advantage and I just didn't know if I had it in me to keep going.

Did I want to do this for the rest of my life? I wasn't even sure I wanted to be a paralegal; it just was something I thought would give me job security. Lawyers are always going to need help and crime wasn't going anywhere, anytime soon. Hell, just on my mother's business alone I'd be set. But was it what I wanted? Who even remembered when the last time was I even thought about what *I wanted*. All I knew was I had no job and very little savings and there was no way I could ask my grandparents for help. It was bad enough they still supported my mother. I couldn't burden them any more than they already were. What was I going to do? I was completely out of ideas.

So rather than compile a plan, I curled up and let the tears and fatigue take me. The solutions would have to wait a few hours; right now misery unfortunately had the spotlight.

six

Rusty

"That was some crazy chick you left with last night."** Joey twirled his stick while we waited on Max to lay down his bass track. "I bet she was all kinds of freaky in between the sheets."

It wasn't a surprise that my sudden exit from the bar would be the topic of conversation. We—Joey, Max and I—had been shooting the breeze with some rather friendly ladies when Alison had shown up. The mouth action that happened soon after hadn't been private. Not that I cared either way.

"Rus, you hooking up with crazy girls again? You really should try regular girls for a change." Angie, our talented and ballsy front woman who'd also known me the longest, usually had something to say. Today was no exception.

"Sure, Angie, let's talk about dating *regular* people. That husband of yours, he's real picket-fence material."

It was an easy comeback. Jason Irwin, aka Mr. Angie, was not only the keyboard player for Power Station—the band we'd been touring with—but also the same dude who'd left her crying and broken hearted ten years earlier. As far as baggage went, the two of them pretty much cornered the market. Not that it stopped the two lovebirds from building a bridge-over-troubled-water. A few months later the knot was tied and boom the chick that used to be shaking her ass all over the stage was now doing it with a waddle.

"Oh shut up, like I would ever date, let alone marry, someone who was going to build me a picket fence." She tossed a guitar pick my way; the grin she was wearing telling me she knew I was right.

"So, you going to tell us what the story is with her?" Max joined in the parade. "That was a pretty sweet pick-up she was working."

Part of me was impressed they'd waited until now to bring it up. We'd been in the studio for the best part of the day recording and re-recording the same damn song. I can only assume frustration was the motivator for the impromptu inquisition.

"You guys really that bored? If there were a story, I wouldn't be sharing. You know I'm more mysterious than that."

Kissing and telling wasn't my thing. For one, I was more a *doer* than a *talker*. Preferring to spend my time actually *being* with a lady rather than sitting around telling my buddies about the size of her tits.

Secondly, I had no interest in sharing. Nope. What the hell for? I wasn't writing a thesis on all the pussy I'd enjoyed, so everyone else could either do their own research or get their rocks off with porn. My lips were staying zipped. My need to not share was especially strong on the subject of Alison. The reasons still not clear as to why.

"Fine, asshole. Keep your mystery. Not like anything went down with us. With fucking Phil on the couch I'm going to be rocking blue balls for a while."

"He'll be gone soon, stop being a whiny bitch about it."

Joey was still moaning about their uninvited houseguest, with Max still defending his wayward brother. Angie and I wisely kept out of the conversation, the whole none-of-our-business being the reason for the silent treatment.

Last night had been different in more ways than one. Sure, I've had girls who have gotten back to my pad and suddenly decided they wanted to cuddle rather than fuck. Their nerve obviously getting lost between the bar and the bed, but with her it wasn't the loss of nerve that was the problem; it was like it would have been a genuinely bad decision.

Maybe I've been soaking up too many of Angie's pregnancy hormones—I took one of her prenatal vitamins by accident a few days ago—but as much as I wanted to get naked with Alison, I wanted her to just be okay more. She seemed like she needed a friend and I was more than happy to play that part, sadly my balls weren't on the same page and I had been rocking a hard-on from hell all night.

Which is why I decided to bail this morning before she woke up. Not my most gentlemanly moment—I'll agree, but a hell of a lot more polite than a big ass erection greeting her good morning. It was a compromise and one I'd hoped she'd understand. Or not.

Who knew if we'd even see each other again, numbers hadn't been exchanged with no talk of *catching up*, so maybe her and I were just a bump in the road. I wasn't entirely pleased at the prospect.

"Rus, you good? We're going to loop it over again." Angie's guitar rang out solo as my rhythm section looked on, my mental vacation catching everyone's attention.

"Uh-oh. Rusty's daydreaming. Can only mean bad things." Joey tapped restlessly on the snare. "Crazy girl must have been pret-ty impressive."

"Hey, we don't know she's crazy." Max grinned as he too weighed in. "Maybe she was foreign and her kissing Rus was her version of a handshake."

"Dude, he was totally gargling her tongue, that wasn't a fucking handshake." Joey bucked out a laugh. I could see this was going to be the source of their entertainment for a while.

"You guys done now? Last time I checked we had a song to lay down, or if you'd prefer we can forget that we have an album to release and get in touch with our inner Oprah. I'm cool either way."

It wasn't like me to get pissed-off—especially not over a girl, but last night hadn't been just about her. It was nice to talk. Most girls weren't interested past whether my dick or my mouth was going to get them off, and for a really long time I was cool with that. But, someone actually being interested in *me* felt kinda nice. I really need to check the label on those prenatals, see if they weren't some jacked-up estrogen supplement. Would explain a lot.

"Hey guys, let's take five. I need to pee anyway." Angie called time out on any further debate. Pulling me with her as we moved out of the booth, the we-need-to-talk look I assumed had nothing to do with her bladder.

"Listen, Ange, you know I love you, but I'm not helping you

pee. You've got a man who signed up for that now. Pretty sure he'd have something to say about it too." I followed her through the narrow corridor to the small courtyard outside.

"You know this isn't about me or my bathroom habits." She sat on an old plastic lawn chair, her eyes staying on me as I planted my ass on the one opposite.

"So, you just want to stare at me for a while. Okay, we can do that. I'll turn for you though, my left side is better."

"You are avoiding."

She was right, I was avoiding. Not because I didn't want to talk about Alison, but more because I really didn't have much to say. She was an awesome chick who unfortunately had drawn the short straw. And I wasn't a heartless bastard who was going to take advantage of that. Sure, I could have slept with her—she repeatedly told me it's what she wanted—but it felt like she needed other things from me instead. Things I was more than happy to give. So as far as discussing her, the topic was closed, even if my curiosity about her wasn't. I always did enjoy a puzzle, which is probably why my brain kept going to the brunette I'd left in my bed rather than the one sitting in front of me.

"Since when have you ever wanted to talk about the girls I bring home, I didn't realize you were so interested."

"I don't care who you bring home, but if something is going on with you, I'd hope you'd still talk to me." Angie reached over and grabbed my hand. "Your head isn't in the game and that's not like you. You've never dropped a note and in the last few hours, you've been playing like shit. And I want to know what is up with that. Just because things are different now doesn't mean I'm not here for you."

Life after the Power Station tour had taken us in different directions, I got that. She more than deserved her happy-ever-after with Jase and seeing her smiling was all I ever wanted for her. She was without a doubt the closest thing I had to family beside my folks, and I didn't need a constant reminder to know that.

"Babe, I would never think that. Look at me. Me and you—we are solid. I will always have your back and I know you aren't afraid to have mine. But your focus has to be on that human you are growing and the dude whose ring you're wearing. I'm all good. The back and forth with Joey and Max sometimes gets a bit old, I didn't get a lot of sleep last night. I'm just being an asshole. Don't mind me."

"You're just tired?" She eyed me suspiciously. I had no idea if she was buying it.

"Yep, I'm just tired."

Not a lie; while Alison passed out sometime in the early morning, I hadn't really gotten much sleep myself. Her rubbing up against me meant *parts* of me stayed awake. The parts that *were* tired not getting much of a choice.

"Well, why don't we wrap for the day. Nothing good is coming anyway and it will give me some time to rework the bridge. I'm not convinced it's sounding tight enough as it is." Thankfully it seemed she was letting it go.

"Yeah, you're probably right. Let's just do that chorus one last time and then we'll bail. Tomorrow's a new day."

•••

Fuck, I could really use a cigarette.

I'd been trying to quit for a few years, but I'd always given it a half-assed effort. Not that I didn't know all the shit it was potentially doing to my body, I just didn't really much care. That changed when Angie got in the family way and smoking around her was banished. I resisted for a while but then finally caved. She didn't lay the guilt on me or anything, but it highlighted my addiction to the Marlboros wasn't doing me any favors. This time round I was convinced I was going to kick it, even if every time I walked past a bar I still got the urge. Twenty-one days to break a habit, my ass. It had been two months, and I still missed it.

One thing that had come with the tossing of the smokes was the fucking constant urge to have something in my mouth. It was that bullshit that had me chowing down on Tootsie Pops like they were heroin. My local bodega supported my newest addiction while more frequent gym visits evened up the extra calories. Both kept me even and in check. Something I needed right now.

As Angie had suggested, we'd pulled the plug on the session and gone our separate ways. I'd headed home wondering if maybe Alison had stuck around, or if at the very least she'd left her number. Part of me was definitely hopeful.

Neither of those things had happened.

No note, no number and no girl—my house completely empty of any traces of her. Even the note I'd written was gone, my unmade bed the only reminder that I'd shared it with anyone. Irrationally, it made me antsy. Disappointed even, which didn't make sense; the need for a cigarette increasing with each passing minute.

Awesome.

And what do you know I was all out of Tootsie Pops. It just kept getting better and better.

God, I would kill for a cigarette. Just one more inhale. No one would even have to know. And I could just quit again tomorrow. What's the harm?

Ah, fuck. I was starting to sound like a junkie, and there was no way I was falling off the wagon. I was just going to have to push through, moody bastard my way through the rest of the day. Thankfully no else had to put up with my bullshit mood. There was a positive.

So rather than risk having a moment of weakness later, I grabbed my keys and my phone and decided to head out the door. Getting my candy stash back up to par was my first objective, and improving my frame of mind came second. Either way, I was done sitting around thinking about a girl I had no business thinking about. That shit was in the past and that's where I intended to leave it.

Things can always get worse. I knew this, my last few weeks had been an exercise in adding a new layer of misery to an already overflowing load—and yet, I was still freaking surprised.

My head hadn't even made a proper indent on my pillow, sleep not coming as I tossed and turned in my bed. The replay of the night's events was still turning in my head, and my eyes still wearing most of last night's make-up when the next bomb dropped. News of my change in employment status had reached my landlord. Specifically that my employment status had been revoked. How? It was still a mystery, although if I had to take a wild stab in the dark I would wager it was my ever-pessimistic neighbor, Joy. Her name was actually ironic because no joy lived in her. Nothing. She was devoid of happiness. Which is why I assume when she saw me crying outside my door carrying a cardboard box housing my prized stapler and coffee mug, she joined the dots. Ratted me out like a second grader vying for the teacher's affection. There was no loyalty among the sexes.

The knock at my door happened around ten a.m., the subsequent questioning happened soon after. My lease had expired last month and with the anticipation of Rob asking me to move in with him, I had yet to renew it. Dumb by all counts. So after informing me that technically I could be tossed out at the end of the month, the demand was made that I pay in advance the next *three* months rent if I wanted to renew my lease. Security and all that, surely I understood. His cheesy smile didn't comfort me nor did his offer that we try to work out *another* arrangement—the fine print being my ass could be used as an acceptable method of payment.

Seemed finding refuge in my apartment was also not in the cards. No—that also had to be taken from me. Instead, I had to focus on how to make some money quick—at this point I was willing to bend on legalities—or find a new place to live. Neither option filled me with excitement or hope. Didn't the universe get the memo that I'd had my share of crap? Obviously not.

It was around two in the afternoon when I'd hit bottom. I'm talking the lowest most desperate place. Darkness, despair, devastation. And they were just the D words. I was slowly working my way through the alphabet, wondering if anyone would actually notice if I was gone. Seriously, notice. I still had Renee's jacket hanging in my closet, so at the very least she'd need me for that. It was a flimsy excuse at best but one I held onto. My untimely death not looking like an option.

So rather than toy with the idea of building a meth lab in my bathroom and becoming a notorious drug lord—what? I got an A in chemistry—I got up off the floor and forced myself to shower. Look at me adulting, all without Renee's threats or a serving of Kung Pao chicken. Maybe I could actually do this. The *this* not thought out beyond getting clean and dressed. Let's not get too crazy now; my life was still in the toilet.

And with my clean, fresh and slightly less manic brain running the show, I'd decided if I was going down in a blaze of glory, it was going to be on my own terms. Thelma and Louise style. No one puts baby in the corner. Or if they did, she certainty didn't have to stay there. I really wished I'd paid more attention to pop culture movies; they seemed like they might have been helpful, or at least I'd get my references straight. Never mind. I was doing this. And I'd be damned if I didn't go down swinging.

•••

Finding a job should have been my first priority, or failing that, a new place to live. Two very good options. Instead, I went with option number three.

Leaving my apartment.

It wasn't going to solve anything, but neither was sitting around obsessing about the series of unfortunate events that was my life. I'd been there, done that, had the souvenir T-shirt annnnnnnnd I was still no better off. My method of *dealing* was clearly flawed. I needed a new plan.

That's what last night had been about. Oh, sure my delusions of freaky, unrestrained sex with Rusty were no longer in play—not that sleeping with him wouldn't have softened the blow. But my main objective now *wasn't* about getting horizontal. Insanity, I know.

It was living up to the list of awesome he had so generously helped me compile that was my main focus. Something that I had all but forgotten this morning when I left, the fragments of the conversation returning now my back was up against the wall. God, I wished I could be more like him. His carefree disposition and confidence would have been an asset. One I could have desperately used.

My pulse raced as I stepped out into the street, my destination not immediately clear but my common sense had sailed right out the window with each passing second.

It was Rusty who dominated my scattered thoughts; my brain auto-directing back to him whenever I was about to panic. The reasons why weren't immediately clear. Was it his calmness, his lack of give-a-fuck that I craved? Maybe it was that he was by far the nicest guy I'd ever met and I just wanted to get to know him better? Who knew? But other than waking up confused and slightly embarrassed, the night with him had been one of my most honest and comforting nights in . . . well in a long time. There was something about him, his energy, his . . . I was really trying hard not to think his cock because that wouldn't be helpful right now but I just knew there was something about him that I couldn't discount. It wasn't even entirely physical, and I just knew I had to see him again. Even if it made it worse, I was willing to take the risk.

My feet moved aimlessly without direction; the store windows I passed not providing anything more than fodder for my already churning mind. I didn't even have to look where I was going, able to navigate my neighborhood purely by memory. The eyes instead inadvertently darting across the street when I caught sight of Rusty slowly emerging from a tiny corner bodega.

My heart skipped a beat like it always did but this time it was more than just the view I was admiring. My insider knowledge added an additional reason for my heart to swoon. Whether or not it was a good idea to see him so soon was quickly tossed around in my head before my feet made the decision for me.

Without crossing a busy intersection into oncoming traffic, or screaming his name at the top of my lungs—both of which I considered—I got my legs moving quickly as I power walked to the crosswalk not far from where I'd been standing.

My hand pumped the button, willing the light to change as I watched him disappear into a drug store further down the road. Crap. *Please don't leave's* were mumbled under my breath as the light finally changed. With my heart in my throat, I sprinted across the street to the other side just in time to see him leave the drug store and wander further down the street. This time into a small bakery, the huge cupcake sign looming above the doorway he'd just walked through.

Without much thought—or common sense it seemed—I took off in a flat out run hoping to catch him before he disappeared again. The alternative of turning up at his house way too stalker-ish, even for me. My feet pounded the pavement as I bounded to where he was. Spoiler alert: I wasn't a runner.

"Hey, Alison." I'd barely jogged through the narrow open doorway when I almost smacked directly into his chest. Not that I would have complained. He had a very nice chest.

"Hey, Rusty." I tried to suck in a breath between words, my fitness clearly on hiatus up until now. "I need to talk to you."

Even I was surprised by my bold request. There was no actual asking of anything. Just a demand for his attention. Who the hell was I?

"I'd say fancy meeting you here but neither of us is surprised." A smile lit up his eyes, the same ones that showed a genuine lack of shock. And if I wasn't mistaken he actually looked glad to see me.

"Did you know . . . I was following you?" I tried to rein in my breathing as my pulse continued to hammer under my skin. Seriously, the treadmill and I were going to be spending some quality time together in the next few weeks. The run wasn't even that far.

"I saw you when I was leaving the bodega. I figured I'd play a little longer, I know how much you love to lurk." His arms folded casually across his chest as the lady behind the glass cake counter looked at us with interest. Yep, we had an audience.

"I was just looking for the right time. I didn't want it to be creepy." I tried unsuccessfully to sound un-creepy, the effort making it worse.

"Ah, babe, that's so sweet. You know I kinda dig creepy. Feeds into my god complex. So unless the shadow-jumping is done with a machete I'm totally cool with it." He motioned toward the door and with a nod of my head, I followed him back out onto the street. Bakery lady not impressed by our lack-of-purchase exit.

"Okay. I'm going to pretend like that statement wasn't just completely nuts, and you basically gave me carte blanche to stalk you." Because we both knew that could be dangerous. Look at what I'd done *without* his permission. Clearly I couldn't be trusted.

"I can put it in writing if you feel more comfortable. I am a man of my word." Another smile and now I was having trouble breathing for an entirely different reason.

"No, that's not necessary." I took a big swallow before continuing. "But I did need something from you."

Asking for help was a huge thing for me. When it came to throwing up a flare or giving someone the 9-1-1, I always chickened out. I figured it was better to slowly sink with my ship than ask anyone to bail me out. Pride, signs of weakness —whatever the reason was, I avoided it like a department store on Black Friday. Yet, there I was. My hand reaching out just hoping another would extend. Petrified wasn't even the half of it.

"Sure, what did you need?" He answered with zero hesitation.

"You're just going to offer, just like that? What if I said I needed a kidney?"

I'd expected my request for help to be met with some resistance or at the very least hesitation. Maybe even a healthy dose of skeptical reservation. What I got from the man in front of me was none of those things. Just an easy, *sure, what did you need.* Like no matter what I'd ask would be no big deal.

"Well, I'd hope if you were angling for body parts you'd at least come and see my band. Oh, and you'd have to wear one of our band shirts. Possibly with the words, *Rusty is the greatest guitarist of all time*, on the front. I figure that's a fair trade." He was no less amused than when we'd started the conversation. Oh, and somehow I'd secured the donation of one of his kidneys.

"You would give someone a kidney just like that?"

"If they needed it and they weren't an asshole. I draw the line at assholes. And people who listen to country music, because that shit ain't right."

I blinked back in confusion. "I don't need a kidney. Or listen to country music."

"You just keep saying all the right things. So, what's this big ask you hunted me down for?"

The street was only a mildly better venue than the bakery, the noise of the road peppering the air around us while we continued this bizarre conversation. The one where I admitted that maybe I didn't know what the hell I was doing.

"I need you to help me be more like you." The words found their way out of my mouth. It seemed even if my mind had no idea, somehow it had formulated the request.

"Alison, I haven't seen you naked, but I can assure you, you would make a terrible guy." He laughed. Not sure if he missed my point, or it was his attempt at humor.

"No, I don't want to be a guy." My head shook as I tried to clarify, realizing how scattered I sounded. "I mean, you. Look at you." My hands waved in front of him animatedly to prove my point. "Nothing fazes you. Before I met you, you said you were playing support to Power Station on a huge tour." I didn't need to hide my admiration. "Destined for greatness. The big time."

"Just because we haven't hit the big time doesn't mean we haven't achieved greatness. I'm here to tell you, greatness was definitely achieved."

"Okay, of course. I mean. Like you weren't a huge success." My stumbling words dug a deeper hole. I truly sucked at this.

"So, are we trying to make *you* feel better or *me* feel inadequate?" He eyed me intently. "Because if it's me, you've got your work cut out for you. I don't buy into that shit."

"Yes!" My hands clapped of their own accord. "That's exactly what I'm talking about. That's what I want. Teach me to be like that. Show me the ways, oh wise one, so I too won't give a shit."

My sudden burst of enthusiasm caught him off guard. It was the first and only time I'd seen him actually surprised.

"You want me to teach you how to not give a shit?"

"Yes . . . Please . . . Yes." Manners were important, especially now.

"Ordinarily I'd say that the responsibility of teaching anybody anything that isn't musical would be a big mistake." His hand rubbed the back of his neck; he was close to agreeing, I could feel it.

"But—" I encouraged him to continue.

"But, given your impassioned plea, I am finding it very hard to say no. Plus, I've always wanted to Mr. Miyagi someone. Sure. Yes. I'll do it."

And just like that, he agreed. I had to fight the urge not to leap into his arms and kiss him. That would have been bad. Especially considering we were embarking on this new relationship which didn't include touching. I was assuming it didn't; it had yet to be discussed.

"Great. I'm so excited. When do we start?"

"We can start tomorrow. You can wax my car."

Wax his car? I wanted inspiration, not manual labor. Even if I did *want* to do it, I could barely wash dishes, detailing a car was . . . no. Just. No.

"Rusty, I am not waxing your car." *Your chest however is another matter. I'd be down for that.*

"This might be a problem then. You have to do whatever I say. That is the deal." His brow furrowed. Oh, wow. He was serious.

"How is waxing your car going to make me not give a shit?" More to the point, why did he want me to do it? Unless waxing his car was code for something else.

"Have you not watched *The Karate Kid* at all?" His eyes widened, throwing out his arms in disbelief. He waited until I shook my head no before continuing. "You are in bigger trouble than I thought. Okay, new plan. You're coming over tonight and we're watching it."

Yes. That's what I had wanted to say but sadly I wasn't going to be able. I had plans tonight. Important ones. Boxes. Packing tape. Sharpies. All of which would be sharing my evening along with the big bottle of wine I'd been saving for a special occasion. The special occasion being that I wasn't living out of a cardboard box just yet.

"Oh, that sounds awesome but I can't tonight. I need to pack." I didn't have to fake the disappointment. That part was real.

"Pack for what? You can't take off on a trip when you are about to start your training."

Explaining my predicament further did not fill me with excitement. The opposite actually. But I wasn't going to lie either. It's not like my over sharing last night hadn't been mortifying enough, no point holding on to something as silly as pride now. Look at me trying new things. It was a revolution.

"Not me, I need to pack my apartment. I'm getting evicted.

Or at least I will be at the end of the month. No point prolonging the inevitable." Or hoping for the miracle that wouldn't be happening.

"So where are you going to live?" The smile he'd been wearing slipped from his face.

"Errr. I can move in with my friend Renee or something." I was almost positive I wouldn't end up on the street. Okay, so maybe not positive but mostly sure. Let's make that probably sure. "It's not going to be a problem. I'll be safely on cloud no-shits-given by then."

"You really *are* in trouble."

He had that look. The one that told me he was feeling sorry for me, the one that I didn't want to see. Not from him.

"No, no pity, remember? I'm not here for that." I waved my hands in front of his face, trying to get back to the happy place.

"Fine, no pity." He sunk his hands into his pockets. "Pack up your shit. How much stuff do you have?"

"Huh?"

Confusion had set in. Why was he asking me how much stuff I had? Was he taking a survey? Now wasn't really the time, I was probably going to be downgrading anyway. That waffle maker I had purchased five years ago that was still in the box probably wasn't going to make the cut.

"Is it just personal belongings or furniture and stuff? Like do we need a U-Haul or can we throw it in the back of my car?"

"Huh?" I repeated again, the words not making any more sense now as he tried to clarify.

"Your *shit*." He annunciated slowly, probably because I was still doing the deer-in-headlights thing. "My house is pretty decked out so if you have furniture we'll have to store it in my basement. Other stuff can just go in your room."

"Rusty, what are you talking about?"

The words *your room* had not escaped me. Nor had the offer to store my things in his basement. It sounded like . . . was he suggesting? . . . no, surely he wasn't asking . . .

"Stick with me, Ali. Try and keep up. Can I call you Ali? I figured we're on nickname basis considering we're about to become roommates."

"Roommates?" I asked barely able to get the word out it sounded so insane. "Are you suggesting? . . . Do you mean? . . . Are you asking me . . . to come live with you?"

Saying it was stating the obvious was an understatement. Offers of storing things, the mention of *my room*, it was all very neatly pointing to that conclusion. The sense it made was zero. No sense at all. As in we'd now taken insanity to a whole new level.

"See, I knew you'd get there in the end." He beamed with pride.

Rusty had seemed perfect. I know I threw around that word a lot but it was the only one that did him justice. Perfect body, perfect face, perfect personality. He was an all-winning combo that would render almost any girl stupid—certainly this one. What I had overlooked was that no one is actually perfect, there has to be a catch. Some defective flaw to confirm they were a member of the human race and not some genetically-advanced alien. And I had at last found the glitch in the Matrix. Rusty—last name unknown—was certifiable.

"I can't come live with you."

I waited patiently for the men in white coats to arrive.

Any second now.

At least they wouldn't be after me this time. Always a plus.

"Well, now you're just being hurtful. First knocking my rise in rock stardom and now turning down my offer of roomies. I know how to put the toilet seat down if that's what you're worried about." Yep, so C.R.A.Z.Y. Beyoncé was going to be singing his theme song.

"Rusty, as generous as that offer is, I can't come live with you. That would be too much. I mean, we barely know each other." That was just for starters. Three weeks ago he had been my illicit fantasy. Then he'd been my failed one-night stand I'd told more of my life story to than my best friend. Now he was offering for us to share a house? If Captain Kirk lost his warp speed for the Enterprise, I'm pretty sure I knew where it was. No one could be that insane, surely. My mind was completely scrambled, any logical thought why he would offer me something so huge couldn't even formulate. BAM. Insta-roomies, who does that? And Why?

Putting aside we were practically strangers, there was also the issue of rent. Or more to the point, my inability to *pay* rent. That pesky little thing called no income hadn't resolved itself.

"You were going to ask me for a kidney, after that I'd say a room isn't that big a deal."

"I wasn't asking for a kidney. I—"

I. That's right—me—was now wordless. I didn't even know how to begin to respond to that.

"Can we argue about this back at my place? Standing on the street is getting kind of old. Loitering is still a crime you know."

I wanted to laugh. The situation so tragically hilarious that laughter would have definitely been acceptable but I didn't because this wasn't a sitcom, it was actually my life. Crazy, unbelievable and improbable—that pretty much summed it up. Which is why I didn't say anything, standing there silent, looking like an idiot. Because that was helpful.

"I get why you're hesitant, we don't know each other but if anyone should be worried it's me, right? You've already admitted to following me, I mean you could be an axe murderer?"

"I'm not an axe murderer." At least I had that going for me.

"All positive things. No reason to hold back then."

One thing I had been good at in school was debating, which is why law seemed like a natural progression. It hadn't been a passion so much as just a talent. The research, justifying the argument—all things I excelled at. Yet with Rusty all that reason I could usually pull together and build a case was lost. He defied logic—his own and mine.

"Assuming I did move in. How would it even work? I'm not after charity." I risked joining him when the men in white coats finally arrived.

"And I'm not in the habit of giving it. You come, you stay, we train like ninjas and get you back on your feet. It makes my job easier, less commuting," he announced matter-of-factly, like it was a done deal.

"I would need to pay rent." My head nodded in assurance.

"Sure, you do. When you get a job. Until then I'll take an I-owe-you. You do whatever you want in your free time. I'll get you a spare key cut and you come and go as you please."

It hadn't escaped my attention that while he was offering very generously to house me and *Mr. Miyagi* me, the sleeping together ship had well and truly sailed. He said it himself; we were going to be roommates. He was inviting me into his house not into his bed. Which could only mean that there would be other girls who would get that privilege. And I was going to be okay with that. Completely. It's not like I had any feelings for him other than physical attraction. That would pass I'm sure. Of course it would. It was going to be completely and utterly cool. Roommates that didn't have sex. Awesome.

"I'm going to pay you back every cent and I'm going to be totally cool if you bring someone home. I don't expect you to change your life for me." I felt the need to prove how cool I was by articulating my stupid thoughts about sex. *Sure, he's not going to think it's weird that you chose to bring that up now.* In the middle of the street. Completely unprompted.

"Sounds to me like we have a deal. You need help boxing stuff? These hands aren't just awesome on guitar; I can handle a box better than UPS." He lifted his hands to demonstrate.

As far as strange days, this one was currently proudly wearing the first-place ribbon. What had started out as hopeless had completely flipped to promising, with a new friend and a new address. And just like that the problem of where I was going to be spending my nights was solved. I was moving in with Rusty I-still-didn't-know-his-last-name. Or as I liked to call him, the hot guy.

Rusty

I'd done a lot of random shit in my time, but asking a girl to move in with me on a whim was up there on my top ten. I didn't regret it though; the words that had come out of my mouth were exactly the ones I had meant to say. Her moving in made all kinds of sense. I had a room and she needed one; it was a simple problem that required a simple solution.

I knew the offer was probably cementing me firmly in friend-zone. The abyss where nice guys were tossed while an asshole came and fucked the girl they wanted. Her comment about being cool with me having other girls over was evident of that. It wasn't an accident that it wasn't a sentiment or statement I reciprocated. Not that she would have to worry about me bringing girls home, pretty sure my dick had lost interest in anyone who wasn't her. The poor bastard not getting the memo it probably wasn't happening.

Of course, I also wasn't a sleazy fucking perv. Able to realize the girl was down on her luck and needed me more as a friend than she needed my penis. Which is why, even though I still wanted her like crazy, I'd made my peace with it. My dick, however, was still in mourning.

Part of me didn't think she would agree. I mean, brought down to its lowest common denominator, it's fucking nuts. And yet here we were sitting in her old apartment boxing up shit and getting it ready to move into mine.

"No, you can't put those in that box. Those go in the kitchen box; you have the bathroom box." She grabbed the roll of paper towels I'd just packed and pulled them out. "It goes in this one." She lowered them into a box that looked identical to the one I had in my hands.

"But isn't it all going to the same place? Bathroom, kitchen—it's just transportation and will all get unpacked, so who cares what box it goes in?" We were moving her paper towels exactly two blocks from where they were sitting now. It's not like we were shipping those bad boys across state lines, the segregation was a little excessive in my opinion.

"You can't just go throwing random things in random boxes." Her head shook in a panic. "No, order must be maintained."

"Wow, you are so anal, do we really need to label everything too?" The packing tape zipping across the now full *kitchen* box as I sealed it closed. Her precious paper towels safe from the riff raff like me.

"Yes, everything needs to be labeled. How will I find anything if it isn't labeled?" More shock, with some disbelief thrown in for good measure.

"We are opening the boxes when we get to my place; it's not hard to open a box and see what's in it." The logic of her process still making no fucking sense.

This shit would go a hell of a lot quicker if we threw everything into boxes and drove the couple of miles to my front door. Instead, we were painstakingly fucking sorting and cataloguing her shit like it was a billion-year-old skeleton of a Tyrannosaurus Rex.

"I just can't work like that." She pulled out more shit I'd apparently mispacked and sorted it into its correct receptacle. "It's just easier my way; please just do it my way."

While the situation at hand seemed absolutely ridiculous, she looked like she was about to pass out from the stress. My help seeming to be more trouble than it was worth.

"You look like you are going to have a panic attack." The box at my feet forgotten as I watched her trying to not hyper-ventilate over my relaxed method of moving.

"No I just need a minute, this is a lot." She sat on the floor and put her head down between her knees for a bit. The deep breaths she was sucking in not convincing me all she needed was a minute.

"Hey, don't freak out on me just yet, we haven't even got to the closet yet. Wait until you see how I'm going to box up your shoes. Can you say scavenger hunt?"

"Great, now I *am* going to have a panic attack." The breaths she was dragging in and out of her lungs getting a little quicker. My attempt at a joke completely missing its mark.

"Maybe give the packing a rest for a bit and just talk to me." I gave up on the packing tape and Sharpie and dropped to my haunches beside her. "Let's just talk through it."

"I'm sorry, I'm just not used to this." She shot me a look of apology. "No one is usually around to help. It's been just me for a long time, so you trying to do things your way is unsettling."

We'd already gone through the rundown. No brothers or sisters, parents who were no more than genetic donors, and elder grandparents who did their best but for the most part weren't around by the time she hit college. All of that added up to the girl doing shit solo; that made sense. But I also knew there had been a dude in the picture, the same waste of space who after dating her for two years decided *they had run their course* or whatever BS he fed her and turned around a put a ring on some other broad's hand. See, photographic memory. None of that shit got past me.

"Didn't you say you had a boyfriend? Didn't he help you?" I dug a little deeper, trying to work out if this was the sort of shit that went down if say . . . someone put a spoon in the wrong section of the dishwasher caddy.

"How do you mean?" She looked at me with genuine confusion, the what-the-fuck ringing loudly in my ears.

"Ok-ay, so you're with a guy for awhile and he's hanging out with you." I tried to be diplomatic as we ventured on our path of discovery. "So maybe you're doing laundry together or maybe you're restocking your refrigerator, or . . . I don't know . . . maybe you're packing a bag to go on a trip somewhere. Did he not get involved in that stuff?"

"Well, no. Not really." She shrugged like it was no big deal. "He'd come over and hang, but he wouldn't stay over. I understood, considering all his stuff was at his apartment, it made sense for him to go home. And we couldn't really go on trips since no one knew we were together."

There was a reason why I hadn't asked for the douchebag's last name and address; the main one being that I was ninety-nine percent positive I would put my boot in his ass and tell him what a sadistic piece of shit he really was. I wasn't usually a violent kind of guy, that chest-thumping macho shit was just an asshole's way of extreme posturing. I didn't have the time for that, but Jesus Christ, this asshole was making me rethink my stance.

"It's not as bad as it sounds, he was just really conservative and I was fine with being alone," she added, needing to fill my silence.

"Yeah, I can see why this is difficult for you." My common sense told me to rein it in. Her ex-boyfriend and their fucked up relationship was none of my business. I also reminded myself that I wouldn't do well in jail, a place I'd find myself if me and this loser ever came face to face.

"You hungry?" She wisely changed the subject. Her hands brushing off her ass as she stood up from the floor; her panic attack no longer in a holding pattern.

"Sounds good. Do you want to go out to eat?"

Me being pissed-off wasn't productive and the smell of cardboard was making me dizzy, so the suggestion of ejecting was a good one. Besides, there was jack to eat at her place and I was starved.

"But if we go out who is going to pack all the boxes?" She looked around at her mostly empty apartment, her concern not justified.

"These boxes aren't going to grow legs and suddenly run into the streets screaming. And you've labeled them so efficiently they're bound to find their way right back if by some miracle they *do* decide to wander. I'm sure they can survive an hour while we go get something to eat."

Two things.

We were going out to eat and it was going to be both delicious and fucking enjoyable, and we were going to have to work on her not being so damn uptight. Hopefully, with some conversation that would be achieved over dinner.

"Fine, we'll go out to eat. But I'm buying." She grabbed her purse as I rose to my feet and joined her at the door.

"Sure, whatever you want." I tried not to laugh as I opened the door. She was not paying. No way in hell that was going down, but if the only way to get her out the door was to let her believe she was covering the check, whatever.

•••

"Batman or Superman? Who do you choose?" She slowly sucked on her soda while we waited for our burgers and fries. Being that she was paying for dinner—not fucking likely—I got the choice of venue, The Juke Joint getting my vote.

"Well that's easy, Superman." I tossed back my answer without even thinking. The classic debate not even a question in my eyes. "Batman has no actual super powers, all he has is a sweet-ass ride and some accessories. He's basically a Barbie."

Alison almost choked on her soda as she weighed my point of view. "How can you say that?" Her laugh not only got my attention but that of the older couple sitting beside us. It was a really nice sound. "He fought crime, he saved lives. He's a superhero." She tried to pursue her argument, her reasoning clearly flawed.

"Ali, if you're going to pick a dude who has a fancy closet, go with Iron Man. Tony Stark. Boom, zero fucks given about the secret identity and he built the freaking suit himself. Batman was a pussy." My latest rebuttal earning me more giggles, her smile lighting up her whole face. And didn't that make me feel like the superhero we were discussing. Seeing that grin and knowing I had something to do with it. Fuck. I'd pretty much do anything to keep that smile firmly in place, outrunning speeding trains totally on the table.

"Strong opinions, good to know." She nodded as the waitress slid her chicken sandwich in front of her before hooking me up with my cheeseburger.

The game of twenty questions had started innocently enough. Like speed dating for a roommate, I thought we should cover the basics to try and alleviate any future concerns. Besides, those questions had melted away any freak out she'd been working up at the apartment with the chick in front of me relaxed and laughing. A far cry from where she'd been an hour ago. The game also had the added advantage of giving me some more insight into the girl I couldn't quite work out.

"My turn." I picked up a fry and popped it into my mouth. "Pancakes or waffles?"

"That's tough." She scrunched up her nose as she gave my question some serious thought. "I sort of love both."

"No fence sitting, Alison. You need to pick a team. Go."

"Waffles." She answered under pressure. Her face not looking entirely convinced.

"Seriously? How can you improve on a pancake? It's light, it's fluffy, so basically you are eating a cloud. A fucking cloud. And you can flavor it however you want." I feigned my disgust. "You and I can't be friends anymore."

"A waffle can be flavored." She threw her hands up in

disbelief. "And it's international. Belgian waffles."

"Hello, International House of Pancakes? Your argument is bogus." No waffle would ever beat a pancake. It just couldn't be done.

"Calling my argument bogus doesn't win the argument but whatever, it's my turn." She conceded, not willing to pursue it further. Probably given she knew I was right. "OOOoooohhhhh I have a good one." Her face beamed with excitement. "Thong or panties."

"On me? Or on a woman? Because you need to clarify if we are talking hypotheticals or probabilities."

"You would consider wearing women's underwear?" She lowered her voice as she moved her head closer.

The direction of the questions had taken a welcome and interesting turn. Certainly not one I had thought it would take, not unless I was the one who was throwing it out there. While our banter had been fun, it had been kept strictly PG-13. And up until this point I'd been a complete gentleman. Her cheeks pinked as I drew out my answer, me—enjoying every single minute of it.

"That's not what I said." I leaned back against the booth, not concerned about lowering my voice. "If we were to assume I was hypothetically female, and which would I prefer to wear there would be a choice. If we were talking about the probability of me preferring either on a woman, then that would be another choice. As for me wearing either as a man, then choice would be none of the above. See? Too many holes, counselor. Requesting a side bar."

"Okay, let me clarify, your honor." She grinned giving up on the dinner she had in front of her in favor of our conversation.

"On a woman, not you—"

"Thank you." I nodded, approving of her amendment.

"—which do you prefer? Panties or a thong?" She cocked her eyebrow as she waited for my response.

"Yes." The answer flew out of my mouth with very little thought, my concern being on which of those two options she was currently wearing and whether or not I would get a chance to find out.

"*Yes* is not an answer, Rusty." She drummed her fingers on the table top, her earlier embarrassment completely forgotten. "I wasn't allowed to fence sit on breakfast food, you can't on this." Her confidence made her even more attractive if that were even possible, ditching the awe shucks routine in favor of grilling me further.

"You want an answer?"

"Yes, I do." She met my eyes without flinching.

"Panties, thong, bare—It's all in the way it's worn." I let the words settle before I went on. "Damn, you could put a girl in granny panties, but if she is working it right, then it's the sexiest thing I've seen. So it's more to do with who is wearing them rather than what they are."

I watched a slow breath blow out from her lips. "Well, that . . . that seems fair." The confidence she'd had a minute ago finding resistance like that long steady exhalation.

"My turn." No way was I giving her a reprieve. "Top or bottom?" An elaboration not needed.

It might have been inappropriate. There we were having a nice dinner, enjoying friendly harmless conversation, and it had disintegrated to talk of underwear and sex. I hadn't started its decline, just merely keeping up. And I was enjoying the hell of it. Pushing her buttons. It was fucking riveting, waiting to see if she'd duck and weave or if she'd meet me head on. I knew which one I wanted and to my absolute delight she didn't let me down.

"Well, Rusty." She cleared her throat before giving me her full attention; her eyes on me giving me a wicked thrill. "In this instance, it's *your* question that is flawed. Are you talking hypothetical's or probabilities?" Her lips twitched at the edges as I enjoyed the show.

Well. Fuck. Me.

"Can I get you anything else?" The waitress, who placed our plates in front of us maybe ten minutes before, interrupted. Her timing, fucking terrible.

"No, we're good." I tried to wave her off, the show of we're-all-good wasted when she didn't leave.

"You want a refill on your drink, honey?" She nodded toward Alison's almost empty glass, clueless as to how much my balls hated her right now.

"Yeah, sure." Alison glanced between the glass and the waitress, the interruption definitely throwing her off.

"I'll be right back." She grabbed the glass off the table, oblivious that had she left shit alone, she probably would have earned that bigger tip she was trying to secure.

With the waitress leaving, so did the happy vibe we had going on, an awkward silence taking its place.

"I'm just going to run to the bathroom." Alison slid out of the booth, clearly needing the time out. *Run* being the operative word. Great. Seriously fucking perfect.

Whatever easy flow we'd had going on left when she'd walked away from the table, and as much as I wanted to dig a little deeper, it wasn't going to happen tonight. If at all. My dick wondered if I'd locked us into a sad situation of endless flirting, while my head told me it was the right thing to do by letting it go.

While Alison was busy in the bathroom, I'd used the time constructively and settled the check. Oh, sure talk had been thrown around about picking up the tab, but she had a better chance of her shit ending up in mismatched, unlabeled boxes than she had of paying for dinner. All of which translated into a whole bunch of never-gonna-happen.

"Sorry." Her constant need to apologize never too far away as she slipped back into her seat. "I'm starving." Her dinner gained the attention she'd previously given me.

"Yeah, me too."

Just not for what was on my plate.

Nine
Rusty

"You are just letting some girl move in with you. Are you insane?"

"Only in the morning." I laughed.

Angie was in fine form today. She'd been pacing in my living room for the last ten minutes, more than a fair share of fucks flying around. It was just like old times.

The chick who'd been my closest friend since tenth grade rarely worried about me and the ladies. Jealousy wasn't her thing, at least not with me. Then again, we'd never been romantically involved, preferring to be the kind of friends who didn't swallow each other's bodily fluids. It just worked. So when she'd stopped by this morning wanting to work on some material before we hit the studio, I had no hesitation sharing the news of my soon-to-be living arrangement. She hadn't shared my enthusiasm.

"Rusty, this isn't a joke. What do you know about this girl?" The twenty questions started.

"Oh, look. You're concerned. That maternal instinct has

kicked in and you haven't even had the baby. I'm so freaking impressed."

As I said, jealously wasn't an issue, if we were going to bump uglies we would have done so by now, but seeing her so wound up was kind of touching.

"Of course I am concerned." She paced some more, her hands just as restless as her feet as she waved them around. "The boys see you hook up with a crazy girl at a bar and then you're shacking up with her. It wasn't so long ago that you were pulling me away from situations like that."

Ordinarily I wouldn't have explained. My need to elaborate nonexistent. But with Angie, I didn't mind. Shit was tight between us and keeping stuff from her wasn't on my agenda.

"I'm not shacking up with her. We haven't even fucked. We're not together like that."

My initial intentions were definitely to fuck her. Every time I saw her, my dick got hard. And as far as looks went, she had it going on. Long brown hair, hazel eyes and legs for fucking days, what's not to like. The awkward crap just made her more endearing, like she wasn't used to the attention. The possibility she wasn't all that experienced kind of excited me. Like climbing Everest, she was begging to be explored. Granted it was a departure from my usual flavor—the girls I usually went home with knew their way around a dick—but she intrigued the hell out of me. And that didn't happen often. Not something to be ignored.

Although chances were the *fucking* was now off the table, it didn't mean that I still wasn't curious on what made her tick. The fact she wanted my help just made it easier. Not that I would ever be a scumbag and use that shit to get her into the sack. I instantly liked her and the more time I spent with her the more I wanted to her be around, so if we just ended up friends who didn't fuck, that would probably be okay too.

"What if she's a psychopath and kills you in your sleep?" Angie was once again dragging up worst-case scenarios.

"At least I wouldn't feel anything, there are worse ways to go." I laughed.

We'd already established Alison wasn't an axe murderer, and she looked like the type of person who would apologize for killing a fly, so I was fairly confident I wasn't going to be rocking a tombstone any time soon.

"Rus, this isn't funny." Angie obviously didn't see the humor or share the sentiment. Marriage had clearly made her boring.

"Sure it is. Do you hear yourself right now? *Oh, what if she kills you in your sleep.* Where's the girl who would walk the streets of NYC with a loaded Glock in her purse? Balls to the wall, no fear?"

"I have more to lose now, and so do you. You're going to be an uncle, damnit. I need you."

"And I'm going nowhere." I threw my arms around her and pulled her into a hug. "Anytime you need me, I'm going to be right here, babe."

It was around that time when I had my arms around Angie that Alison came stumbling through the door. Her arms stacked with as many boxes as she could carry.

"Oh, hey. Sorry, I just wanted to drop the last of this stuff off." Her eyes widened as she looked from Angie to me. Assumptions clearly made.

"That's cool, Ali. This is a good time actually 'cause I can introduce you to Angie. She's the singer in the band but more importantly, my best friend."

"Hi, Ali." Angie moved from my side and held out her hand. Whatever she thought she was doing, she was failing miserably. Her voice was devoid of warmth.

"Hi," Alison blinked, lifting the box higher—her excuse for not reciprocating the greeting. The handshake wasn't happening. Great. This was going to be fun.

Silence.

And wasn't this fucking heartwarming, the two of them eyeing each other like they were about to step into a ring. Just all kinds of loved-up feelings radiated from both of them as the temperature in the room dropped below zero. Awesome.

"Well, I'm going to go. See you at the studio, Rus." Angie gave me a hug followed by one of her death stares before moving to the door. Not sure if it was for mine or Alison's benefit, the conversation and her objection, far from over.

"She seems nice." Alison waited until the door had slammed before giving a half-assed smile, walking past me to get to her room. Her feelings for Angie, pretty evident.

"You are a really bad liar. And for the record, Angie and I aren't together. She's a friend—we're tight, but she is also pregnant and married to someone else." The need to set it straight was pretty high, not because I owed her anything but because I didn't want it to turn into an epic misunderstanding. The kind that promotes ideas about me being an asshole who knocks up a woman and then invites another to share his house.

"You don't have to explain stuff to me, remember? Just roommates." The fake smile got a little bit crazier. She wasn't even halfway convincing, her face telling me that she wasn't feeling the *all-good* she was trying to convey.

"It's okay if she pissed you off. She can be abrasive sometimes." And that was putting it mildly, but saying Angie could be a bitch behind her back wasn't productive and not conducive to the conversation either.

"What? Angie? No. I don't even know her. She was fine." She scoffed like I was talking out of my ass. Her hands hugged the box still locked in her mitts.

Fine. That was bullshit if ever I'd heard it. And I'd heard some shit in my time, so I would know. Alison, fine. Yeah, I didn't think so.

If I didn't know better I might have thought it was jealously, but I unfortunately *did* know better. Her chill directed at Angie's resting bitch face, not a pissing contest over me.

"Put the boxes down, Alison. I think we should start your training right now. Yeah, actually this is a good opportunity."

If we were ever going to get past the charade she seemed to play, we needed to start it now. She was so tightly wound I wasn't sure she wasn't going to levitate off the floor and bounce off the walls. That was going to have to go.

"Rusty, I've got to get these things put away. I'm fine—" She shoved past me as she made a move for her room, the path cut off by yours truly. She wasn't getting out of it that easily.

"You agreed, remember? Whatever I said, you would do. So put the boxes down." Her resistance eased on her prized cubes of cardboard so that I was able to pull them from her hands. The floor, their next destination.

"Okay." Her arms limbered up in front of her. "What is it you want me to do? Sand the floor? Or paint the house?"

"Sarcasm, I like it." Was a hell of a lot better than the

passive shit she had going on. "But, no. I've got something else in mind."

Alison had a chip on her shoulder. I knew her for all of five minutes and I could see it. Whether she wanted to admit it or not, it was there—hanging out, making shit harder than it had to be. That had to stop. Immediately.

"Then what is it?" she asked impatiently, the foot tapping thrown in for good measure.

"You have this whole holding back thing happening and it needs to stop. You're so tightly wound, one of these days you're going to snap. If you are truly going to not give a shit, you actually have to *not give a shit.*"

There wasn't a doubt she had it in her. I'd seen a glimpse of it when she came into the bar and made out with me and then again in the street when she'd asked for help. Of course last night it had shone through as well, right before she clammed up again. Underneath the restraint was the real her trying to get out, the one who would be kicking ass and taking names. The Alison she deserved to be.

"Is this about Angie?" She wrongly assumed, her hands on her hips as she waited for my instruction. "Because I told you it was fine."

"If you're going to lie at least make it convincing. But no it's not about Angie. You were pissed-off just now and what did you do? Pretend that you weren't. If you're pissed-off, get pissed-off." I moved closer getting toe to toe, needing to be right there with her.

She took a step back, putting some distance between us. "I thought the idea was for me not to give a shit, not get upset over trivial stuff."

"Here's the thing. And it's a radical idea so you're going to have to trust me on this. But, in order to not give a shit you have to accept your feelings as they are. Meaning if you want to get angry then get angry. Then it's done. No more holding onto it. What you're doing—shoving it down—is not doing you or anyone else any good."

"So what, you're a psychologist now? Your advice sounds questionable at best. Get upset to free yourself? How would that even work?"

There was no reason for me to be involved in any of this. Asking her to come live with me, agreeing to help her be more like me—whatever that meant—made zero fucking sense. This whole situation was an exercise in what-the-fuck. And I wasn't the type of guy who liked a project, so the fact that I was doing this was baffling. Yet, here I was. Fucking compelled.

"Let me ask you something. When your boyfriend dumped you and then fired you, what did you do?" I was fairly sure I knew the answer. Her kicking his ass was probably not what went down.

"What do you mean, what did I do?" She looked at me indignant. "I left. I wasn't going to beg."

Well halleluiah for that.

"You didn't even suggest that maybe there were *two* of you involved and you shouldn't be losing your job because he couldn't keep his dick in his pants?"

The guy clearly had no sack. Letting her take the fall, and then dropping her like a bad habit. How he slept at night was beyond me.

"He is a lawyer, I'm a paralegal. They wouldn't have fired him."

I couldn't believe she was defending him, that she didn't see he'd used her. Treated her like shit and then left as soon as he was bored.

"Says who? You broke your contract; I'm sure he broke his too. You're a smart girl, why didn't you take it to someone above him?"

"Because I didn't want to make a scene. It probably wouldn't have changed anything anyway." Her voice got a little more edgy.

"Make a fucking scene, damn it. That's what not giving a shit is. It's about you not caring what other people think of you and doing what you need to do. For you."

The vibe had started to get heated. My needling her, trying to get a reaction was exactly the plan. It wasn't just about the dumbass who had his fingerprints all over this mess, it was about her seeing that she could stand up for herself. That the world wouldn't fall apart if she suddenly made a fucking fuss.

The back and fro escalated. Not that I assumed that it wouldn't. Her claiming it wouldn't have achieved anything just made me beg to differ. Of course I was going to need to pull out some big guns given I was pushing the hell out of her buttons and she still wasn't yelling in my face like I assumed she would. Which is why I pushed a little further. Explosion pretty much guaranteed.

"Okay, Alison, we'll just agree you're a fucking doormat and call it a day shall we. I mean it's cool, just as long as you can admit it. "

Something inside her snapped. Whatever trigger I'd hit, there was no turning back. Regardless of the fallout, I was seeing this baby all the way through to detonation.

"I'm not a fucking doormat," she barely spat out through clenched teeth.

"I don't know, kind of feels like you are." I shrugged, my indifference pushing her a little further.

"I. Am. Not." It was the first time she yelled, her fists curled up by her side so tightly her knuckles were white.

"You angry?" I moved closer to her, my body towering over hers. She didn't move.

"Yes, I am." Her face red with freaking fury. Her tightly balled fists glued to her side as her back jacked her straight. Her shoulders squared off as she met my *eyeball* and matched it.

"Good, so get angry." I brought my face in closer. If we weren't in the middle of a heated discussion, I would have bent down and kissed her.

"I *am* angry," she bit back, the fire burning in her eyes. Her body a contradiction as it fought to stay in place, her fight for control evident as her arms twitched by her sides.

"No, I mean really angry. Get that shit off the leash and let go."

I wanted her angry; I wanted her furious because she deserved better. I wanted her to see she could fly off the handle. That she had a right to do that. Which is when I came up with another of my bright ideas. "I know, punch me."

"What?" She pulled back in horror. "I can't punch you."

"Why, because you're a girl? Save us both the time, girls can punch too." My arms opened wide giving her access to my body, in case she thought it was some bullshit bluff.

"You're crazy. I'm not punching you." She pushed me back, my offer obviously not being taken seriously.

"One punch, Ali. It will make you feel better and I can take the hit. Get it out. C'mon. Let go." It was going to take a lot more than a fucking shove to end this.

"No. I don't want to do this. The whole idea is dumb. I'm not a freaking Neanderthal." Another shove, this time a little harder. Still not what I was looking for.

"I said, punch me. Do it." My hand grabbed hers, forcing her to thump my chest. To my disappointment it wasn't anything more than a tap.

"Let me go, you're being stupid." She pushed me away, trying to fake to the right before going left. Not quick enough though, as my body got between her and the path to her bedroom. Our conversation and the exercise far from over.

I'm not sure why this shit was so important to me. Common sense should have kicked in by now, i.e. it wasn't going to happen. But something inside me wouldn't let it go. And I rarely disagreed with my gut. Which is why I went to the one place I knew would get her swinging like a champ.

"Well, I guess I can see why your boyfriend left you."

She stopped dead in her tracks, her urge to push me away or slip past me suddenly disappearing as her feet stayed glued to the floor. "What's that supposed to mean?" Her eyes on me as they tried to make sense of what I was saying.

It killed me to take it there; to know what kind of ass I was being in saying those words. The ones I knew would hurt her but also set her free. The inevitable hurt minor compared to the relief she would get if she just fucking let go.

Time to go all in.

"Means if you fuck like you fight, he might as well be doing it solo."

There was no lead up. No slow-mo fist flying toward me, no opened-handed slap bouncing across my jaw. All of which would have been acceptable. It was, after all, what I'd been begging her to do. What I hadn't planned on, and therefore prepared myself for, was the punch right to my fucking balls.

BOOM, right to my nuts.

I dropped like a sack of shit.

My body got cozy with the floor as I rolled into a fetal position trying to breathe, my effort coming up short. Every muscle tensed as it tried to absorb the unimaginable pain ripping through me. The urge to puke so freaking strong I wasn't sure I was going to keep it down. I couldn't move, the blood roaring in my ears. Lights out would have been welcomed, but instead of going nite-nite, my brain and lungs checked out instead. The paralyzed meat bag that was my body, unable to do much more than cough out *fuck* a few times as I laid on the floor.

"Oh my God, I'm sorry, I didn't mean it." Alison dropped to her knees beside me. At least I think it was her; it could have been the Virgin Mary coming to take what was left of my stones, but I wasn't opening my eyes to check. "I'm sorry."

It would have been good at this time to let her know it was okay, that I'd be fine and she didn't have to worry. The problem was that forming sentences wasn't happening—my mouth unable to multitask with the breathing and the talking. That, and I had no idea if I was actually okay.

"I'm sorry. What can I do?" Her hands moved to my back, as my face maintained its newfound relationship with the carpet.

"Just . . . give . . . me . . . a . . . minute." The best I could do under the circumstances. The minute I was asking for was going to be more like an hour. Maybe longer. This floor was pretty impressive; lets just make it an even day.

Ten solid minutes. That's how long it took before I was able to roll back into a sitting position and grunt more than "I'm fine" to every one of her "I'm sorry." The pain slowly dulled to an ache.

"Rusty, I—"

"If you say sorry one more time, I'm going to punch *myself* in the balls. And neither of us wants to relive that, right?"

"Okay, but I feel terrible. Why the hell did you make me do that?" She sunk to her ass on the floor beside me.

"I said punch me, Alison, not clock me in the sack. In case you were wondering, huge difference."

I tried to lift slightly off the floor. Nope, too soon. Guess I was going to be chilling a while longer.

"Can I get you anything?" Her hand resting on my thigh made my junk tingle. I wasn't sure if it was from the trauma it had just suffered or something else. Maybe a little of both. Reassuring I guess that shit still worked down there.

"Nope, I'm just going to hang here for awhile. You good? Didn't that make you feel better?"

"Feel better? No, I feel fucking worse." She lifted her fist and popped me right in the arm.

"See, that's what you should have done the first time." I rubbed my arm, her hand barely leaving a mark. "If nothing else, at least now you are punching properly *and* you're saying fuck, that's an improvement. And the feeling good will come soon. Trust me."

"Well, this lesson sucked." She gave me another punch. The second a little bit harder than her last. The smile that came with it was really nice too.

"Anytime you want to stop would be good." I chuckled, slowly rising to my feet. The pain not gone, just less noticeable. "I think I'm going to go piss blood or something. Say goodbye to my chance at having kids." The smile she was wearing evaporated.

"Please tell me you're not serious." She got off the floor in a hurry, her legs straightening beside me.

"Relax, there will be little Rusty Crawford's someday. The world didn't get that lucky."

"Your last name is Crawford?" Her head tilted to the side. I guess we'd never gotten to the full intro part. Sort of redundant now.

"Yeah, it's not your last name too is it? 'Cause it would suck if we ended up being cousins." She was definitely not kin. No branches of my family tree producing fruit like that—I was a hundred percent sure.

"No, it's Williams." The smile was back; the tension in her eyes easing a little too. "We probably should have done that a few days ago."

"Nah, it's all good. Look at all the fun we're having."

If I hadn't just been clocked in the balls I might have said there was something there. She was beautiful and the way she was looking at me, kissing her would have been an easy thing to do. But she wasn't here for that and I wasn't going to be a jackass, even if my dick didn't agree. It wasn't about working the long game either. For the first time in a long time, I had no strategy when it came to a girl.

Well, shit. Looks like we both were learning new things.

Punching Rusty in the man parts was not something I wanted to do. He provoked me. Got me so fired up, I had no idea what I was doing. My hand leapt from my side, where it was hanging idly, and of its own accord clocked him in his . . . uh-hum.

I felt terrible.

Honestly, who does that?

His version of getting a reaction out of me was not what either of us had planned, but unfortunately that's how it went when I was around him, brain cells just got up and left. It wasn't hard to understand why.

Rusty Crawford was hot. Not just hot, but smoldering sexy. You know the kind, where you are sitting there casually minding your own business and you suddenly smell smoke? Oh, look. My panties are on fire. That's how hot Rusty was. Not that anything was ever going to happen. No. Of course not. We were just friends. Who also happened to be roommates. How lovely for us both.

After Rusty spent more than just a few minutes in the bathroom—God, I hope I didn't do any permanent damage— he said a goodbye and went to the studio. He had work to do and I didn't expect his plans to change because I was now sharing his living space, but part of me mourned the loss. Not because he was hot but because for the first time someone had actually looked beyond my layers and saw me. *Me.* It was both amazing and terrifying that a complete stranger seemed to know me better than I knew myself. That being around him made me feel excited. It was stupid. Absolutely made no sense, but here I was sad anyway.

Issues was my middle name.

So rather than sitting around being unreasonably emotional —I was dangerously close to exceeding my limit on that—I unpacked. Look at me being productive. I was a regular modern marvel.

Moving hadn't been hard. My tiny apartment had come furnished so packing took no time at all. It was comforting that my life was so easily boxed up. Small blessing I guess. While I lost whatever money I'd already paid on the month's rent, I didn't have to deal with my sleazy landlord. Oh, and I got my security deposit back too which meant I had—albeit limited— cash.

Another positive. See, no reason to be sad. Ugh. Rusty was right, I was a terrible liar.

By the time I had unboxed all my worldly belongings, and enjoyed a tasteless but strangely satisfying frozen TV dinner, it was already dark outside. Rusty hadn't come back and I didn't have any idea when he'd be home. The time ticked along so slow I ended up giving up and going to bed. Not the bed I wanted to be in either. Lord, it was going to be a long night.

It was some time later that night or early morning that I heard noises coming from inside the house. Sleep had obviously come at some point, but as I woke up from a weird, hazy dream I heard the distinct sound of . . . moaning?

Not loud enough for me to be sure, I jumped out of bed to investigate. Because obviously *that* was the smart thing to do in someone else's house, at an unspecified hour of night. *Shut up logic, I'm curious.* And with as much stealth as I could muster I crept out of my dark bedroom and into the main living space.

Darkness.

Silence.

Maybe I dreamed it?

And just when I was about to turn around and give myself a firm talking to about my vivid imagination—and overactive hormones—I heard it again. Just as faint as the first time but this time more prolonged. Whoever it was, *she* was either in severe pain or extreme pleasure. Obviously I couldn't go to bed now.

My feet tiptoed across the dimly lit living room as I followed the intermittent low moans, my ear straining as I tried to decipher the direction. Left—no right, the noise getting louder as my feet crept across the carpet. God, I hoped the floor didn't squeak, the strains of her voice getting louder the closer I moved to the bathroom door. The location of Ms. Moan-a-lot no longer a mystery.

"Yeah baby, like that." The voice spoke for the first time. "God, you are so good at this." A louder audible moan followed soon after. *I guess we can safely rule out pain.*

Pleasure it was then. While the door was closed I was able to draw my own conclusions. Rusty was obviously home and entertaining in his bathroom. How lovely. And by all accounts he sounded rather talented. Lucky her.

Whore.

I knew it wasn't fair of me to call the poor lady a whore; after all I had no basis for my argument. Other than having parts of Rusty in her, she could have potentially been a lovely girl. Not that I cared. I was too busy hating her. Her constant screams of "yeah, baby" not doing her any favors either. I seriously needed to stop.

Because I apparently enjoyed listening to the man I had a serious lady-boner for pleasuring someone else, I pressed my ear to the door a little more. You know, in case I missed something important like the impending orgasm she was working up.

Issues. Major, major issues, and I had all of them.

My breath slowed while my heart rate increased as my illicit eavesdropping continued. The ecstasy-laden cries got louder and more frequent with each passing minute. Her encouragement was increasing too, with repeated *yeses* also thrown into the mix. She was certainly appreciative; at least she had that going for her. Not that she needed any approval from me, by the sounds of things she had her own positive reinforcement going on. Oh, and I still hated her.

The thunderstorm of moans was just about to reach its spectacular crescendo when I realized I wasn't alone. I— standing in my faded *Marvel* pajamas that were too tight across the bust—turned my head to come face to face with the one and only Rusty Crawford.

Oh, shit.

Busted.

"Crap," I whispered, my already accelerated pulse skyrocketed into the danger zone as I tried to rein in my breathing. "You scared me."

"Sorry. Late night call of nature?" He casually asked like he hadn't just caught me listening in on someone else's sexy time. The big grin on his face telling me otherwise.

"Um, yeah." My eyes now fully adjusted to the dimness scanned him up and down. My heart rate elevated for an entirely different reason.

"So how are you finding the acoustics? They don't build rooms like they used to." Another smile. Not that I was paying much attention given he was wearing just shorts and no shirt. The streetlight that streamed through the drapes gave me just enough light to appreciate the view. That chest of his, just as impressive the second time around.

"Yeah, the sound really carries. Must be the high ceiling." Sadly I didn't stop there. "I thought it was you." My mouth unwisely offered. Because listening hadn't been bad enough, I had to volunteer that it was him I suspected getting jiggy with it.

"Nah, the bathroom poses too many hazards, slippery surfaces being what they are. Besides, I've got a perfectly good bedroom at my disposal." A rational explanation, one I probably should have come up with myself.

It didn't escape my attention that we were having a full conversation in front of his bathroom door. The occupants and their sexy antics no longer held my attention. Nor did I care if they heard us. Sort of tit-for-tat really, we'd heard them now they'd have to hear us.

"Oh, I don't know. The chance of falling adds another element don't you think? Like bungee jumping without the rope." Seriously, who was I right now?

"Hmm. I see where you're going with that. Though if you were going to attempt either of those two things I think bathroom sex is where your efforts should be. A rope-less jump isn't going to end well." His arm leaned up against the doorframe giving me an ever better view of his naked and toned torso. The Chinese dragon tattoo that featured grinning right back.

Gulp. Licking him right now would not be out of the question.

Pity it was completely inappropriate.

It would be, right?

"So who—" I didn't get to finish my sentence about who was in the bathroom with the door flying open to reveal a very satisfied busty brunette and a tall, dark-headed rocker looking dude. His pants still undone at the fly.

"Hey, crazy bar chick. I heard you moved in, nice." Rocker dude looked down at my pajamas or maybe it was my breasts, I couldn't be sure. "Wow, *nerdy* crazy bar chick. You just keep getting hotter."

Ummm. Huh?

While Rusty and I had been discussing the merits of bathroom sex and cathedral ceilings, rocker dude and his lady friend had received their happy ending. And while they had been rather taken with each other around twenty minutes ago, it seemed busty brunette had now turned her attention to Rusty while the object of her affection was now looking at me.

Obviously, their super hot encounter not one to stand the test of time or exclusivity.

"Hey Rusty, you look great tonight." Busty brunette ran her fingers over his chest. "You need anything, baby? Before I go."

Did she just . . . after she just . . . No, surely I misunderstood.

"I'm good, Rochelle." Rusty smirked without missing a beat. "Maybe next time."

God, I hoped he wasn't serious.

"So, you need me to tuck you in?" Rocker dude ignored the busty brunette/Rusty exchange, keeping his eyes on my boobs. The lack of bra not escaping his attention.

"I'm going to go with no. I mean you seem nice and everything but I've got the tucking in thing down and I'd hate for someone to mess with my system." I didn't add there also needed to be a cold day in hell. Rudeness wouldn't solve anything at the moment.

"Hey, Joey. Not happening." Rusty eyed him hard. "Say goodnight to Alison and leave the spare key on the coffee table. Alison, this is my drummer, Joey and his charming date is Rochelle. She's . . ."

"I'm a stripper," she finished off, her smile widening proudly.

"Wow, a stripper. I never would have guessed." That rudeness I was trying to avoid wasn't doing a good enough job being avoided. "Okay, it's been awesome. Need to pee. Goodnight." I took the three steps that were needed to get into the bathroom and shut the door behind me. The safety of four walls had never been such a welcomed relief, leaning against the wall in the dark.

"Bye, Alison," Rocker dude, Joey, called through the door.

"See you soon."

Not too soon I hope, my mind churned out with my mouth going the diplomatic route of "Uh-huh, yep you too." Whatever that meant.

The voices soon shifted away from the bathroom as I sat on the closed toilet, the need to pee fabricated. Rusty's front door slamming was hopefully a sign that the company had left.

"Alison?" The knock at the door had me leaping off the toilet, almost hitting the tub. Rusty was right; bathroom sex would be difficult. The counter would be the only viable spot, which is why I was avoiding touching it. At least until I could get my hands on some Clorox.

"Yeah almost done." I hit the flush as I went through with the charade. Next came the water running. No need for him to know I was actually hiding out.

"All yours." I stood proudly in the now open doorway.

He didn't answer. Instead he moved closer, his eyes completely unreadable. Pity my mind had decided bathroom sex wasn't an option. That had been hasty, not at all smart.

"Joey had a spare key, he crashed here a couple of days last week but that won't be happening anymore."

Problem here was that even though those words weren't even close to being sexy, they were sending tingles to parts of me that had no business tingling. I was still amazed my ill-fitting pajamas hadn't spontaneously combusted. Damn, I really should have slept with him when I had the chance.

"I'm going back to bed." The mouth that had been playing mute while I eye-fucked him *finally* got on the same page.

And while part of me wanted to wait and see if he'd stop me, the smarter part—*the one hopefully running the show right now*— knew that would be dangerous. As would be standing there any longer, which is why no sooner had I announced my departure that I turned my happy self around and retreated to my bedroom. Alone.

Knowing Rusty hadn't been in that bathroom filled me with more happiness than it should have. He wasn't dating me so was free to see other people, but because he was allowed to didn't mean I wanted him too. It didn't get more irrational than that.

I hated it, the thought and myself for feeling that way. That someone that wonderful would be with someone else; that they would be on the receiving end of his kindness and his amazing sense of humor. I had no right to feel anything for him other than gratitude and yet feelings, welcomed or not were seeping in. My mind was complete mush and I didn't know whether to rejoice in the freedom or be petrified of the uncertainty. Either way, I needed new pajamas and a solid plan. One that didn't involve me throwing myself at his feet or admitting I had feelings that made no sense. The new pajamas were definitely going to be the easier of the two.

As my eyes closed and my brain tried to will itself to sleep, I made myself a resolution—one where I stopped living in fear. That's why I was here, so that I could be a better me, not give my heart to someone who didn't want it. The unknown would no longer paralyze me and I was going to try new things. A world of discovery was just waiting for me. It was going to be amazing, and if nothing else it would stop me thinking about whether Rusty thought about me as anything other than a friend. Maybe my solid plan wasn't going to be so hard after all.

Slide

But all my new adventures could wait until tomorrow. Right after I bought new pajamas.

Eleven
Rusty

Fuck I was tired. I'd tossed and turned the whole night wondering whether or not I should have thrown the game plan out the window and knocked on her door. Not like it would have been difficult, my door being a full four feet away.

"Crazy chick keep you up last night?" Joey twirled his stick while hitting the bass drum. "Congrats on tapping that. Those tits, pretty impressive."

"Yeah, about that. Her name is Alison and she's a no-go zone."

I wasn't in the mood to hear his shit this morning. Despite him just having blown his load in some other girl, it took two seconds to wise up and see Alison was fucking stunning. Not in the typical way either. She had something else.

Unpolluted by the world, her look was a cross between girl-next-door and classic beauty. Her hair was probably the same color Mother Nature had given her; she hadn't caved to enhance herself with unnecessary shit. And her body was freaking amazing. A combination of soft lines and curves, she looked every bit the woman that she was. That kind of body made it hard for guys like me to keep their hands off.

And as much as I hated to admit it, Joey wasn't lying about the tits—impressive was an understatement. Their superb perfection gave me a hard-on for the better part of the night. And those fucking Captain America pajamas she'd been wearing, I was nominating for an academy award. Not that any of that mattered, neither of us was getting anywhere near her, especially not him.

"I mean it, completely out of bounds." I repeated in case he hadn't heard me the first time. Or in case anyone else had any ideas.

"Easy there, Rus, I was only playing. I don't want your leftovers." He turned his attention back to his kit.

"Ha! Since when? Every girl he's screwed you've wanted a piece of." Max added some gasoline. Not unexpected, not much was off limits with those two.

When it came to Joey, he had trouble playing with his own toys. Whatever either of us had, he usually wanted a part of. And as conceited as it might sound, I'd never had trouble finding people to play with. If they happened to decide that when the game was up they wanted to continue with Joey, well that was none of my concern. I wasn't the possessive type. Alison, however, wasn't up for the taking.

"You guys gossip more than old ladies. You know we have our first gig in forever next week and it's bad enough I look like the Michelin man, I don't want us to sound like shit too." Thankfully Angie chimed in, changing the topic.

"Come on, Angie, you look fantastic, babe. Besides no one is going to be looking at you, they're going to be too distracted by the three of us." My arm pulled her into an awkward side hug, that belly of hers hindering my effort.

"Yeah, yeah. So let's stop jerking around and play." She slapped me across the chest, the feel-good moment obviously running its course.

"Sounds perfect to me." Anything to stop me from thinking about Alison and what she looked like last night.

We'd never been a studio band. We'd earned our chops playing night after night in shitty bars and broken down dives and we'd been holed in a room playing to a bunch of dials for too long. Which is why some asshole—me—had the bright idea that we needed to get back on a stage; give the songs airtime. Our front woman being currently more roll than rock wasn't an issue, her assuring me that the extra cargo could take the stage without breaking a sweat, and I was itching to play. One small local gig for old time's sake. It might have been my suggestion, but we all agreed it was needed.

Unfortunately, it was going to take a lot more than playing guitar and preparing for a show to get my new roomie out of my head. My reasons for wanting to gig nowhere near as urgent as they'd been a few weeks ago. I'd even stopped sucking down Tootsie Pops like a two-year-old. Guess the distraction was good for something. Cigarettes were the last thing on my mind.

Just like Alison, I'd been woken by the Joey appreciation club early this morning. Like an idiot, I'd completely forgotten the dickhead had keys, acquired when he guilted me with the whole Phil situation. *That* asshole was causing more than just a few headaches, his domestic situation cock-blocking my boys. Of course ordinarily I wouldn't have cared about the guys using my pad to get some much needed relief, but now that shit was off the table.

If I hadn't walked out and caught Alison with her ear pressed to the door, I might have gone full-metal jacket on Joe. His timing fucking horrible. But seeing her with messed up bed hair listening to the two dumbasses getting-it-on thawed any homicidal tendencies I had brewing. She was fucking adorable.

Halfway between curious and confused, she'd been stuck to that door like it was going to start spewing out dollar bills. The image alone gave me a hard-on from hell, the conversation that followed made me wonder why the fuck we weren't in my bed getting horizontal.

Pity I was the only one jiving that way, with her taking off like her ass was on fire the minute we were alone. Guess the question of whether she was into it was answered.

"Hey, Rus? Can you drop D on the last bit? Needs to be dirtier." Angie paused on her vocals as her eyes met mine, none of the words sticking in my short-term memory.

"What, babe? Sorry, was in the zone." My lame-ass excuse a quick save for my mind going off reservation—my head not in the game.

"Drop D. On the last bit you played. I think it will sound better." She repeated slowly, clueing me in that she didn't buy my in-the-zone bullshit. Figures, bullshit and me weren't usually a package deal.

"Yep. All over it. Let's do that bit again."

Giving myself a shake wasn't out of the question. But being that my hands were otherwise occupied and I was already getting more than my share of attention, I settled for pushing all things Alison to the back of my mind and played the fuck out of the riff we'd be trying to nail. I'd get to all my thoughts about her later. Maybe tonight. Hopefully she'd be wearing those pajamas again.

Fuck.

This shit was not helping.

It was going to be a long ass day.

• • •

I'd never been that dude to think too much about the big picture. The future was going to do what it was going to do, all I needed to do was handle today and the rest would take care of itself.

The band—it was a matter of time before we were back in the spotlight. And I was all about biding my time. No longer having to work day jobs was a big fucking win, so who cared if we had to wait a few more months for the Billboard charts. It would just make it all the sweeter when we got there.

So being that I didn't need to crystal-ball my fate, my usual demeanor was pretty damn chilled. Add in the plentiful female attention that seemed to come my way and I'd go on a limb and say my life was fairly fucking spectacular. No shit, if I wasn't already living it—*I'd* want my life. But the shopping list of awesome didn't do jack to stop the edgy-as-hell that was breathing down my neck. Knowing she was going to be waiting when I got home got me so juiced up I could barely sit straight.

Oh, I knew why. I wasn't one of these clueless shitheads who didn't know when their ass had been handed to them. It was just unexpected. Me and long-term didn't usually belong in the same sentence, not unless you were talking about my guitars. So imagine my fucking bewilderment when I had zero interest in any other girl that wasn't currently living out of my spare room.

Narrowed that shit right down, didn't it?

My long day was going to be an equally long night.

And there she was. Wearing a pair of old jeans like she was doing them a favor with a T-shirt that was doing little to hinder my view. No make-up, no shoes and probably the most beautiful woman I'd ever seen.

"Rusty." Alison looked up from her computer as I walked through the doorway. "I was about to order some takeout, you want in?"

Hells yeah I did. Pity we were reading off a different menu.

"Sounds good. I'll buy." My ass hit the couch as I tried to focus on something other than how beautiful she was. It was a tough ask.

"You're not paying for dinner. You've done enough. I'll buy, you choose." She twisted her hair into a messy bun and came over to where I was sitting. "What do you feel like?"

These fucking questions were the work of the devil. I kid you not, somewhere in my living room Satan himself was sitting around giggling his scorching red ass off.

"Whatever you want is good, but you paying isn't in the cards. So I can buy or we can both go hungry tonight." I shot the idea of using her pennies down pretty quickly. Just like us fucking tonight, her paying for dinner wasn't happening.

"Fine, thank you." She gave me a shoulder bump, wisely not arguing. "How are you with hot and spicy?"

Are you shitting me right now? My pants suddenly felt tighter in the crotch.

"I'm cool with whatever." I prayed to God she was done asking questions, especially ones that got me thinking about her naked. On second thought, that was pretty much a done deal regardless of what we talked about, her double entendres were just speeding up the process.

"Oh, there's a new Burmese place that just opened up." Her face lit up with excitement.

"If that's what you want. Sounds good." And no innuendo, always a plus.

"Awesome, I'll order then."

She leapt out of the chair and grabbed her phone, her other hand picking up a flyer that was sitting on my kitchen counter. The big ass grin continued as she read out our order to the person on the other end of the phone.

Well at least someone was happy. Either that or she was really fucking hungry. Whatever the reason, the worry that usually clouded her eyes wasn't there, and I really liked this new development.

With the task of takeout all sorted, she went back to her laptop while we waited for the food to arrive. Which gave me the opportunity to go grab a quick shower. Me wanting to be clean was only half of the reason I was desperate to get under the spray. The cold water required for the other purpose.

I'd managed just enough time to clean up and grabbed an ice-cold beer from the fridge when the delivery guy started rapping at the door. The timing outstanding.

My interest in getting comfortable on the couch was higher than moving to the kitchen, so the executive decision was made to eat in the living room. A plan Alison seemed on board with as she unpacked the plastic containers of whatever it was she ordered and settled on the floor beside me. Her happy mood took a nosedive as she opened one of the lids.

"Oh. My. God. What is this?" She threw her hand around her mouth like she was going to puke. "Why does it smell like that?" The container dropped on the coffee table in favor of her pinching her nose.

Her horror made me interested in the square piece of plastic that had provoked the reaction, my hand picking it up as I gave it a sniff. The smell not tickling my fancy as I tried to work out what was housed in mystery box number one. "It's some kind of curried fish."

"Ew. This stuff looks gross." She unpacked mystery box number two, her look of wanting to gag no less than the first.

We didn't bother with mystery box number three, its weird and wonderful secrets probably joining the other two in the trash.

"Don't you know what you ordered?"

I'm sure I didn't imagine the part where she'd suggested what we ate and then proceeded to order it. Which should have made the game of peek-a-boo unnecessary.

"No, the menu didn't have any pictures." She kept her hands up near her mouth, the smell not getting any better. "I took a guess. I've never eaten this stuff before."

It would have been easy to laugh, her horrified face surveying the mess that was our dinner. But the last thing I wanted was for her to feel any worse. The *sorry* no doubt already working it's way up her throat as she looked at me with those big sad hazel eyes. Damn, it just made her look more adorable.

"So I'm guessing I'm getting pizza." I fished out my cell from my pocket and started dialing. My back-up plan sounded better by the second as I watched her wriggle out of her seat.

"No." She tried to grab the phone out of my hand. "I'll eat this. I can do it." Her horror-filled eyes turned to the coffee table of doom as I attempt to work out who she was trying to convince.

"You're not eating that, we'll get pizza. It's fine." My fingers started dialing, wondering why the hell she was acting so weird.

"No, I'll do this. I can eat it." She rehashed the argument, the second time making no more sense than the first.

Whatever was going down here wasn't about the food. An obviously bigger issue had to be the reason why she was refusing to order something else. It was like she was playing some stupid game of dare, and she couldn't back down. She was going to force the food and the point, regardless of what her gag reflex was saying. Her doing that to herself didn't sit right with me, and being such a caring and concerned citizen I wasn't going to sit by and watch it happen.

"Why would you eat something you don't like?" I had no intention of letting it go.

Her eyes shot me a look of sadness that made my insides hurt.

"Because I've never had it before. I wanted to try something new."

And there it was. The reason why instead of chowing down on pie from Mario's we were looking at a bunch of containers neither of us wanted to eat. All of it orchestrated to prove—either to herself or to me—she could try *something new.* Except it didn't prove shit and we were both still hungry.

"Trying new things doesn't mean making yourself do something you hate. Pushing yourself out of your comfort zone is a good thing, I'm glad you want to try new stuff, but its cool if you don't like it."

"I suck at this." She huffed in frustration. "All of this." She motioned at the graveyard of dinner on the coffee table. "Sucks."

"Hey, come here."

And just like magic, I pulled her out of her chair and into my lap. It was a neat trick too, because one minute she was cursing under her breath and the next the smile had crept back on her face. Which was a good thing because my next move was putting my arms around her and giving her a hug. Her body tight against mine as her head rested against my shoulder, both of us even managed a laugh.

Dangerous territory.

Did I stop?

Hell no.

Friends hug. Yep, they sure do. I'd hugged plenty. And we *were* friends so the fact I had my hands around her was totally fine. My hand moving down her back—not so much. She could have stopped it any time. A simple *hey, what are you doing* would have put the brakes on with no questions asked. Lucky for me, those words weren't spoken so I kept my palms right where they wanted to be—on her. My dick on the other hand wasn't happy with just touching, the son-of-a-bitch taking a very keen interest in what was going down.

Ali on my lap just felt right, which is why I pulled her right back into it as soon as the pizza I ordered arrived. She didn't protest either, her ass not moving as we ate dinner. One of my hands staying on her the whole time while the other was used to balance a slice of pie.

Probably the best pizza I'd ever eaten, and it had nothing to do with what had been in the box. The company far outshone the five-cheese special, with more than half of it remaining uneaten on the coffee table.

The after-dinner cuddling in front of the television was also something special. Her head nestled against my neck while my hand stayed busy locked against her hip. Her gentle breathing against my skin made me feel so relaxed I could have stayed in that chair for a week and not complained.

And while *I* wasn't disappointed with the way the evening turned, my dick wasn't so understanding. The need to kiss her so strong, I had to stop myself no less than five times.

The *goodnight* was bittersweet. My arms no longer having a reason to be around her, gave her one last hug. Her head fit so perfectly against my chest that I had to wonder if holding a woman had ever felt this good, but when I let go, she went to her room and I went to mine. The part where I was able to touch her came to a very quick finale.

That part wasn't so great.

It was going to be another restless night—just me and my hand.

Good times.

This shit was not getting easier.

No matter what I thought was going on between the two of us, I was mistaken. By the two of us I meant Rusty and I. The lack of the *Us*—the saddest part.

Being around him didn't make things easier. He was so kind to me, just so sweet and the more he gave me, the more I craved. Sadly, the sexual attraction didn't diminish either. A couple of nights ago I was convinced something was going to happen. He pulled me into his arms and we were so close I could almost taste the kiss. Turned out, it was just a false alarm.

In fact he hadn't tried to kiss me at all in the week I'd been living with him. Or sneak into my bedroom like I'd been telepathically commanding him to do. I'd left the door slightly ajar and everything. I was hopeful.

But no. Nothing. Not even a peep. No interest it seemed as I embarked on my journey into discovery. Apparently I had a lot to learn. Sadly, not all of it fun.

Somewhere in my fucked-up beginnings I'd decided I

needed to be someone else. Live someone else's life, and I didn't really know who I was anymore. I'd been so pre-occupied with not turning into my mother that I forget to work out who I wanted to be. It was criminal how much wasted energy I'd expended and all it achieved was to screw me up more than I already was. It was acceptable to say *screw* in that context apparently.

Screw, screw, screw.

Unfortunately not the screw I wanted.

Ugh. I mentally wanted to shake myself.

So I'd learned a lot about myself in the last few days. One, I was a little uptight. Okay, maybe more than just a little. Fine! A lot. I was a lot uptight. And secondly, I was horny as hell.

All the devastation, my life is ending crap, didn't kill my libido which was comforting. Thus proving that your sexual organs are not attached in any way to your brain. The part of my body I should have been thinking with. Yep. Uptight was definitely going to be easier to fix.

It was in the spirit of my new awakening that Rusty set me a new task. Me—the consummate control freak—needed to push myself out of my comfort zone and to try something new. Burmese food didn't count apparently and that was a disaster I would happily forget.

No, I wanted my out-of-the-zone experience to be completely reckless, something so crazy my hair would curl. So for now it was back to the drawing board.

Rather than worry about what I needed to be a silly and fruitless exercise, and convinced that my opportunity to hang from the chandeliers would eventually reveal itself, I concentrated my efforts on finding a job.

Well. That's what I was trying to do.

The problem was, the internet was a minefield. A sea of distraction and procrastination. I'd go on to check job vacancies and I'd end up pinning Crockpot recipes for three hours. No one who lived at this address owned a Crockpot. Which should have been my wake-up call and yet, that five-ingredient barbeque chicken looked delicious.

You know what else was on the internet?

Porn.

Not that I didn't already know that, but I'd never had much time to look. Too busy being uptight and working. And boy, had I been missing out. Seriously.

I don't know how I even ended up there, I just clicked here and then clicked there and before you know it, I was looking at naked people.

Porn. It's not just for creepy dudes with comb-overs that's for sure. And not just your run-of-the-mill type stuff either. I'm talking hard, pummeling, holy-shit-he's-going-to-rip-her-in-half type porn. I had to be thorough. Of course I did. My research abilities had always been my strongest asset. Strangely —or maybe not—I was aroused.

But more than aroused I was actually curious, the mechanics of it all just seemed freaking fascinating. How the body could bend and contort in so many ways to accommodate things that large was truly amazing. I was impressed.

It got me thinking about my homework assignment. The pushing my boundaries thing. Me, being uptight. Which lead to other thoughts about what I'd like to do. Out of the comfort zone. Which made me wonder.

Could I be less anal, by actually having *anal*?

It was bound to get messy.

My ass had always been strictly an exit only. I didn't mind some non-penetrative play, quite the opposite—I welcomed it. But when it came to going *down that road*, I didn't. Ever. Not even a possibility.

Maybe I'd been missing out? Those girls online seemed to build a solid case if their euphoric ohhh's and ahhh's were anything to go by. I'd never orgasmed that hard when a man was in my vagina, let alone . . . out of it.

It was settled. I had to do it.

Without going all-out crazy and asking some random guy to put his penis in my out-hole—I still had some sanity left—I decided that I could achieve all of this solo. Yes, ladies and gentlemen, I was going to attempt to screw *myself* in the ass.

As hilarious as it sounded, it wasn't nearly as easy as I thought. You just can't ram a sixteen-inch dildo up your pooper. Well, not unless you wanted to do some serious damage and possibly be rocking a colostomy bag for a while. The problem with matching it with your shoes an obvious concern. But as I came to find out, there is an actual process that is required, whereby you train your butt. Like minoring in Spanish, I was signing up to butt-sex 101.

A website I discovered was not only extremely informative, but very conveniently had all the tools required. Like a Home Depot of deviancy, advice with an impressive product line. It was more than just a little overwhelming.

There were ones that boasted about their hospital grade materials, others claimed to be more resilient than the Space Shuttle and finally some that had more parts than an Ikea storage center—some assembly was required. Who knew screwing yourself in the ass was such an in depth process. Certainly not me.

On a whim—and with as much knowledge as I was able to gather—I purchased a few things on my overused and probably soon-to-be-canceled credit card. I was both excited and terrified.

Please God; don't let me end up in an emergency room.

The wait for the package was excruciating.

The longer I waited the more I worried I'd lose my nerve. And I was determined to follow through with it. For whatever reason, this was very important.

It was my saving grace that Rusty wasn't home when my coveted box arrived. I smiled at the delivery guy as he handed me a non-descript harmless looking package, the contents of which would soon be getting very intimate with my exit anatomy. Poor guy smiled back. He had no idea.

The front door had just slammed shut when I took off in a power walk to my bedroom. Running was still out given I hadn't had my date with the treadmill yet and *my room* was the designated place for the magic to happen. It had been a tough decision between it and the bathroom. I still wasn't sure I'd made the right choice. Too late now.

My nondescript, harmless box was ripped open with a wild abandon that would give six-year-olds on Christmas morning a run for their money. The journey of ass-funary had waited long enough.

And there it all was. Lined up neatly on my bed. Ready for me to try. Lube, butt plugs and anal beads. Like a delightful kinky buffet.

I had no idea what to try first.

So with my cheat sheet handy—I'd downloaded some notes from the website—I started with the lube.

It was cold and slippery.

And not in a good way.

Flashbacks of gynecological visits and pap smears raced through my mind as I got the area well prepared. God, I hoped this was worth it.

Next I needed to choose my instrument of pleasure. This was harder than I thought. Everything I'd bought looked larger than it had on the website and slightly less comfortable. Still with me being naked from the waist down and with my ass full of lube, it was probably too late to be having second thoughts. I was just going to need to push through—literally.

Eeny, meeny, miny, moe ended up making the decision for me.

Anal beads.

At least they looked pretty, their purple bulbs of wonder just waiting to give me pleasure. I was going in, or at least they were.

My eyes bulged as I slowly pushed in the first bead, its entry met with resistance. It didn't feel good and I immediately wanted to pull it out but I wasn't a quitter. Nope, I was staying the course. So I tried to push in another two. Yep, now it just felt worse. Something was definitely wrong.

The instructions didn't seem complicated—they were anal beads not Pythagoras' theorem—but reading over them again highlighted that I skipped a step. An apparently important one, and one that I thought would be pretty impossible now.

Getting aroused.

Awesome.

So while the beads were left abandoned in my ass, I turned my attention to my clitoris as I tried to summon anything that would get me even the slightest bit turned on.

Utterly ridiculous.

I should have bought a vibrator as well.

Masturbation wasn't something foreign to me. In fact the only orgasms I'd had over the last two years with Rob were courtesy of my own hands, so reaching down and touching myself wasn't weird for me at all. What was *weird* was being bent at the waist with stuff hanging out of my ass while I slowly circled my clit in a strange bedroom. I wasn't even completely undressed, which further illustrated how crazy this was.

Clearly I hadn't thought this through, my excitement diminishing with each passing second. Candles might have been good, music too but despite all the enthusiastic rubbing and stroking I was doing, my libido had hit the snooze button. Not even conjuring images of what Rusty might have looked like naked worked.

Nothing.

My vagina was broken.

Frustrated, and losing sensation in my lube-covered fingers, I'd decided the effort was a bust. Of course in my battle of will trying to get to my happy place, I had momentarily forgotten about the tail of beads still happily lodged in my butt. Something I was reminded of when I sat heavily on the bedroom floor.

"Crap," I screamed, the words flying out of my mouth automatically.

I'm not sure why I anticipated the end of this pathetic mess to be any better than it was, but me on the floor in a puddle of lube and anal beads was really far worse than I imagined. That was until I heard the knock at my door.

"Hey, Alison, are you all right in there?"

Great, because the situation wasn't mortifying enough, I now needed to share it with a friend, namely the guy I'd been trying to imagine naked not even ten minutes ago. Any time the universe wants to throw me a bone would be a good time. Honestly, hadn't I suffered enough?

"I—I'm okay. Just fell off the bed." I shuffled back up to my feet. It wasn't even close to the truth but it was as much as Rusty was getting. This was an afternoon I was happily taking to my grave.

"Do you need help?" The door pushed opened a crack.

HOLY SHIT! So in addition to the vibrator I'd forgotten to purchase I'd also completely neglected to barricade the door as well. The absence of a lock should have been the deciding factor in doing this in the bathroom. A little late now.

"Noooooooooooo." The scream leapt out of my mouth as I slammed the door back shut before it had a chance to open any more.

"What the fuck?" Rusty called through the wood, obviously not expecting a face full of door as his greeting.

"You. Cannot. Come. In. Here." My pulse raced as my breathing increased. My eyes frantically tried to locate my panties and jeans as my legs stayed rooted in their spot. Too far—my wayward clothes taunted me from the edge of my bed.

"Why not?" He wasn't giving up, possibly looking for an explanation as to why his roommate had lost her damn mind.

Valid at this point.

"Because you can't." I prayed for my mouth to say something plausible as my brain struggled to kick into gear. "My room's a mess, you can't see it like this." That will do.

"I don't care about a mess, just open the door."

"Please. I am begging you. Do not open this door."

If I were certain he wouldn't fling the door open the minute I moved, I honestly would have dropped to my knees at this point. Pray to whoever was up there to save me from the embarrassment I was literally ass deep in. Sadly, I think God had more pressing issues than me and my butt.

"What are you doing in there?" His voice sounded less mad and more curious. The change did not help my cause.

"Nothing. Who says I'm doing anything?" Nice. Solid. Convincing. It didn't even sound like I was lying unless he could hear my heartbeat hammering away in my chest.

"Because you're acting weird."

The man had a point. As far as acting like a lunatic was concerned, I was currently its poster child. Not that I had displayed many moments of sanity since our first meeting—oh no, I was happily tumbling down the rabbit hole headfirst. Pants apparently optional.

"I'm naked. I just had a shower." Thank you, brain. Nice of you to show up, could have used you about an hour ago before I started this mess.

"So hurry up and throw some clothes on. It's no big deal."

That would be perfectly logical. Of course it would. I was in my room after all, so clothes shouldn't have been an issue. The issue was, however, the collection of sex toys on my bed—not even counting the one still in me. Yeah, I really, really need to take that out.

"I'm fine, Rusty. You don't need to come in." My hand reached around the back and yanked on the rubber ring. "Oh, shiiiit." My body tingled as the offending beads slid out of my butt. Wow. Those girls weren't lying; it felt pretty damn good actually.

"What now? Did you fall again? Alison, just put some clothes on and open the damn door."

"Okay. Just give me a minute. Do not open the door."

Unable to bask in the strangely nice sensation for long, I grabbed the beads, lube and butt plugs and shoved them in the top drawer of my nightstand. Hopefully where they would stay undiscovered. Next on the agenda were panties and jeans, which I pulled on after a quick clean up with some tissues. The lack of hand sanitizer was still bugging me as I pulled open my door.

"Heeeyyyy." I stood with my hip against the doorjamb, hoping like hell he would see me in one piece and move on.

"Hey." Rusty eyed me curiously as he looked me over, my enthusiastic *hey* not enough to appease him. "Can I come in?" His eyes moved from me to the rest of my room.

"Sure, sure. Come on in." It was his place after all, not like he didn't have every right to inspect it.

"Messy huh?" He scanned my neat and tidy room. "I'd hate for you to see mine."

Thankfully my mouth didn't spill that I'd love the chance to see it too. "Messy for me." I casually leaned against the wall; if I was trying to act nonchalant I was failing miserably.

Like he possessed some innate sixth-sense his eyes moved to my bed, which up until a few moments ago hadn't been as sweet and innocent as my Pottery Barn comforter suggested. It was when I followed his line of sight that I saw it.

A rogue.

Obviously missed in my hurry to get the others into my drawer, the lone black, large instrument of torture—it was too big for much else—sat at the end of my bed where it had rolled, conspicuously mocking me.

"Well, well you didn't tell me you were having a party." He didn't even try and hide his grin.

"Oh fuck."

I officially wanted to die.

"By the looks of things, it seems to be the case." He laughed, thoroughly enjoying himself at my expense. No need to ask me what I had been doing, I think the evidence spoke for itself.

"It's not what it looks like." Yeah, let's pretend it doesn't look like a large rubber anal fist. Don't know why I even bothered.

"Really? Because that looks like a butt plug." The grin got wider, as did my shame. Every. Single. Time. It always got worse.

So instead of pretending like I hadn't been doing what we both knew I had, I decided to throw caution to the wind and own it. Stop being the doormat he wrongly accused me off.

"So, yeah, it's mine." I pushed my shoulders back proudly as I retrieved the offending object and tossed it the drawer with the others. "I was following your lead."

"Whoa, my lead? Please enlighten me, because this is interesting the hell out me right now." He took a seat uninvited on my bed, his eyes on the open drawer that housed my paraphernalia. No point hiding it, seen one ass toy, you've seen them all.

"You told me I had to get out of my comfort zone. That's what I was trying to do here." There I was—owning it.

"Hey, I'm not disapproving. I think this initiative is fucking fantastic. Honestly, great work, wish I had been here to see it." He laughed. Not just any laugh, a big throaty laugh that moved his whole delicious body. The visual could have been useful earlier, might have to save it for later.

"Yeah, laugh away. Nothing happened, it didn't get that far."

"Hmmm the open lube would hint otherwise."

"You can leave anytime, Rusty. The show is over." I moved off the bed and pointed to the door.

"Ali, all jokes aside, are you good?" He stopped laughing as he followed my lead and joined me at the door. "You didn't hurt yourself with anything did you?"

If this had happened with any other guy I probably would have been mortified. Not that I would have even attempted this type of shenanigans with any other guy—but with Rusty, it actually wasn't that bad. Any embarrassment I initially felt was gone now it was all out in the open, and even I was starting to see the funny side. His concern for my ass was also remarkably touching.

"I'm fine. You can go." Not that I really wanted him to go but he really didn't have a reason to stay. Not unless he wanted to . . . no he probably didn't.

"Well if you need me, I'll be jamming in my room." He stopped short of leaving, and gave me a warm smile. "You're doing great."

The need for him to explain the *great* wasn't required. In the short few days I'd met him I was slowly changing. Not because of him but because I was finally in an environment where I wasn't trying to be something else. And I loved the freedom. The chance to explore with no boundaries made me feel strong—something I sadly hadn't felt, maybe ever.

It was while I was exploring these feelings of empowerment that I decided what my next task would be. I'd just stuffed a foreign object up my ass so surely this would be easier. I was done with waiting. Tonight, I was finally going to do what I'd wanted to for a long time. I wasn't going to wait anymore.

Thirteen
Rusty

Coming home early had been the best thing ever.

No shit, I still couldn't wipe the smile from my face.

We'd wrapped at the studio like usual, but instead of heading straight to the bar with Max and Joe, I went home instead. Yep, call me boring or whipped but I'd rather chill with a girl who I wasn't sleeping with than fuck someone I had no interest in. Besides she probably needed someone to pull her out of her room, where she spent most days burning up the Wi-Fi. A beer and some friendly conversation were definitely required.

What I hadn't expected was hearing her curse like she'd fallen on her ass and then refuse to open the door. Came to find out, my initial assessment of the situation wasn't too far off the mark, with her ass definitely involved. Wow. Never dreamt that me telling her to let shit go and try something new would have resulted in butt plugs and lube. Her dedication to the task was motherfucking admirable.

Unfortunately, the whole idea had me rock-fucking-hard.

Can't tell you how easily it would have been to rip off those jeans and show her exactly how anal was done. I'd barely been able to walk out of her room with the hard-on I'd worked up; how she'd missed it was beyond me. Still, the fact that I'd jerked off twice and *still* had an erection that could take out an eye, proved how much that girl turned me on. It was torture. Sweet, slow and amazing torture.

Pursuing something with her would be wrong, right? That hadn't been my intention at all. Hell, if it was just sex I was after I would have fucked her the first night she'd been in my bed. It didn't happen and now we had a different arrangement. One where she lived in my house, and I didn't bend her over the couch. Still, given half a chance I would be so into it.

Fuck. I was going to have to jerk off again.

I rolled onto my back as I went for a new record; my hand sliding down my stomach and hitting my waiting cock for the third time that night. And just like I was fourteen, the bastard stirred the minute my fingers curved around the shaft. It—like me—couldn't get enough of the visual.

My brain flipped into autopilot as I recalled every single inch of that beautiful body. *God, I'd love to see more of it, and work it over nice and slow, starting with her perfect mouth.* Slowly my hand pumped, moving up and down as my hips got in on the action. Yeah, that's it. That felt sensational. My imagination took it a little further, forgetting it was my hand around my dick as I pictured her lips stretched around my cock, sucking me hard as I pumped into her mouth. Yeah. Wow. That was so good. So fucking close.

"Would you like me to do that?"

"Ali?" My hand froze mid-stoke.

"Um . . . Yeah?" She stood beside my open door, the one I hadn't heard her open because I'd been busy doing other things. "Seeing as the anal sex didn't work out so well for me. I figured I'd rather do something else. Something I know I can do. I think I'm pretty good at it too."

Saying no is what should have happened. Given her the speech that I had it covered, and we could each go back to sleep. But damn, as she stood in my doorway in her bra and her panties there was no way I could send her packing. I wasn't that strong a man. And I really wanted to see what she had in mind.

"Show me."

On my word, she sauntered over from the door to my bed. Her hips swaying with confidence as she lifted up onto the bed and straddled me, putting her knees on either side.

She glanced down at the hand that was still locked around my cock, her eyes opening a little wider in surprise. The confidence she'd shown at the door slipped a little as she brought her own smaller hand to take over. Her other hand joining the first as they wrapped around my dick and slowly started to stroke. At first her hand struggled to get into a rhythm, with the slow and rough slide feeling uncoordinated and awkward. But it didn't take too long for her strokes to even out to a smoother glide. The end result made me buck my hips in appreciation. She wasn't lying when she said she was good at it, her hands were fucking magic.

"Yeah, baby. That feels good." My head, which had been previously resting on the pillow, lifted up as I strained to see, watching her work—getting me even harder.

Asking what provoked the change in her attitude wasn't

happening, with the thought this was a dream still very much on the table. But whether she'd suddenly had a revelation, or my jerking off had just entered a new level where I was hallucinating, I was not about to stop it. Not. A. Chance.

"It's even better than I imaged it." Her lop-sided smile hinted she'd at least thought about it, that alone making it hard to keep my control. "You have a very impressive cock." She threw me a wicked smile as she twisted her hands up and down my shaft slow and tight. Mother-fucking-mind-blowing.

"I'm so glad you approve. I'll show you any time you want, after all, sharing is caring." And I meant it too, if this is what the end result was I'd pretty much give up wearing pants while I was home. Fucking overrated if you asked me.

"Really? You probably shouldn't have said that, Rusty." Her hand moved a little faster. "I'm going to want to see it every day, you know."

"Ah, Alison." My body got even more juiced up "Every day." I struggled not to blow my load in her hand. "I'll show you . . . every day."

"I'm going to want to do more than just look, though. Is that going to be okay?" She stopped mid-stroke and clocked me with the sexiest look I'd ever seen. Seriously, this girl was fucking insanely hot and I couldn't believe she currently had my dick in her hand. Not to mention I was sure this would *never* happen. Screw Powerball, my lucky number had definitely come up.

"Sure. I'm sure we can work something out. What were you thinking?"

"Like maybe this?" She slid down my body; her neck bent down to allow her mouth to swirl the head of my cock. Her tongue took over from her hand as it worked up and down my length.

"God, yes." I was torn between wanting to watch and needing to lay my head back down on the pillow. "I give you complete permission to do that. Anytime you want."

Dear God in Heaven, or anyone else up there willing to listen. If some spirit of porno queen past has taken up residence in Ali's body, I thank you.

Seriously, what the fuck was happening right now?

If the hand action had been good, the blowjob was fucking better. Her lips and tongue licking and sucking me like a pro, as I watched her freaking mesmerized. Yeah, this was definitely better.

"Some days I might want to mix things up and do this." My eyes stayed glued on her as she flicked off her bra. Just one fucking maneuver and the thing was gone, giving me the best view of her gorgeous tits. Thinking it was going to end with a blowjob had been definitely premature with the show taking a new direction. Her tits now the star attraction as she leaned forward and sat my dick in between them, continuing to lick the head while she moved up and down.

"Yes. Yes. You can do that too. All the time, Alison. Do that."

I could have let it gone on longer, the jerking off, the blowjob even the tit fucking was beyond freaking awesome. And I would have happily blown my load either onto her stunning looking tits or possibly into her mouth. Either of those options would have been a fucking winner. But I wasn't happy to be sitting there as a spectator any more. Nope, that part was done. And as much as I didn't want her to stop, my hands needed to get on her and make this a two-person participation thing. It was only fair after all.

"Take off your panties," I gritted out through my teeth.

"I'm kind of busy." She gave me a flick of her tongue.

"Yeah, it can wait. Take them off."

She hesitated for a second and then moved her hands to her hips. Slowly, she slipped them off her body, kicking them off to reveal her beautiful pussy. It was perfect.

"So here's what I was thinking." My hand moved in between her legs, my fingers instantly coated as they slid inside her.

"Yeah?" She moaned as I gave her another finger.

"That some days it shouldn't be your hands, mouth and tits who get to have all the fun. I think that this beautiful pussy should get a turn too." My fingers got deeper as I watched her ride my hand.

"That is such a good idea." She moaned as her eyes struggled to stay open.

She twisted her hips in time with my fingers as they slid in and out of her, my thumb rubbing small circles at her opening.

"I'm glad you like it because I think some days it should be my cock in here and not my hands." My fingers continued to move in and out, picking up a little more speed. "I'm desperate to get inside of you."

"Me too." Her hips rocked against my hand. "I want that impressive cock in me."

"Ali, today is that day. I want to fuck you."

"Yes. Please. Yes."

My back jacked up off the mattress as I took her mouth and kissed her hard. She had said yes and that's all I needed; I wanted to kiss her so badly my balls ached. My lips crushed hers as I positioned her on top of me; my cock sliding against her pussy as we made out, my tongue doing the fucking my dick was desperate to do. It was hot, her hands clawing at my chest with freaking need as I palmed her ass to bring her even closer. One slip and I was inside. Keeping out was the ultimate test in restraint.

"Rusty," she moaned as my fingers slid up and down the seam of her ass. "Please. I really, really need you inside of me."

Hearing her beg sent me off on a frenzy. My cock was also begging, wanting me to do whatever I had to do to get inside her. We were all on the same page as I fumbled single-handed in my nightstand for a condom, the mind and body so juiced up I wasn't sure I was going to be able to put it on.

"Give me a minute, babe."

My fingers leaving her ass was fucking tragic, both my hands required in getting the rubber out of the packet and onto my cock. The operation taking less than the minute I'd asked for.

With all systems go, I moved back into position, needing more than anything to take this to the next level. Both of us had waited long enough.

"Alison." The tip of my dick slid inside of her and I lost any control. "Fuck." My teeth gritted as I pushed all the way in unable to stop.

"Oh. Wow." She gripped my shoulders in a panic as I gave her a second to get used to me. I'd given her my whole length a lot quicker than I'd meant too. I couldn't have held back even if I'd tried.

"You good?" My mouth reached up and kissed her tits.

"Ah-ha." She nodded, her eyes peeled back wide.

"Good, because I need to keep moving."

"Yes. I think you should do that too."

It was a good thing that she was agreeable on the subject because stopping now would have sucked. And staying still wasn't working much for me either, as I pulled slowly out and then moved right back to where I wanted to be.

"You feel so fucking good." My hips moved a little faster, each drag in and out getting slightly easier.

"Thank you, you do too." She matched my thrusts with some of her own.

"No need to thank me, sweetheart. It really is my pleasure."

"Oh God, your cock is so amazing." Her hands reached up and played with her tits as she rode me. "So much better than butt sex."

I was expecting to wake up any minute, as my mind tried to reconcile this wasn't a fantasy resulting from jacking off too many times. But there was no way this wasn't real, my thanks going to whatever force of nature made it happen.

"My cock thanks you." My hands palmed her ass as I pushed in deeper. "But talking about fucking your ass is going to make me come."

"Rusty, I'm so close."

"Yeah? Let's get you there then."

"Yes. Don't stop."

"I won't."

It didn't take long, just a few more thrusts and I felt her tighten around my cock. Her body shook as she unraveled around me, my resolve flying out the window as I watched her come. I'd wanted to hold back, enjoy the feeling just a bit longer but my dick had other ideas. In this case I didn't mind him taking over, liking the direction he had taken us as I exploded into her. There was nothing gentle about it as my body pumped hard while I spilled my load, her body collapsing on me as I continued to come.

"Hey." My lips moved to her neck while we both breathed out of control.

"Hey." She slowly lifted her head, giving me an awesome smile.

"Well, that was unexpected. You want to tell me what inspired that?"

Having sex with Alison hadn't even been on my radar tonight. I was going to jerk off again and hopefully get some sleep, but the way it all worked out was utterly sensational. The reality was even better than I thought it would be, and I'd imagined it plenty good.

"I just wanted to." A shy smile spread across her face. "I just thought I'd try and be more assertive."

"Hmm. I like you assertive. You should be like that every day." My eyes stayed locked on hers as my grin widened.

"Yeah, I really liked having sex with you, so if we're taking a vote, I think we should be doing *that* every day." She gave me a cute smile, wrinkling her nose as she slid off me and onto the mattress beside me.

"Oh you do, do you? You sure about that?"

"Yep. Consider it my extra credit."

Can't say I disagreed. While she may have seemed locked up tighter than a drum, she loosened up the reins pretty damn quick. The Ali I was currently in bed with more confident than I'd ever seen. And fuck me if that wasn't an even bigger turn on. As for that blowjob—fucking stellar. I'd love to have those lips around my cock on a daily basis.

Besides, now that I'd had a taste, I was a hundred percent sure I wasn't going to be able to keep my hands off or her.

Fuck. That.

No, seriously, given the chance I was going to be in her every opportunity I got. She was my new addiction.

My arm curved around her, bringing her closer to me. I liked her there. Tucked up tight as her breathing evened up. Her freaking satisfied and relaxed smile making me feel more like a rock star than I ever did on stage.

"So, we going to talk about your foray into anal sex?" I pulled off the condom and threw it into the waste paper basket beside my bed. "Because I have to tell you, I jerked off twice before you came into the room on that thought alone." My hand slowly moved down her back as my fingertips gently brushed her ass. My cock already stirring despite having blown my load only a few minutes a go.

"Oh, it was horrible." She lifted her head to look at me as she kissed my neck. "I was trying to shove these beads in my ass while fingering myself. I could have used an extra hand and stirrups and it still wouldn't have happened. Nothing that is supposed to make you feel good should be that complicated."

Hmmm. Yep. I was definitely getting hard again. Between the kissing and her recount of her afternoon I was pretty sure I was ready for round two.

"You know, purely in the interest of you seeing this thing through—I would totally endure the hardship—I could take care of all of that for you. I'm pretty good with my hands." Said hands demonstrated their agility as they moved up and down the crease of her ass. I was a giver and this was not a hard ask. Not. At. All.

"You want to shove something in my ass." She smiled wrapping her leg around me giving me better access, totally into what I was doing.

"Babe, my dick is already hard just thinking about it and this is the third time I've come tonight. What do you think?" It wasn't even a question. Hell I'd put my dick anywhere she asked me to, as much as she wanted. That's how committed I was to this cause.

"Okay. But it might take some time though. I have notes." She shot me a slight look of concern. "I mean if you want to follow through and actually do *it*. We need to build up to that." The *it* not needing to be defined.

"Trust me when I say I don't need the notes, babe. But thanks." I couldn't help but grin. "And yes, Ali. I very much want to do *it*. Whatever you want to do and as long as it takes is fine by me."

That shit about me not liking a project was clearly bullshit. Just thinking about the lead up had me fired up.

"I'm kind of excited." Her face beamed in case there was any doubt.

"I guarantee you're not as much as I am."

She slid her fingers up and down my chest, my ink work getting most of her attention.

"Not to inflate your already huge ego, but that was kind of amazing." She peeked up at me from under her lashes. "I haven't orgasmed like that in a while. At least not with a guy. I was beginning to wonder if my vagina was broken."

"So glad we were able to clear that up for you. If there is anything else I can do, please don't hesitate to let me know."

Literally anything. Given she had concerns about her pussy

maybe we should continue to test it. To be sure. I'd hate for there to be any doubt.

"Um . . . I'm good for right now." She glanced around the room before her eyes came back to me. "Should I go back to my room?"

Yeah, not if I could help it. Her, leaving my bed tonight—not happening.

"Well that depends. You *could* go back to your room, or—here's a radical idea—you can stay here, I can get another condom and we can fuck some more. Ass play included."

"You would have made a really good lawyer."

"I make a better guitarist. So what are you thinking? Sleep or sex?"

It was my attempt at being a gentleman by giving her a choice, but make no mistake, I would *not* have been fine with her walking out the door. If sleep is what she chose, then she was going to be doing it right next to me, hopefully after more sex. I wasn't worried, though. I could be very convincing.

"Sex." She grinned like she knew there had been no other option. "I need you to make me come again in case the first time was a fluke. You can never be too sure."

Ab-so-fucking-lutely. I completely agreed with her plan and I was going to enjoy proving my point.

"Agreed. Now lay down, I'm going to go down on you first."

Holy **mother of God, last night had been awesome.** Seriously. If I wasn't still sore this morning I would have been convinced it was a dream. Some crazy manifestation of my horniness that conjured up some wild and wonderful sex dream. But it wasn't.

Oh hell no.

So rather than lay in my bed frustrated and unsure about whether or not Rusty felt the same attraction I did, I took matters into my own hands. Like a sexual vigilante on a mission, I stormed into his room and saw he had a mission of his own happening. Wow.

Possessing bravery I'd never even known existed, I left any second thoughts at the door as I took over for his busy hand. The sight of him jerking off was almost enough to make me orgasm. I was not disappointed.

Not. One. Little. Bit.

His cock was impressive. And considering the amount of porn I'd watched in the past few days, I'd say I was extremely qualified to make that statement. Lord knows I'd seen more *dick* recently flashing across my laptop screen than I had in my entire life. Big ones, wide ones, ones that bent to the left and right, and yet Rusty's cock blew—no pun intended—them all away.

It wasn't so much big, as it was *freaking* huge. And I would be lying if I didn't say that a slight moment of panic flashed through my mind when I first saw it, all erect and ready in his hand. But I wasn't a quitter. Nope, and after the lackluster sex I'd had over the last two years, I deserved some big cock porno sex. Rusty's *cock* was more than up for the challenge.

Oh, and he totally knew what to do with all of that equipment. No "hey, baby, shuffle this way" or "hey, baby, tell me what you like." No directions required. Just voilà. Instant orgasm. Renee was right. I felt like a million bucks.

I hadn't given it all very much thought to be honest— shocking I know. But lying beside him in post-sex bliss brought up a slightly new panic. *One* harder to manage than just a sizable penis. The pesky little chestnut of *well, what do we do now?* Rusty didn't share the same concerns.

Assuming I'd have to do the undignified march back to my bed and chalk our encounter up to a one-time deal, I'd thrown it out there rather than suffer in uncertain self-doubt. What happened next floored me more than sex.

He wanted me to stay.

Crazy, right?

He actually wanted me to stick around.

While we didn't gaze meaningfully into each other's eyes and declare our undying love, whatever was going on between us wasn't purely a physical attraction. Rusty had to have felt it too. That maybe, just maybe, apart from amazing sex, he might like me as much as I liked him. Did I dare to hope?

The whole night he worshipped me like a goddess, making me come so many times I was convinced that I was either dreaming or having an out-of-body experience. He wasn't even weird about it. No talk of one-night stands, no friends-with-benefits, no that-was-great-now-get-out-of-my-life. Instead, he held me all night long. And even if it was temporary, I felt more wanted and cherished than I had in the whole time I'd been with Rob, and *that* was even better than the sex.

When I finally allowed myself to open my eyes, hoping that it wouldn't bring with it a horrible reality that we'd made a mistake, he just smiled and told me to get more sleep while he got a shower. His arms wrapped me in a warm hug as he kissed me deeply, almost as if we were already a couple. All completed with no freak-out. Well, none by him. Me on the other hand. I was still not convinced.

"Hey, baby." Rusty walked back into the bedroom, his towel slung low around his waist. "I want you to come hang out with me tonight. You have to be sick of sitting around this house." He dropped the towel with absolutely no warning, my eyes widening at the sight of him in the daylight. How the hell did we even get that in me last night? Did it get even bigger?

"Ummm." I tried to form words while my eyes stayed on his very ready penis. "Errr." Nope, no good. My brain waved the white flag signaling my mouth was on its own.

"You using me just for sex?" He moved closer to the bed not bothering to hide the now massive erection he was packing. "Or we going to date? I know you've probably been wondering, being that you tend to overanalyze everything, so I thought we should just get it out in the open and clear it up right now."

Silence. I blinked back, still unable to speak as I tried to reconcile what the hell just happened.

Did I just get a boyfriend?

"Okay, so we'll date then." He smiled, completely unfazed by my lack of response as he continued to talk. "Good choice. I'm an awesome boyfriend just so you know and even though you aren't crazy about Angie, having a girl best friend has had its benefits. I'm not great with chick-flicks but I'm happy to comfort you after and I can buy a pack of tampons without breaking a sweat. If you could just give me a heads up when you are going to have a period, that would be cool. As for me being on the road, you don't have to worry about that either. I'm over the groupie thing, so keeping my dick in my pants isn't an issue. Anything else?"

It's like he could read my mind. Like somehow he just knew everything I needed to hear and said it. Completely unprompted. No holding back, no second guessing—nothing. It was a freedom I could only dream of possessing.

"We're dating?" I really wished I could say something more intelligent, something that didn't make me sound so inept, but given the turn of events, I didn't hold out much hope. At least I was talking now, an obvious improvement from just staring at his penis. Small steps.

"Yep, sure are. Look how happy you are already. You can barely stop looking at my cock. Got to admit that kind of makes me happy too. We make such a great couple."

It was just as well I wasn't wearing panties because with that smile of his they'd be in some serious danger. He was also a master negotiator, and I wasn't going to argue.

"I guess we're dating then." My head nodded in a mix of disbelief and happiness. Look at that. I'm dating a rock star.

"Knew you would see it my way." He crawled onto the bed and tipped my chin. "Not to push the issue, but now that you're my girlfriend you are going to have to come see me play. You don't have to make a big deal about me being on stage right away but wearing the T-shirt isn't debatable." His lips found their way back onto my skin. I was totally digging this boyfriend thing. Oh yes I was.

Enjoying the moment would have been awesome, but sadly self-doubt crept back in. And as wonderful as his cock had been, it couldn't just wave away my insecurities. If only it were that simple. I'd be up for trying though. His cock was most definitely magic; maybe it just took a few turns?

"I'm good with T-shirt wearing, and band seeing but I have a few conditions of my own."

"Sure, go ahead. I already said I'm down with anal so anything else you've got lay it on me." His hand moved down my shoulder and across to my breast, his fingers not making it easy for me to concentrate.

"I can be neurotic and I overthink things. Sometimes I'm not great at communicating," I blurted out. He was going to run, any minute now.

"Ah, babe. It's kind of adorable that you think I don't know all that, but none of that shit matters to me." His kisses barely interrupted as he shook off my first point of concern.

"You have to be honest with me, always. No matter what happens, I need to know. If you accidentally do something with someone else or you suddenly decide you're not into me anymore, I want to know." I added, because obviously I hadn't scared him off yet. I needed to try harder.

In truth it was better we put it all on the table now, so he knew what he was getting into. I wasn't delusional enough to think he was offering me a forever here but I needed to know that when it ended, he would treat me with respect not blindside me and toss me aside. I wouldn't go through that again, even with the promise of really great sex.

"That's not going to happen. I'm not the type of guy who does shit like that, so it's not an issue for me." Tiny kisses skated across my collarbone, his lips doing their best to convince me before he stopped to look me in the eyes.

Almost as if he knew how important it was for me, keeping us right there. Connected.

My silly verbal spillage could have easily been shaken off. Dismissing my feelings as insecurities or being overly emotional. I'd been there before, the asshole who had tossed me aside so easily, had been great at minimizing my feelings and I had been too dumb to see it. In the end it didn't matter. I wasn't good enough which only reinforced what I had been feeling from the start.

Rusty was right. I deserved better than that.

"There's something else I need to tell you."

Apart from watching porn and sitting in my room wondering what it would feel like to run my tongue along Rusty's abs, I had spent some time—all right limited time—job hunting. The problem was that I didn't want to go back. Not just because I didn't want to start over at some new law firm, but because I honestly didn't know what I wanted to do for the rest of my life. Being a paralegal wasn't it.

He nodded waiting for me to go on, "So tell me."

"I'm not sure what I want to do." I took a deep breath and thought about how much easier this would have been without all my hang-ups. "I have never loved my work, and the more time goes by, the more I realize it was just a job for me. I did it because I felt I had to, but it didn't excite me. I want to do something that I love. Like you do. Which is dumb considering I have no money and I'm not really qualified for anything else."

And as if I hadn't just told him that I was probably going to be an unemployed loser for an indefinite period of time, he kissed me. Not those sweet kisses he'd been teasing with across my skin, a kiss that left no doubt that he wanted me. An involuntarily moan bubbled from my throat as he deepened the kiss, his hands pulling me closer as his mouth explored mine. Tingles traveled all over my body as I desperately needed more contact, my fingers feeling their way over his skin like they'd discovered muscles for the first time. I was almost positive I'd be able to pick him in a line up purely by touch.

"That's awesome." He smiled after he finally pulled his lips from mine. "'Cause I don't want you to get a job that you hate just because you *think* you should. No problems here, babe. And don't worry about money; it's not an issue. The house is mine and while I'm not tossing Benjamin's around like a pimp, I've got it covered." That mouth that had been so attentive earlier moved dangerously close to mine. "Anything else? Because I need to be in the studio in an hour and I want to make sweet, sweet love to my new girlfriend before I have to leave."

I didn't understand how he could be so cool with it all. Me, a complete mess with hardly any prospects and here he was signing up for it. And because I couldn't leave well enough alone, it really was a talent how argumentative I was, I had to ask why my laundry list of flaws didn't bother him.

"Alison, I'm plenty bothered. The fact I'm standing here naked and we're still not having sex is a problem. Don't make an issue where there isn't one."

Well, wasn't that just the revelation of the century. Don't make an issue where there isn't one. And without even trying he was teaching me something else.

"Make sweet, sweet love to me, Rusty." I stopped fighting and let go.

He smiled as he traced the outline of my breasts. His mouth slowly gliding down past my belly; it's journey ending between my legs. "Best girlfriend ever."

...

"You were supposed to fuck him, not date him. Have I taught you nothing? You are like a serial relationship-er." Renee stormed inside. "I guess at least *this* guy is hot. Tell me about the sex, on a scale of one to amazing, how good was it? Am I going to cry? Because you know I practically gave him to you." She barely took a breath as she collapsed onto the couch.

"Renee, you aren't even dating men right now remember? What happened to all that *dicks are so last week and pussy is where it's at?*"

Renee was my best friend, no question, but she was also completely scattered. Her mind was like a game of Jenga, which is why when my eviction notice was delivered I didn't immediately jump at the idea of moving in with her. Of course she would have offered, and I would have had a lovely sofa to spend my nights on, but her crazy antics would have made me more neurotic than I already was. Oh and she slept with everything that moved. Men, women—she didn't discriminate. Love was love and she had a lot to give. There were some things I just didn't need to see. My best friend in a threesome on her kitchen table was one of them.

"I'm not dating anyone right now, girl or guy." She dismissed me with the wave of her hand. "But I can appreciate a decent penis even if I'm currently on a girl streak. FYI this is what your problem is, you could learn a lot from me." She glanced around the room like it might hold some magical clues as to what Rusty's penis might look like.

"Well out of the two of us, I'm sure I'm the only one who came five times last night so I really don't think I need any lessons."

Sure it was crass. The whole kiss-and-tell wasn't my usual MO but as it stood now I was currently floating on cloud sixty-nine—something else we did last night—and I didn't care who knew it.

"Five times!" Renee almost fell of the couch, her eyes peeled back to straining proportions. "Holy hell, I take back what I said. Fuck dating the man, get a ring on it. Any man that makes you come five times you're going to want to keep around."

"We're not getting married but we are dating. He even called me his girlfriend without totally freaking out. I know usually you're supposed to date the guy *before* sleeping with him but the doing things backwards is sort of working out for us. I'm rolling with it."

I had fully expected Rusty to want to keep us low key. After all, I'd seen his reputation first hand. The continuous line of gorgeous women. He didn't strike me as someone who was itching to settle down. Not to say that I wasn't absolutely floored and excited beyond belief that he did want to do the let's-be-exclusive-thing, but I would have understood easing into it. Dipping a toe into couple-dom. Rusty Crawford however, eases into nothing.

Instead of slowly emerging as a pair, maybe changing his relationship status on Facebook or waiting until Christmas and posing for a joint Christmas card, we—the collective of him and I—were going out tonight with his band.

As a couple.

Together.

Around other people.

I had to fight the urge not to throw up.

Not only did I have maybe twelve or so hours to get used to the fact I was no longer single, but we were going to have to broadcast it publicly.

"Oh, God. I'm going to throw up."

Because I didn't want to share my wonderful spew-tastic moment with Renee, I ran my not-so-single ass to the bathroom and slammed the door. My body just making it to the toilet bowl in time for my undignified heave. Gross. This was not a good thing.

"Hey, you used protection right? Five-times-lover boy didn't knock you up already did he?" My beautiful yet not so wise bestie called through the door.

"Yes, we were careful and no one gets morning sickness that fast," I hollered back as I tried to win a war with the impending nausea. *Please don't throw up again, please don't throw up again.* And . . . too late, my body once again doubled over as what little had been in my stomach came back up for a revisit.

Ugh. This was not good.

"Why are you puking? Please don't tell me you are allergic to good sex. You'll break my heart." Renee's face greeted me when I finally opened the door.

"It's not the sex I'm worried about, it's his friends." The enormity of what I was about to do hitting me. "I was dating someone in secret for two whole years, I don't know how to do this in public. Plus, you've seen him. I'm going to be around all *that* where people can see. Judging me with their *judging.*" I waved my hands in front of me for effect.

I could see them now wondering what the hell a guy like him was doing with a girl like me. Talk about punching above my weight, I was going to be slaughtered.

"What are you talking about?" Renee slapped me across the shoulder. "You're gorgeous and if he didn't want to be seen with you he wouldn't have asked you out. He isn't anything like the loser you used to date who wanted you only as his dirty little secret. As for his friends, if they are judging you, it's because they are narrow-minded bastards who know nothing. Their opinion should mean nothing."

Easy for her to say, she wasn't the one who was going into the lion's den. God, that asshole really messed with my head. Thanks a lot, Rob—my mental fist shook in the air. I hope his new wife-to-be was a terrible lay.

"I can do this," I said out loud, under no delusions that I was the only one I was trying to convince. "I can totally do this."

"Of course you can. You are going to be brilliant." Renee

pulled me into a hug. "Just don't puke on him; that would be bad."

"Thanks for the vote of confidence."

Continuing to talk about it wasn't the solution. Nope. All it had done was give me a panic attack and made me lose breakfast. I needed action. Yes, that's what I needed to do. Push myself out of my comfort zone. Be strong. Be brave. Be . . . insert another motivating adjective.

So with my mind firmly set that I wasn't going to look like a loser, I pushed Renee out the door with a promise to give her a full report. I stopped short of photos because we both knew I sucked at selfies. The angle, trying to look sexy and not constipated, holding the camera with one hand and pressing the button—it was just beyond me. She would have to take my word for it.

First things first, I needed to decide what I was going to wear. I could already feel the panic starting to build again as I walked back into my room and started to rummage through my closet. It was seriously lacking in the rock and roll department with the main concentration of my wardrobe being corporate attire. Awesome, if we were going to take a deposition I'd be rocking it, but hanging with his friends—not so much.

Okay, Okay. Let's not panic. I have jeans. Cute tops. I have stuff to wear, I just needed to coordinate it all together. Oh and makeup too. And hair. Fuck. I was going to need a paper bag to blow into. Or a shot of Valium. Maybe both.

It was while searching for the paper bag—I was almost positive that looking for Valium would be a fruitless exercise—that I found something else which might be helpful. Something to calm my nerves.

No, not alcohol, I'd already established I wasn't a great drinker. But in the top-right hand kitchen cabinet housed in an old-school cookie container I found a very small bag of what I knew to be weed.

Ah, the flashbacks. Fond memories of my mother stashing her *baggies* in my Barbie's dream house, me wondering why Barbie needed dried oregano. It was such a joyous time.

In any case, I was going to get high. Not get so wasted that all I wanted to do was sit around in my underwear eating cold pizza, just enough of a buzz that the anxiety I was feeling wouldn't be an issue. What could possibly go wrong?

Trying to find rolling papers was another story. No amount of drawer rummaging turned up anything remotely useful. So rather than turn the whole house upside down in search of a smoking device, I decided to embrace my domestic goddess and have an afternoon date with my good old friend *Betty Crocker.*

Excellent. I was going to get high and eat brownies; just an average afternoon.

After I'd carefully measured out the ingredients, and added a liberal dose of herb, I put the pan in to bake. I was feeling relaxed already. This was the best idea I'd had all day. There was a little rock star in all of us and mine was just dying to come out.

And while my pockets of goodness were getting baked—the irony that I soon would be, wasn't lost on me—I returned to my closet with a new perspective and fresh pair of eyes.

I had plenty to wear. Heaps even. I have no idea why I was even worried in the first place. Totally unnecessary. I was going to look awesome.

The buzzer from the oven sounded as I'd finally decided on a pair of skinny jeans and a corset. The corset being from a leftover Halloween costume when I had insisted on going as Scarlett O'Hara. My frankly-my-dear-I don't-give-a-damn not getting anywhere near the acclaim it deserved and I was thankful I hadn't tossed the beautifully made undergarments away with the hideously hooped skirt.

See, everything had a purpose, and finally I was being rewarded. Rusty wasn't going to believe his eyes when he saw me; I was going to look sensational.

All I needed now was to get high, get showered, get dressed and get sexy—and I couldn't wait. This was going to be the best night ever.

Fifteen

Rusty

"**R**us, I'm in way over my head."

Max wasn't the type of guy to deal out the drama. He was your classic, laid back dude. More reliable than Joey but nowhere near as high strung as Angie, he was an easy fit in the caravan of crazy that was Black Addiction. So his current mood was completely out of character when he was pacing, wearing a hole in the floor and acting like the Po-Po just took his last dime bag. I had to wonder what the fuck was going on.

"Dude, whatever it is, we'll work it out." It couldn't be that bad, maybe Angie's pregnancy hormones were just getting to everyone.

"Yeah, it's that fucking bad." He pushed his ass into the seat beside me.

"So lay it on me, what's going down?"

There wasn't a lot that could have killed my mood. After finally getting Alison into my bed and having more sex in the last twenty-four hours than I'd had since she moved in, I was happily in bliss-town.

While the first time we'd had sex had been pretty damn awesome, it wasn't even close to what the rest of the night ended up producing. The douchebag she'd been with before hadn't made her come properly in the two years which meant she had turned into the perfect lady-in-the-streets-and-a-freak-in-the sheets combo, willing to try almost anything. She was an enigma and there wasn't a chance in hell I was letting anyone else get a taste.

Fuck. That.

I was locking it down, happily doing the couple thing. It was an easy choice.

Unfortunately, while I was fantasizing about my hot new girlfriend, Max was spilling his guts about his fucktard of a brother. The piece of shit douchebag who had been mooching off Joey and Max, had also been up to some shady behavior. Max overheard some cryptic late-night phone calls, Phil also being evasive on his whereabouts when leaving the house. His long-suffering wife was completely done with his stoner ways and wanted to make the split permanent.

"Some serious shit is going down. Nicole, Phil's wife, didn't just kick him out. She's divorcing him. I went to her house to see if I could patch things up between the two of them, smooth some shit over. And instead I came face to face with a dude who is almost as wide as he is tall wearing Phil's fucking robe." He dragged his hands through his hair. "She said he'd been hiding something their whole marriage. Like epic shit that even she couldn't believe. She told me she was done with him; that she couldn't believe he'd buried the secret for all these years."

"What the hell could Phil have done? Another woman? It's

not like he's smart enough to do much else?" Phil putting his dick where it didn't belong was plausible, but other than that I came up empty. Last time I checked the US government had stopped using monkeys so CIA operative wasn't even in contention.

"Dude, she wouldn't tell me, just kept going on and on about the emails she found. Years of correspondence that confirmed he had some kind of double life. Something bad apparently happened before they even met and he's kept it hidden all these years. Thank fuck they never had kids."

"Surely she's exaggerating? Double life? Unless he's been going to Thailand and entertaining lady boys, it has to be an affair. Do you have any idea what she could be talking about? He isn't rocking some deep desire to suck dick is he?" I bucked out a laugh wondering how *that* asshole shared the same DNA as the standup guy in front of me. Maybe he'd been switched at birth. That could qualify as the deep, dark secret and surely a fantasy we'd all hoped for.

"It's not funny." He huffed out a breath before continuing. "Problem is that Phil knows I went over there. He thinks me talking to Nicole was going to work shit out for him. And there lies the dilemma. I have no idea what I'm dealing with, what if he's dying or something? And how to tell him that not only is there no hope but there's some other guy in his house taking care of his old lady."

I was trying to be sympathetic. Really, I was, but the fact Phil contributed nothing to society other than trouble for his brother made it really freaking hard for me to dig deep and give a fuck.

"Ah fuck, Max. That sucks but you're just going to have to

tell him, no point in prolonging that shit. Like a Band-aid—boom, your Mrs. is shacked-up with someone else and by the way, she found out about your fetish for lady's lingerie." No shit, I gave zero fucks.

"Are you kidding me?" Max clocked me with a stare, my lack of fucks multiplied by a million by him. "He's already talking the *I've-got-nothing-to-live-for* shit, I don't want him to off himself while I'm gone."

"He doesn't mean that stuff, he's just being dramatic. You're going to find out this BS secret is going to be lame and all this worry was over nothing. Trust me, he is a grown ass man, he'll deal." Phil was slowly climbing to the top of my shit list. Right after the limp-dick who'd messed with my girl.

"And what if he doesn't *deal*? That's the kind of guilt I don't want to be carrying for the rest of my life."

Max had a point. While I might not have lost any sleep over the oxygen thief's demise, his kid brother would have life-longed that burden. Max was one of the few dudes I'd take a bullet for so the problem that hadn't been mine was suddenly moving into my mental space. Like it or not, this shit wasn't going away.

"So what's the alternative? Let him believe he has a chance? It will just be worse for him in the long run. Get him drunk and get him laid and hopefully he'll come clean or if nothing else, find someone else to be his new personal Jesus. There are plenty of dumbasses that will still find your loser brother attractive. Why, is still a mystery, but you give him two weeks and he will be all wrapped up in some other set of pretty legs. It's Phil, if the man didn't think with his dick, he wouldn't think at all."

We just needed to keep him drunk enough and whatever shit he'd been hiding would find its way to the surface. Then Max and the rest of us could move on with our lives. It would also serve to distract him from the fact his wife had moved on to greener pastures, tired of his BS and was ready to sign paperwork to make it legal. Perhaps she'd just been sober enough for the first time and realized what a dickwad she'd actually married, hate to break it to her but that wasn't much of a secret.

"You think that would work? We take him out, get him talking and set him up with someone?" Max was slowly coming around to my way of thinking.

"Well it's an option, less chance of you finding him in your bathroom with slit wrists if his dick's getting sucked." Problem fucking solved. Honestly, I could totally moonlight as a hostage negotiator. Now, if everyone was off the ledge maybe we could wrap this up so I could go home to my girl.

"You know what? I think that might work." Max relaxed for the first time since we'd started the conversation. "We get him out, meeting girls and convince him he doesn't want to be married. Show him what he's been missing. He'll come clean about whatever it is and be begging for the divorce."

"That's the spirit. All good things. Glad we had this talk." I gave him a tap on the shoulder as I grabbed my keys and phone. Now we could move on to more important things, like me getting home.

"Wait, where are you going?" Max grabbed my arm stopping me from walking out the door.

"Um, home. You know that place that I live, pay the bills for. Figured that was a good place to go." Did I really have to explain this? Last thing I needed was to be late when I promised to take Alison out. She'd been unsure it actually counted as a first date but whatever it was, I didn't need Alison already pissed at me before it began.

"No, you can't leave me with this." Max shook his head while his body blocked the door. Me, leaving any time soon, not happening. "This is a team effort, you need to come with us. Besides no one gets the kind of girls you can."

"Dude, I'm seeing Alison now." I didn't think the elaboration was needed but threw it in for good measure. "So in the spirit of dating, I'm not fucking anyone else. I know it's old fashioned of me but I'm kicking it retro for a bit and seeing how it feels."

Whatever the plan was, I wanted no part of it. A month ago, there would have been no problem. We could have all gone out, gotten hammered and gotten laid. As far as good times went, I knew exactly where to get them. But no fucking way was I going out on the town looking for pussy after I just told a girl we were going to be doing the couple thing. Max had a better chance of me sucking his brother's dick than me letting some girl suck mine. Not happening.

"So don't fuck them." He stepped in front of me again as I tried to pull a dodge and make for the door. "I'm sure you've spoken to girls you didn't fuck."

"Well, yeah . . ." I wasn't an animal; there were plenty of girls I spoke to who I didn't end up in. Difference was, the types of girls we were going to need to lock up this deal weren't the kind that wanted conversation. Unless by conversation you meant talking to their pussy, then they were all about it.

"So that's easy, just don't tell them you're not going to fuck them." He shrugged impassively like it was no big deal.

Max had to be desperate. Seriously these were words of a man doing that final death walk and hoping like hell his last Hail Mary was going to stick. No crystal ball was needed to know this was going to end badly.

"Oh, no. This is where I go out with you, and then Alison sees or hears about me with a girl and thinks I'm cheating. Then Phil's drama becomes my fucking drama. I'm not interested in the misunderstanding fall out. Seriously, you tell me how this all plays out in your head where *I* don't end being screwed over."

It was a sure thing. A bonafide cluster fuck waiting to happen, where all the good intentions in the world wouldn't count for jack.

"I will talk to Alison, I will tell her the whole thing," Max offered, not willing to let it go.

"How about you *don't* talk to her and do what you need to do and leave me out of it."

I was all ready to leave, to tell Max good luck with his quest for pussy and go home to my girl, but the utter defeat in his face stopped me walking out the door.

"Rus, please. I know I'm asking a lot but I need your help. Not for Phil, for me. Don't fucking hang me out to dry, okay? I know you don't give a shit because your life is so fucking perfect right now but not all of us are riding that wave. He does something stupid or gets into trouble and I'll be the one wearing that. He's my family, same as the band is. I would never turn my back on any of you but if shit goes south I won't be able to leave him either. Please don't make me fucking choose."

Well. Fuck.

Every reason I had not to help him was negated by those four fucking words—*I need your help*. If Joey or Angie came to me, it would be the same thing, no questions asked. Just tell me what you need and it would be done, so whether or not it was going to mean a lot of heat for me, there was no longer a choice to make.

"You had to go there and throw in that *Nicholas Sparks* shit?" My hand smacked him across the back.

"If that's what I need to do to get you in on this, then yes."

"Fine, but *I'm* the one who tells Alison." I was already regretting my decision. "Let me be clear, there will be no fucking on my part. Nor any shit that is going to impact what I am trying to get going with my girl."

No, really. If this ended up the way that had me losing my girl, Max wasn't going to have to worry about his brother killing himself, I'd take care of that for him.

"Wow Rusty, reformed and everything. Who knew you had it in you?" Max laughed as he followed me out the door.

"It's done. I like her. Do not fuck this up for me."

"I swear, Rus, nothing bad will happen."

Famous. Last. Words.

●●●

The drive took longer than expected. My little heart-to-heart with Max meant I got caught right in the middle of peak hour traffic. Not that there was ever a time where driving on the roads in New York was clear, but even giving my Camaro a few extra taps on the gas pedal still wasn't getting me home on time. Utter bullshit.

When I finally pulled up into the driveway I was half an hour later than I wanted to be and I was hoping my later arrival didn't mean I'd missed anything good. She still had those anal beads and a healthy curiosity. Man, I could only hope.

"Hey, baby." Alison ambled over wearing a corset and a thong. "Ready to go out?" Her body struggled to remain upright.

Gravity wasn't her only problem. Her arms and legs weren't doing much better at being operational, her eyes struggling to remain open as she mumbled an affectionate hello. Her mouth was still talking nonsense as she pulled me into a kiss, her hands all over my ass.

"Alison?" I peeled my mouth away from hers long enough to ask. "Have you been drinking?"

While the smell of alcohol was noticeably absent so was her sobriety. The under-the-influence part of the equation fairly evident—the "*with what*", my only question.

"Not. One. Little. Drop." She tapped me on the nose before collapsing into my arms and exploding into spontaneous giggles.

"What the hell happened to you?" Considering her pants were MIA and she had less muscle control than a newborn giraffe, I'd say something wasn't right. Also in the mix were her hands that were alternating between grabbing my ass and trying to unbuckle my belt and her mouth trying to touch any of my skin it could catch between laughing. "Baby? What's going on?"

More giggling, this time followed up by her lips sucking on

my neck.

"Rusty, can we have sex? I'm really, really horny." Her hand grabbed at my crotch and yanked at my dick, her tits doing their best to rub up and down my chest.

"Jesus Christ, are you high?"

Unless someone had taken an overdose of Benadryl followed with a vodka chaser, the confirmation wasn't required. And color me surprised because instead of walking in and seeing Ali with an ass full of butt plugs, she was as high as a kite. Not something I was expecting to see today. Or ever.

"I may have had a teensy, tiny bit of your weed." Her hand gave up trying to work me through my jeans and instead dove into my pants, her fingers grazing my skin as they made contact with my cock.

"My weed? I don't have any weed."

While the hand job she was currently trying to work was sloppy and uncoordinated, my dick didn't care. Nope, not at all. He was happy for her to get her experimentation on and let her *Helen Keller* her way however she saw fit. And as for being high, while unexpected, I had no problem with it. Not sure if it was residual boredom or an extension of her *trying something new*, but there was nothing wrong with a little medicinal relaxation. Had partaken in it myself from time to time. Always ended with a good time, much like where this one was headed. So other than trying to be responsible and not just fuck her like she was asking me to do, her buzz didn't worry me. Not in the slightest.

What did have me perplexed beyond measure was the fact she'd said it was *my weed*. *My* weed did not exist. I'd cleaned house in an effort to keep me on the wagon, one cigarette *usually* lead to the other, which meant my time worshiping the ganja gods came to an end. So as far as anything of *that* nature being mine, we had a problem.

"Alison, I don't have any weed. What are you talking about?" She moved awkwardly in my arms as she undid my belt.

"Ha-har," she mock laughed. "Of course you do. I found it in the kitchen. I couldn't find any papers though so I had to bake it." She laughed legitimately this time; her words obviously being hilarious. "I baked it to get baked." She laughed again. "Oh my God, I'm so hungry. I don't want any more brownies though; we're going to need to find something else to eat. Are we still going out to dinner? I just need shoes." She stopped working my cock and whipped around to look at her bare feet.

"You're going to need more than shoes, babe." I wondered if any further effort to gain information was going to be futile. Whatever she'd found in my kitchen hadn't been mine.

While the slow dance with flailing arms and legs was a good time, I figured getting her to the bedroom was a better plan. It would also give me a chance to investigate the mystery that was my stoned girlfriend. Her horizontal meant less chance she'd hurt herself, not that I wasn't enjoying the random cock grabs and neck sucks.

"Just taking you to bed, babe." I gave up on the assisted walk and picked her up instead, her relaxed body easing into my arms as I made the short walk to the bedroom. "I'll get you something to eat if you lay down like a good girl." Her body sunk into the mattress as I lowered her slowly, her arms staying locked around my neck.

"Cheetos. Can you get Cheetos? And a Diet Coke. Maybe ice

cream," she mumbled into my neck as she tried to pull me down with her. "And M&Ms, I want those too." She slurred, giving up on me and rolling onto her side, the food obviously more important than my dick. Awesome. This was going to be a fun night.

"Yep, I can get all that stuff, but you need to not get up," I warned her, giving her a kiss on the cheek. "I'll bring it all to you."

"God, I love you," she blurted out as she flipped onto her back. "Love you so much. And your penis. I *really* love him too."

Completely toasted. The come down was going to be a bitch.

"He's glad, we're both ecstatic. So let me do what I need to do so I can get back and we can enjoy each other."

While my penis was happy for the love and adoration, the rest of me knew she didn't mean it. Her mind was so clouded she had no idea what she was saying, and if I had produced a bag of Cheetos like she wanted, they too would have gotten an I-love-you. Not to say it wasn't nice hearing it, even if it would be forgotten by morning.

Leaving Alison in my bed, hopefully where she wouldn't get into any more trouble, I went back into the kitchen to hunt and gather. Clues being the first objective, junk food and soda being the second. Handy that they'd both be in the one place.

Obviously she'd cleaned the kitchen before getting wasted with the place spotless, the mixing bowl and brownie pan already chilling in the dish rack. The only evidence of any foul play being the plate of innocent looking baked goods sitting on the kitchen counter. Me, no more informed than when I'd left the bedroom. Where the hell did she get the drugs? My eyes scanned the room until they settled on an unfamiliar ceramic cookie jar still on the counter. It's ownership, not mine.

Motherfucker.

It took me about ten seconds to join the dots, my hand reaching for my cell and dialing Max before it even reached my ear. My anger playing catch up to the fucking disbelief.

"Dude, you want to go tonight? We can be ready in thirty?" Max started talking without the obligatory hello.

"Which one of you assholes put Phil's stash in my kitchen?" I followed suit, my greeting also missing in action.

"Oh, yeah. Forgot about that. Just leave it and I'll pick it up later. Just don't smoke it. It's hella strong—messed Phil up—which is why I took it and hid it at yours. He was strung out for fucking hours."

No shit. Watching Alison trying to stay upright was like trying to nail Jell-O to the wall, I didn't need the "it's strong" disclaimer.

"Well, it's a bit late for that. Tell me it's not fucking laced." I pinched the bridge of my nose hoping we were dealing with straight weed.

"Huh? You smoking again?"

"No, not me."

My patience had already gone beyond its expiration date so I nixed any further of the back and forth. Filling Max in on the wonderful housewarming I'd received when I walked through my front door. My new girlfriend stoned out of her mind in case he didn't pick up the hints.

"Holy shit, how much did she have?" He laughed into the phone, his enjoyment of the situation not pleasing me.

"Considering I don't know how much there was to start

with, it would be an estimation at best. Let's say enough to take down an elephant." My hands squeezed the phone as I heard Alison calling from the bedroom. Her words nothing more than random sounds.

"It's un-doctored, medical grade with a kick. She'll be fine." His laughter continued, mine still missing in action.

After giving Max a few stern *fuck you's* and gaining an apology, I ditched the call and the phone, my plans for the evening now in desperate need of rearranging.

Loaded up with some chips and a Diet Coke—the best I could improvise without heading to the store—I made my way back to my bedroom where sleeping beauty was passed out with her legs wide open. Oh . . . that's right, she was also wearing a thong, my dick taking a sudden interest in what was happening on my bed.

"Babe?" I dumped the food and drink on my nightstand before giving her a gentle shake. "You still hungry?" I was literally shaking my head.

"Heeeyyyy." An eye slowly cracked open, being chased up by a beautiful smile. "You're back." Her arms spaghettied in front of her as she reached for me.

"Sure am beautiful girl. I brought snacks too but we're going to have a little chat first." I kicked off my shoes and crawled onto the bed beside her. "You want to explain how this all happened?"

Expecting any logical or coherent explanation was ambitious at best, but questions still had to be asked. Her choice in wardrobe was also another flashing neon sign. None of it made sense.

"I'm not cool enough . . . your . . .friends . . ." Was as far as she got before another eruption of giggles, her hands doing their best to undo my belt.

Her sentence—and I use that term loosely—didn't offer up too much. A bunch of garbled, random words and frequent pauses meant I had more chance of deciphering da Vinci's code than I did of understanding her.

"Okay, babe. Let's just hang here tonight. We'll do the date thing tomorrow." Hopefully when she could pass a clear urine sample and connect two words together without the added laugh track.

"Rusty, you need to fuck me now." Her mouth fumbled over the letters but surprisingly strung them all together.

Yeah, can't say I disagreed, my jeans were about to choke out my dick while my mind was weighing the options.

"Babe, you want sex, you need to be conscious. It's a funny rule I have, so you're going to have to humor me on it." I pulled off my shirt and jeans as she struggled to sit up.

"I'm awake. Look at me." Her hand tried to smack her face but ended up flying past and hitting her shoulder.

"Yeah, I'm looking." I laughed; my eyes watching her flop around on the bed while I ditched the rest of my clothes.

"You are sooooo hot." She jacked up of the mattress and started making out with my pecs. "We are so having sex right now." Her fingers gripped my dick and started to stroke.

"You sure that's what you want?" My mouth kept talking despite my balls wanting it to shut the fuck up. "I thought you wanted to eat?" My hand did its own exploring and found that beneath the thong, she was already wet.

"I do want to eat." Her mouth moved further down my abs. "You." She barely got the word out of her mouth before it was replaced by my cock.

"Jesus." I held her head while she shoved it deeper into her throat, the whole gag reflex obviously not an issue today.

"Mmm. Hmm," she mumbled while she sucked me, the vibrations traveling down my length making it feel insane. Her hand joined the party keeping time with her mouth.

"If you're eating, it's only fair I should be too."

I was a team player, and liked to give as much as I liked to receive. Given our plans for tonight involved staying within the four walls we found ourselves in, I was all about making the most of it.

It only took me a second to maneuver her the way I wanted. Alison protested as I pulled my dick from her mouth, the award winning blowjob continuing the minute we were both lying on the mattress side by side. Panties were torn off her and thrown to the floor in an effort to gain better access. Her top was left on after I gave up trying to unhook the piece of shit, my patience for the stupid thing being tossed out the window. It took a few tries—her body rag-dolling this way and that—but finally I'd spun us around so that all the bits that matter matched up, my tongue dragging across the entire length of her pussy in one long continuous lick.

"Holy shit." She pulled my dick out of her mouth as she realized what was going down. Namely, me.

"Yeah? You want me to do that again?" I didn't wait as I repeated the action, this time my fingers giving a little love too.

"It feels . . ." She didn't finish, her eyes glossing over as my tongue got busy again, my dick getting some vice action from her hand.

"Easy there, baby. He likes to get squeezed, not suffocated."

The sweet feeling danced between pleasure and pain.

"Yes."

Just one single word passed through those beautiful swollen lips and then her mouth got busy doing something else. Her hand continued to stroke me while her lips and tongue choreographed a dance of kissing, sucking and licking—all of which was driving me insane.

Not to be outdone, I had a floorshow of my own happening. My mouth feasting on her while my fingers stretched her out, my hand fucking her in the absence of my dick. Her squirms giving me all the signals I needed that she was close.

We were both close.

The more I concentrated on what I was doing the more my body took over, my dick screaming on the urge to come as I felt her clamp around my hand and still for minute. There was no need for a verbal confirmation, her pussy giving me all the intel I needed as I shoved a finger in her ass while she rode against my hand. Her body bucked out of control against my mouth as I refused to let up, teasing every inch of pleasure out of her.

I couldn't hold back as whatever resolve I had went flying out the window. Her hand griped me tighter as a silent scream vibrated against my shaft, my hot load squirting into her mouth and face as she continued to jerk me off. Our bodies falling apart from each other in one big, hot, sweaty, out of breath mess.

"Rusty. That was—"

"Fucking outstanding." I didn't give her a chance to finish, my own natural high getting close to her synthetic one.

"Yeah." She nodded, her body worming its way down the

bed to where I was laying, the sheets underneath us completely saturated.

"I take it you've never had sex while under the influence."

"Um. That would be a no." She laughed her head moving across to my chest as I played with her hair.

"A whole new world. We can make it just as good without though, that I can promise." And was going to have a hell of a lot of fun proving.

A few more giggles shook her before she drifted off to sleep, her body wrapped around mine the entire time. Her quest for Cheetos forgotten while she dozed in my arms, sleep not on the cards for me, being it was only seven thirty.

A couple of hours were spent in snoozeland before she finally woke, her arm stretching and slapping me in the face as she tried to clear her bloodshot eyes. Come down's weren't ever great and hers was no exception.

"My mouth feels funny." She smacked her lips together as she slowly sat up in bed. Her hair looked like a tornado and whatever makeup she'd been wearing was now gracing my sheets.

"Happens. Have something to drink, you'll be fine." I handed her the Diet Coke she'd forgotten about, the can losing its chill hours ago.

"I think I must have added too much weed to the brownies. I only ate one but I still feel weird." She scratched her head as she took in her surroundings, not sure how much recall was actually connecting.

"It was a strong batch. It was Max's brother's. God only knows where he got it. Guy is a certified stoner." I shuffled up the bed to join her and pulled her into a hug.

"Yeah, that wasn't my smartest idea." She nodded against my skin, her hand on me like she didn't want to let go.

"Nope, I'd say probably not. I guess boredom is a killer." It was the only excuse I could come up with why the girl who'd been seriously straitlaced would even think of toking up. Sitting at home day in and day out couldn't be easy; eventually you're going to look for some form of entertainment.

"Not boredom. Nerves. I almost had a panic attack over us going out with your friends. I know it's stupid, but even when I was in a relationship it was sort of in the shadows. We dated each other, no one else was really involved so I'm not used to the extended circle. People judging me. And you're you. There are definitely going to be questions asked." She barely took a breath getting all her words out, her need to explain fighting against her urge to shut up.

"You were worried about my friends?" I shook my head in disbelief. "Even if I did care what they thought, you're with me and that's all that would matter to them. But this other stuff, I'm me? What do you even mean?"

Never had it occurred to me that hanging with me and the band would make her feel inadequate. I was actually hoping for the opposite, pushing her out of her shell a little to show her how much I wanted her in my world. I wasn't even sure why, I just did and that was enough for me.

"I mean, look at you." Her fingers circled the muscles in my chest while she kept her head down. "You don't think they aren't going to wonder what the hell you are doing with me? Like whatever possessed you to date me?"

"Have you looked in a fucking mirror recently?" My head snapped around as I forced her to look me in the eye. "Fuck,

Alison. You're beautiful. Any one of those assholes would kill to have you as their girlfriend, that's what they are going to be thinking. If anyone is going to be wondering anything it will be how the hell did I land you?"

Joey had already shown his appreciation, not so subtly hinting that he would happily take her off my hands. Max had more class so he wouldn't say anything but the fucker wasn't blind. Angie would be Angie but eventually she'd come around too. What was there not to like? She was a fireball wrapped up in a sexy package and in the space of a few short weeks had knocked me on my ass.

She didn't answer, her silence disagreeing as she snuggled closer to my body, her inability to see what a catch she was, unable to make sense in my head.

"You know what, let's go anyway." My need to prove her wrong higher than my need to stay in bed and cuddle. "Let's get you cleaned up and go meet them. Obviously you aren't taking my word for it. Best you see it first-hand." My arms and legs untangled from her as I lifted myself off the bed.

"You want to go? Now?" She resisted as I yanked on her arm, trying to pull her off the mattress with me.

"Yep, no more thinking about it. Shower, change and out the door. We can grab some dinner on the way."

"Rus—" I didn't wait for the excuse.

"Don't think about it, you're giving that shit too much power. Just walk to the edge of that cliff and take a leap. Nothing bad is going to happen."

Not sure if it was her loser mother, the loser ex-boyfriend or something else—but her perception of herself was seriously messed up. Stuck in a world where she didn't think she was good enough and believed she somehow deserved—and worse than that, expected—bad shit to happen.

While she wasn't totally on board, she didn't fight me either. My offer to shower with her met with a smile that told me she knew it wasn't only hair washing I had on my mind. And being that we weren't in a hurry I made sure we were both good and clean before getting our clothes on.

Her earlier choice of outfit abandoned as she grabbed a pair of jeans and top. Much better.

"You ready?" I grabbed my phone, my keys and her hand and opened the front door.

"Sure, but don't tell me I didn't warn you."

As his old 1960's something Camaro sped down the road, my brain slowly flicked into focus, the residual high taking longer to fade. He was right. He was *always* right. I gave the opinions of others way too much power.

Controlling people's thoughts was a super power I'd never possess, sad I know. Even trying to change their perceptions was a fruitless exercise, so I needed to stop. Take responsibility, and own it. Own who I was without the thousand apologies. I was good enough.

All of this had been a catalyst, like being shot out of a cannon. It was crazy but I had needed to hit my bottom. To reach absolute saturation of shit before I could finally wake up. I had been a doormat. I had allowed people to treat me a certain way, excused their behavior. It was a pattern and one I desperately needed—and for the first time *wanted*—to break.

"You nervous?" Rusty turned his head as the car pulled up at the front of the bar. My restless knee bouncing on the seat a dead giveaway.

"Yep, but I'll be fine." No point lying, we both knew I wasn't doing great.

"Own it, Alison. Don't let anyone tell you, you aren't good enough. They do and you push your shoulders back and flip them the bird." He pulled the keys out of the ignition, his hand just stopping short of opening the driver's side door.

"Consider it owned." I smiled back, hoping my resolve would kick in.

He had jumped out of the car and was at the passenger side door before I'd had a chance to even climb out, his arm slipping around my waist the minute my feet hit the gravel.

His hands on me sent waves of excitement through me. My nerves tried to not short circuit as we walked into the crowded bar. The same bar where we had our very first conversation, and the one I had waltzed into and made out with him shamelessly. The bar definitely had history.

Pushing through the throng of people was difficult, it seemed like we had to stop every two steps for people to say hello to Rusty, their interest in me ranging from none at all to friendly hellos. To my surprise no one cowered away in gasped shock, Rusty's hand on mine earning not even so much as a stare. Hmmm.

"Crazy bar girl." The guy who had been having sex in the bathroom called out as soon as he saw us. His beer lifted almost as high as his smug grin. Ugh, I dug deep hoping to find a pocket of bravado still left in me so I wouldn't have to hide behind my boyfriend. Gah, it was still weird saying it.

"Hi, rocker dude with questionable judgment." My mouth shot out before my brain had registered, Rusty giving me a squeeze of encouragement as we got closer.

"Wow, she's got your number." The other rocker dude shoved original rocker dude's shoulder. "I'm Max, nice to finally meet you."

"Oh, yeah?" It hadn't meant to sound like a question but my surprise overrode my mouth. "I'm Alison." I held out my hand awkwardly wondering if handshaking was no longer cool. There really wasn't an acceptable alternative, hugging was definitely not happening.

"I know." Max winked, thankfully returning my handshake so my hand wasn't sticking out there like a loser. He was a good guy I'd decided. I wouldn't plot his demise, at least not today.

"Angie and Jase will be here soon." Original rocker dude waved over the bartender. I struggled to recall his name. "Just a heads up."

"Thanks, Joe." Rusty pulled me closer to his side thankfully saying the rocker dude's name so I wouldn't look lame by asking. Joey, my recall making the connection thanks to the prompt. Maybe this wasn't going to be so bad.

I'm not sure if it was his faith in me or my commitment to change which made me relax, but like a strange and wonderful miracle it all made sense. There was a reason I had sought him out in the first place. That when my life was crumbling and I was drowning in misery, the road had led to him. My subconscious putting me on the path I knew would shatter the walls I'd spent years building up. And I wasn't going to disappoint either of us.

"So, Alison." Max rolled the bottle of beer slowly in his hand. "Heard you had some fun this afternoon." He and Rusty having some eyeball, non-verbal exchange. Tales of my adventurous afternoon obviously had been recounted.

That was exactly the kind of confrontation that in the past would have sent me running. Flimsy excuses about needing a bathroom would have been made and possibly a few "I'm sorrys" would have been thrown in. Anything that would have secured my exit and driven the attention away from me would have been my strategy, but instead of going down my well-worn path I tried something new. I didn't run, I didn't make excuses and I didn't apologize. It felt incredibly liberating as I shucked my previous MO.

"Yeah, I got white trash wasted on some special brownies." A voice I barely recognized as my own spilled out of my mouth. "I heard it was your brother's; kudos to his dealer." A newfound freedom exploded within me, no idea where any of it had come from.

"You made pot brownies?" Joey asked, obviously not having heard about my wayward afternoon where I got high in my underwear. It had all been pretty impressive, I'm sure he was sad to have missed it.

It was a shame for him really, because it sounded like I was a riot high. Pity only snippets of it actually stayed with me. Other than the incredible sex, which was out of this world amazing.

Instead of stopping my out of control mouth that was currently operating without my usual hesitations, I just shrugged and kept going. "Yeah, I had to improvise. I know brownies are a bit of a throwback, I would have preferred to make fudge. Possibly macaroons? You can connect with your inner Jim Morrison and still be classy." Who the hell was I right now?

"Whoa, you need to ditch your boyfriend and come hang with me. Your talents would be more appreciated." Joey's eyes widened, obviously appreciating my culinary skills or the fact my mouth was spewing out whatever popped into my head.

"Ah thanks, but I'm not your type. You like strippers and I can't dance, so we'd have never worked out."

Whoever was talking wasn't Alison Williams. She looked like me and sounded like me, but it was surely someone else. Maybe a random bored spirit that was tired of circling purgatory jumped in and possessed me, but whatever the reason, I liked it. The freedom of saying whatever I wanted dizzying me in exhilaration.

"That's my girl." Rusty nuzzled my neck in appreciation, kissing me right there for everyone to see. I liked it. Both my loose mouth and his public display of affection. We made such a great team.

"Your girl is awesome." Max nodded, handing me a beer. "You don't have a sister do you?"

"Nope, just me." I accepted the beer I hadn't ordered and lifted it to my lips. "Thanks for the drink."

Wonders would never cease. Here I was having a conversation with people I didn't know and there was no need for a paper bag or drugs. I could actually do this, who knew. Celebrations were definitely on the cards.

"You're welcome." Max shot me a wink, his smile widening.

"Dude, I know you aren't hitting on my girlfriend right in front of me. 'Cause if you are, you should just save your time, she's pretty taken with me." Rusty gave Max a friendly tap on the arm.

"If he gets to flirt with her, I do too." Joey added into the mix. "Guitarists have big egos but not much else, everyone knows the drummer is the star of the band." His brow rose in suggestion.

"Don't mind Joey, babe, he is obviously high as well." Rusty mock whispered in my ear earning him a finger from the drummer in question.

Ah, it was all just going so well. My fears slowly dissolving with a *pfft, what were we worried about*, the conversation as easy as the view. Not that I'd ever consider defecting, but every one of those Black Addiction boys were attractive—all that *good looking* had to be dangerous on stage. I was definitely going to see them play.

But like all tests—ones we give ourselves or prescribed by others— inevitably a wave of panic rolls in. Like sitting in an exam and not noticing you forgot to fill out a page until the last dying ten minutes. That was exactly the feeling that washed over me as I saw a very pregnant, heavily-tattooed badass who I'd already met—Angie. And here we go.

Round two.

"Hello, Angie." My hand shot out offering her the handshake I'd denied her when we first met, my smile hopefully not looking as fake as it felt.

"Hello, Alison." She reached for my hand, her smile just as manufactured as mine. Oh, goodie. We were going to be such good friends. Not.

"Well I'm glad everyone could make it." Rusty's hand returned to my waist in a show of affection. "I know it's all about me showing off and you're all awesome to humor me. This is my girl Alison and she has excellent taste in men."

Angie looked at the arm he had around me and gave him a

not so subtle glare. She was going to be a harder nut to crack.

"Hi, I'm Jason." The guy who had his arms solidly locked around Angie volunteered. "I'm the husband." His muscular arms just as inked as his wife's.

"Don't let him fool you, Ali." Rusty brought me in closer, giving me a kiss on the neck. "He's the keyboard player for Power Station. It would be good if you can pretend they're a big deal, even if you don't know who they are. They aren't as humble as us."

The introduction wasn't necessary. Unless you'd been living on Mars for the last ten years, everyone knew who Power Station were. Especially if you had a New York zip code, the local guys who were catapulted into international rock stardom were a household name. And while Rusty had mentioned they'd toured with them previously, I hadn't realized they were all good friends. It was sort of weird seeing a celebrity up close. I am fairly sure Rusty never mentioned Angie was married to one of them.

"I know who Power Station are." I smiled, trying to not to sound like a moron in front of the famous guy. "I saw you guys play at a club a few years ago, some kind of surprise performance. It was great."

"I said acknowledge them, I didn't mean inflate his already huge ego. You'll give me a complex." Rusty squeezed me tighter, his grin hinting he wasn't serious.

"Well, thanks. I'm glad you had a good time and in case you didn't already know, Rusty couldn't get a complex if he tried." Jason's conversation continued despite his wife not looking impressed. "And it's good to finally meet you too. Rusty likes to talk, I wasn't sure you were real."

Everyone laughed except for Angie. Her steely disposition not changing since she'd walked in. To be honest, I didn't understand the girl/guy best friend dynamic. Not saying that it wasn't possible to have a platonic meaningful relationship with a member of the opposite sex, but in my experience it just didn't work out that way. And even though Rusty assured me nothing had ever happened between them, I wasn't crazy about another girl being that close to a guy who I had just started dating. My feelings had already started to develop into something other than just lust. I really, really liked him.

"Angie, can I get you something to drink? A juice or something?" While I was sure I was fighting a losing battle, I tried again to be polite. Ordinarily I would have happily let it go, allowed the two of us to continue to give each other the evil eye, but if she was important to Rusty then we'd somehow have to find a way to be in the same room together. I could be the bigger person. Hopefully my effort wouldn't be tossed back at me.

"Sure, let's go to the bar." Angie agreed with very little enthusiasm. She might not have been happy about it, but perhaps a middle ground could be reached. If only because we both cared for the same guy.

There were a lot of things I didn't want to do tonight, heading to the bar with a girl who clearly couldn't stand me was on that list. Maybe that had been her plan, expecting me to say no. But failure wasn't an option, so the bar was where I was heading.

"Do you want me to come with you?" Rusty grabbed my arm before I could leave.

See, this is where Rusty was different, why my heart just

grew a little bigger every day I was around him. Most guys would have either ignored the tension, played it off like two emotional women or been excited by the prospect of a catfight. Rusty wasn't interested in doing any of those things. He was smart enough to know that while I'd been *owning it* like a champ tonight, I might still need some reassurance.

"No, it's okay, we're just going to go the bar. We won't be long."

He hesitated but he let me go, but not before giving Angie a firm no bullshit look—another silent conversation being exchanged.

The *drink* was an excuse. She knew it and I knew it, so we didn't bother with the pretense. Angie followed me as I led the way, passing the bar completely as we walked to a quiet corner on the other side.

"I know you don't like me and that's okay, but I really like Rusty and I think we owe it to him to be civil when we're together."

I'm not sure what I was hoping to achieve, but the guy who had brought me to meet his friends meant more to me than any other guy I'd ever been with. For a reason I couldn't quite understand, he wanted me to be a part of his life. A life that included all these extra people and I wasn't going to be pushed out.

"Is that what you think, that I don't like you?" Angie's face softened for the first time since I'd met her. "Alison, I don't know you, how can I have any feelings about you?" She held her hand up to stop me before I could argue. "But he's known you for five minutes and you've moved in? You can't blame me for being cautious. That guy right there is one of the best guys I know. He got me through a lot of shit, so I know that when it comes to being a hero, he is more than qualified. I just don't want him taken advantage of."

"I'm not taking advantage of him, I would never do that. I know you don't know me and my word means nothing, but I'm not that kind of girl."

From the outside in, it looked bad. Girl meets guy, girl has nothing, girl moves in with guy. The word gold digger wasn't thrown around but I could read the subtext. Rusty Crawford wasn't flashing a Rolex and a Benz but he wasn't hurting either. The house he lived in was mortgage-free, his prized vintage Camaro needed no payments and his band had signed a lucrative deal that would probably make them a lot of money. I, on the other hand, had no car, no job, no savings and not a lot to offer. On paper we made no sense but in some crazy way in the real world we did.

"I care about him, Angie. Not because of what he has, but how he makes me feel."

"Just don't hurt him, okay?" Her arctic chill thawed a little more. "I know he seems tough but he has a huge heart, which can mean an epic heartbreak."

"If anyone's heart is going to be broken, trust me it will be mine. I would sooner die than hurt him and I mean that."

My honesty had been more than I'd wanted to give. Admitting to her how much he meant to me before I'd even admitted it to Rusty felt wrong, all those feelings of vulnerability swirling around for the world to see. We had just started something amazing and the last thing I wanted to think about was it possibly ending. Another wake-up call thanks to my stupid mouth, highlighting that maybe being with Rusty wouldn't last forever.

"I'm sorry." She whispered her voice so soft I'd barely heard it over the noise of the bar. And if it hadn't been for the tears welling in her eyes, I'd have probably just assumed I'd imagined it.

"For what?"

She took a long deep breath, the air slowly passing through her lips as her shoulders slumped. "I was the girl people made assumptions about, the girl they whispered in the corner about, and up until recently I'd never had female friends. I was a bitch to you and you didn't deserve that."

As much as I wanted to dislike her, I couldn't. We were as different as we were the same. Sure, I wasn't sporting tattoos and piercings nor could I sing in key but neither of us had been prom queen. And maybe she had some of her own insecurities just like I did. In the end we both cared for the same man.

"I get it, Angie. You wanted to protect Rusty. He's a special guy. Not saying I'm happy about being not liked but I understand."

"I'm just crazy hormonal at the moment and I have no idea whether I want to laugh, cry or punch a wall." She wiped away a stray tear. "He's family to me, Alison and I don't want anyone to mess with my family."

Those words chilled me to my core. Family. Something else I didn't have. While I had two grandparents who no doubt loved me and I loved them, they'd been absent from my life for a long time. And if I had what she had I would have fought for it just as fiercely. And well . . . shit . . . I just couldn't hate her for that.

"You have a real problem with locating the bar in this

place." Rusty materialized by my side, his eyes glancing between Angie and me. "Everything okay here?"

"Yep, all good." Angie gave him a smile before turning back to me. "Thanks for the chat."

"Anytime." And just like that, the first real smile was exchanged between us. Wonders would never cease.

Angie gave Rusty a friendly squeeze on the arm and then walked away, waddling off to her husband while leaving us in our secluded corner.

"Anything you want to share?" Rusty leaned in brushing his lips against my nose. "Or is it secret women's business?"

Instead of answering, I kissed him. Not sweetly like he'd just kissed me but a real kiss. Deep. On the mouth.

"I really like you," I mumbled against his lips.

"I'm glad, 'cause it would suck immensely if you didn't," he mumbled against mine.

"No, I mean I *really* like you." My arms wrapped around him as I struggled to get close enough.

"And I *really* like you." He kissed the top of my head. "You want to go back and hang with the band or do you want to make out some more? Just putting it out there that I'm good with either."

"I want to make out with my hot boyfriend and *then* we can go back."

"Best. Plan. Ever."

Seventeen
Rusty

"**So I need to tell you something and you need to listen** all the way through before you freak out."

There were about five hundred other conversations I would rather be having but unfortunately here we were—having this one.

"It's bad, right? Just tell me, I'm already imagining bad, bad things." Alison sat up in bed, the sheet slipping down to show me a spectacular morning view. Her bedroom was going to be strictly for show from here on out, no way I was ever going to be sleeping alone.

"It's not bad but it's going to take some understanding on your part."

Last night had gone a long way in us moving forward. The guys loved her just as I knew they would and even Angie let go of the hesitation. My girl, however, was the star of the show. Trading barbs with Max and Joey, she eased right into the group. The springs had definitely been loosened and this version of her was way more relaxed. Had to admit, seeing her confident like that made me all kinds of proud.

"O-kay. So what is it?" While her voice wavered slightly, she didn't give me the same look of hesitation I assumed she would. And other than assuming it was bad when I said I needed to tell her something, she hadn't jumped to worst-case scenario just yet. All in all, a massive improvement from what I thought I'd be facing.

"I need to go out tonight with the band." I hoped like hell the calm was going to last. "A seedy bar which means there are going to be girls that are possibly not interested in my new off-the-market status. But I promised you I'd be honest so rather than bullshit and tell you I'm going somewhere else, you need to know. You also need to know nothing is going to happen with any of them, I'm with you and I mean it."

It would have been easy to give her some line about needing to stay late in the studio, or maybe some BS about having a band meeting. Official business would have been the easy way out. Probably would have saved us both a lot of heartache. But I wasn't in the habit of lying to the people I cared about so I wasn't about to start now. Not to mention she already had massive trust issues, me adding to them—wasn't happening.

"Oh." The one word enough to prove she wasn't cool with it.

"Max's brother is still giving him headaches. I came up with the bright idea that if we get him out and get him laid he won't be worrying about all the other shit. Somewhere in that discussion, I got tasked to help. But I'm telling you because I didn't want you to get the wrong idea."

I wasn't the kind of guy who asked for permission. I wanted something; I went and did it, which is probably why I had been playing musical chairs with the ladies in recent times. Easy. No questions. Freedom. But what all that shit didn't give me were the feelings I was starting to muster up for this girl. Shit that went beyond just a good time. And I sure as shit wasn't looking to give that up.

"I see." She drew her knees up to her chest, my perfect view now hindered by her legs. That wall that had been lowered last night started to creep its way back up again.

"No, you don't see." I moved closer not allowing her to shut me out. "Whatever you have going on in your head right now, isn't going to happen. My dick isn't going to accidently slip into someone else. I'm not going to suddenly see a pair of tits and forget about you. Look at me, that isn't going to happen."

"You're so sure?" Those eyes of hers unable to hide the vulnerability she'd been trying to keep under wraps.

"Yes, I'm sure. I know that I'm not fucking someone else just because there isn't the opportunity, it's because I don't want to be with anyone else."

Who knew when it all happened, but my script had definitely been flipped. What possibly started as attraction and fascination, quickly changed to something else. Maybe it's because she wanted something from me other than sex, maybe it's because she wasn't impressed by the fact I played six-string with a band. Maybe it's because she had been dragged through shit and was still one of the sweetest girls I'd ever met. All I knew was that the kind of crap that had landed in her lap would have justified crazy-evil-bitch-from-hell being unleashed and yet she didn't.

"You always tell me to let go, that I'm too uptight. So here you go." She steadied herself before taking a deep breath. "I hate it. I really do. But I also know that if I'm ever going to trust someone, it needs to be now."

"Do you trust me, Alison?" It killed me to even ask and I hoped like hell the answer was going to be yes.

"Yes, I do. I know that if you want to cheat on me, you're going to do it. If the only reason you're faithful is lack of opportunity then it doesn't mean much. I also know that I can't be scared of that stuff anymore. I have to be enough."

"You are enough. More than enough. Trust me, and I promise I won't let you down."

Never needed a rubber stamp of approval from anyone. My folks had been so cool about everything I'd just expected them to be supportive and proud. I lived my life without the safety net and just knew I'd be fine. A healthy dose of arrogance and an inflated sense of self-assurance have always been the only tools I needed. Those days were done. See ya later, bye-bye. What I wanted instead, for maybe the first time ever, was to have actually earned the fucking praise. To know the person clapping their hands was doing it for the right reasons. Not because I *felt* I'd earned it but because I actually had.

"Don't break my heart, Rusty. I'm not that strong." She shot me a look that just about killed me.

"It's not going to happen." I'd rather die than disappoint her, that much I knew for sure.

"Good. Don't kiss them either. Those lips are mine." The first sign of a smile started to play at the edge of her lips.

"All yours, along with the rest of me." I planted my lips on hers seeing as she'd been so keen to take ownership; the kissing that followed an added bonus.

"Go to work, rock star. You have an album to finish and I

have a busy day of watching porn." She playfully pushed my chest, her words making me stop more than the shove.

"You watch porn when I'm not around? Why is this the first I'm hearing about it?" My chances of being late today were getting higher by the second.

"Yep, sure do. I'm getting all kinds of ideas too so you might want to not come home too late." She was so fucking sexy, grinning like she knew what kind of trouble she was causing.

"Ah babe, you're making it really difficult for me to get out the door. I'm not saying lie to me, but maybe work on your timing when you tell me these things."

"Nah. I like it better this way. It makes me feel less inadequate to know you're antsy. Consider it your gift to me." Her amusement growing by the second.

"I've been *antsy* since the minute I laid eyes on you, Alison. Enjoy your porn, sweetheart. I'll expect a full report the minute I walk in the door." I laughed, only half joking. "Oh and feel free to send me pictures of anything that strikes your fancy. As well as being antsy, I'm a sucker for a pop-quiz."

●●●

It was our final day in the studio. All the songs had been wrapped and we were just adding the finishing touches. I couldn't have been more proud of the work we'd done—the music, the sound—all if it, us completely unfiltered. I fucking loved it.

"FUCK YEAH." Joey tossed his sticks in the air as our sound engineer gave us the thumbs up, the last note locked and loaded.

"Well gentleman, it's been an honor." Angie gave her swollen belly a rub, junior obviously giving us a standing ovation. "As much as I would love to go out and celebrate with you, my plans include a tub of ice cream and a nap."

"There is so much wrong with that, I don't even know where to begin." I slid my guitar off my shoulder, the relief washing over me. "I'm going to have serious words with your kid when he or she is born. Someone needs to instill good rock values seeing as you've gone soft."

"Yeah, yeah." Angie flipped me off proving there was still some badass left in her. "Let's hope he or she can hold off until after our gig. I'd rather not give birth on stage."

Suggestions of how cool it would be for Angie's baby to make their entrance at a rock show were tossed through the air. Only to be overruled by our adamant front woman who was going traditional and having the kid in a hospital. And after packing up our equipment for the last time, we thanked our sound guys and went home.

The evening designated for operation *get Phil laid* had me lacking excitement. I was even less enthused when returning home to take a quick shower and change, and I found the house empty—Alison MIA. Of course I wasn't expecting her to be thrilled about my impending night, but I had hoped she'd be around for my honey-I'm-home entrance. My words unfortunately hit empty air as I walked from room to room without finding the hot brunette I'd recently grown pretty attached to. My mood sunk further as I went and got ready.

I'd half expected her to come waltzing in while I was getting my shit together, but as I was heading out the door, there was still no sign of her. The earlier two text messages I'd sent were also left unanswered.

This night was so going to suck.

Chasers was the name of the fine establishment we'd decided was getting our coin tonight, the vibe just as sleazy as the interior. Funnily enough I'd never noticed up until now.

"What up?" Max greeted me as I walked through the door. My entrance delayed by the need to find a park for my ride.

"Not much. You guys already drinking?" My head tilted to the three empty shot glasses on the table in front of them with the half drunk beers chilling right next door. It was going to be one of those nights.

"Yep, cabbed it in. Everyone is getting hammered." Joey raised his long neck in a mock toast before taking a swallow. His reason for the celebration a little different than the douchebag sitting next to him. Fucking Phil.

The dude who shared DNA with my bass player and good friend had thankfully cleaned himself up. While he still looked like a class-A dipshit, he at least didn't look like the stoner, unemployed loser that he was. Ah, the power of a pair of new jeans and a button down. False advertising at its finest.

"Rusty!" Phil pulled out the chair beside him and invited me to sit down. The asshole completely ignoring the fact we'd never been friends. "Fucking ecstatic you could join us. Nobody goes on the prowl quite like you. Hope you're ready for some superfine ass."

The man was fucking clueless. Not only was I not ready for some *superfine ass,* but I never went on the *prowl* and wasn't about to start tonight. His definition of getting a girl vastly different from mine.

"It's all about you tonight. You and the boys, I'm here

strictly in a wingman capacity." Best we clear up any mis-understandings from the start. Me hooking up with anyone wasn't happening. Nothing even remotely that looked like hooking up was happening. Lines were drawn, and here I was nowhere fucking near it.

"Oh, come on, Rusty. Don't tell me you're settling down. You boys are about to hit the big time. Pussy for days. Relation-ships are traps, man. Nothing good can come of them." The asshole dished out his advice even though I hadn't asked. If he and Max didn't share the same last name, I'd think for sure this clown wasn't his kin. No wonder his parents disowned him.

"Well you keep singing your tune and I'll sing mine. We can sit here and have a drink or not, I'm cool either way. But my interaction with the ladies is going to be strictly hands off. Not interested in pussy for days."

It was already pissing me off that I'd agreed to this, the fact I hadn't seen or spoken to Alison since this morning was also another reason my mood wasn't cheery. Add the extra element of a dude pushing forty trying to relive his glory days and it was a bonafide guarantee to make the night blow.

"Your loss. More for me then." He took another drink, tapping his glass noisily on the bar after he'd finished.

"So, Phil." My curiosity got the better of me. "Anything new going on in your world? Got any plans other than couch surfing at Max and Joe's?" Max shot me a what-the-fuck look I was a hundred percent expecting.

"Yeah, I'm working on something. Just seeing how it pans out." Phil swallowed the shot I had conveniently lined up in front of him.

"Hmmm. Sounds interesting. Anything you need help with?

You know—in case you've missed it—we're pretty good at getting shit to come together." I waved the bartender over for yet another drink. Phil was a big dude; it was going to take more than a couple of tequilas to get him talking.

"Don't think so, buddy." He tapped me on the shoulder as he happily accepted the beer the waitress had brought over. "There's a girl from my past, and I have some catching up I need to do."

So that would explain why his wife was going *Call of Duty* on his ass. The dumbass was trying to relive his glory days and connect with some chick from his past. I fucking knew his double life BS was going to be tied up with pussy. With Phil there weren't many other options.

"You know bro, you can talk to me. This girl? She someone special?" Max followed my lead, putting another shot in front of his brother as we continued with the interrogation.

"I don't know. Maybe? I just know I need to see her. Wow. This conversation is getting too heavy. I thought we were looking for ass, not sitting around having deep and meaning-fuls. Step back, gentleman and watch the master work his magic." He downed the newest shot before getting up from the table. I guess to go looking for ass. Or scratch his balls. With his game, it could really go either way.

"I really appreciate this, Rus." Max leaned in as we watched Phil work the room. "I knew if anyone could get him talking it was you. You were right. The asshole was obviously having an affair. No wonder Nicole wants done with him."

"Yeah, we can dial down the crisis now. Looks like he's less suicidal and more than ready to get his dick wet. At least the night wasn't a total wash."

Funny how this used to be our usual routine and yet right now I would have traded it for a night on the couch with Alison. Maybe Max's dumbass brother was right and I'd gotten soft. Who gave a shit, if I had? In fact, I welcomed it.

"How did she take it?" Max asked, pulling a mind-read and knowing exactly where my thoughts were at.

"She wasn't crazy about it but she understands." I sipped my beer as a tall leggy blonde shot me a wave from the bar. "Of course that was this morning before I left. When I got home she'd ghosted so who knows." The same blonde started her walk to the table. Annnnd here we go.

"Hi." Blondie gave me a big smile as she pushed out her tits. "You're Rusty Crawford, right? From Black Addiction. I'm a big fan." She didn't wait for an invitation, just slid into the seat vacated by Phil. Just another reason to hate him.

"Yep, that's me. And here is Max and Joey." I pointed to the boys opposite me hoping one of them would catch her interest.

"Hi." She waved in their general direction while her eyes stayed on me, my effort to divert her attention not sticking. "I saw you guys on the Power Station tour. You were amazing on stage."

Ordinarily this was the point where I'd do my thing. She was pretty and seemed more than game for some private adulation, which in the past would have been my green light. Usually I'd suggest we take it somewhere a little more private or even let her sit in my lap, my willingness to please the fans legendary. But seeing the shit play out on the other side made me realize what a cock I'd been. I wanted none of it.

"I'm glad you enjoyed the show, we had a lot of fun on that tour." My diplomacy kicked in as I took a swig of my beer. "Will be good to get back on the road." A better alternative than the not-interested-in-the-dog-and-pony-show-sweetheart-it's-best-you-get-a-steppin.

"So . . . Rusty." And here we go, the *can I have your dick in my vagina* speech I was a hundred percent sure would come next. "Do you play any other *instruments*?"

I didn't miss the eyebrow raise or emphasis on the word, both of which I probably would have found cute a few months ago. Now. Not so much, her lip biting also not doing her any favors.

While being an asshole wasn't the plan, letting the charade continue wasn't going to happen either. "Hey, you seem like a nice girl but I'm just hanging with my boys tonight." My head tipped toward the two morons in my rhythm section who had been unhelpful in the unwanted advances.

"Oh, I'm sorry." The blonde who hadn't bothered to introduce herself looked over at Max and Joe. "Umm. I'll go then?" She waited, hoping I might change my mind.

"Why don't you come over here and talk to me instead?" Joey offered. "Rus is in a bad mood. He broke a guitar string or two today." The dumbass's excuse making me sound like an award-winning crybaby not helping the cause.

"Well, I'm good at cheering people up."

I had to hand it to her, she was fucking persistent. She was going to try and work herself in there until she had no hope. Little did she know that she'd had no chance from the minute she sat down.

"Going to go check on your brother. Nice meeting you."

When I needed to use Phil as an excuse, I was really scraping the bottom of the barrel. But as I pushed away from the table, leaving the leggy blonde to try her luck with the other two, the objective of why we're here was highlighted. The sooner we got the moron a girl, the sooner we could all leave. The sooner the fucking better. Oh, and my phone still hadn't lit up with any incoming messages, in case I needed even more reason to be pissed.

"Rusty!" Phil waved me over to where he was perched at the bar, the two ladies he'd been chatting to looked toward me with promise. Here we go again.

"How you doing, buddy?" I gave his shoulder a shake as I signaled the bartender for another beer. "You having fun yet?" Translation—are you going to score with either of these two so we can wrap this up?

"Having a ball, champ." The genuine pleasure lit up his face as he forgot about the mystery girl from his past and apparently his wife. "This is Lori and Mercedes." He introduced his two friends while I grabbed a fresh microbrew. "Can you believe they're cousins? Born only a day apart. How cool is that?"

"Pretty amazing." My head nodded as I lifted the beer to my lips. *Oh God, just let this night end.*

"Are you Phil's brother?" Either Lori or Mercedes asked. I didn't care enough to know which. "We hear you're famous."

It was no surprise that in Phil's effort to score he'd used his brother as bait. It's not like he wasn't already mooching off the kid, nope—he had to use his name as well. I seriously didn't know whether to take him out the back and beat him to death with his own hand or put him out of his misery and pay a girl to go home with him.

"Nope, I'm not Max." And thank fuck for that. "Just making

sure everyone was having a good time. Looks like you have a handle on it so I'll leave you to it." My goodbye waved as I excused myself, the need to prolong the agony nonexistent. Phil's new friends not so pleased by my hasty departure.

"She didn't stick around?" My chin tipped to the vacant chair, the leggy blonde no longer occupying it. "Such a shame, she seemed nice." Unable to disguise my utter delight as I re-took my seat.

"Yeah, she's into guitarists. Her need to stick around vanished when you did. Funny how that works." Max grinned as he played with his phone. "He getting any closer?" His eyes went to Phil who was now flying solo, the cousins he'd been so impressed with no longer in sight.

"Dude, you know I say this with all the fucking love in my heart. But your brother is fucked. He has zero game, no charisma and acts like an asshole. I'm not sure how he gets chicks which is probably why he's chasing up this blast-from-the-past. Tell me again how he convinced Nicole to marry him? Were you actually at the wedding? Was she fully conscious when those I-dos were exchanged?"

"I know." His fingers played with the label on his beer. "Hey, if I didn't already say so, I really appreciate this. I owe you, big time."

"You don't owe me shit, but make no mistake I'm doing this for you—not for him."

"Well I'm done sitting around," Joey announced as he rose to his feet. "I should be able to at least get a hand job in a place like this, I'm going to hunt and gather, my friends." His mouth not even finished with the goodbye as his feet moved toward the redhead on the opposite couch.

"Good luck," Max called after him, his attention distracted by the brunette walking toward him with yet another beer. "Feel free to take a walk, Rus. I think she likes me." A wink shot in her direction as she got closer to the table.

"And on that note, I'm going to take a piss." My feet once again hitting the floor as I made for the bathroom door. The musical chairs routine had already gotten old.

The bathroom brought a welcome reprieve. The place deserted except for the urinals and the stalls, my need to piss no longer hypothetical as I unzipped my pants and pulled out my cock. The stream of pee hit the metal just as I heard the door behind me open. The moment of solitude short-lived as someone walked in.

"You need a hand with that?" The voice called from over my shoulder, the shock cutting me off midstream.

"What the fuck?" I'd said it as well as I thought it as I spun around ready to unleash hell on whoever the bitch who was invading my personal space. "Alison?"

"Hey." A shy smile teased at her lips as her fingers waved a hello. "For the record, I don't usually hang out in men's bathrooms."

"What are you doing here?" The question was ambiguous. Here in the bathroom? In the club? It could really be asked of any of those and in reality I didn't really care what the answer was. "Let me just zip up."

"Oh!" Her eyes widened as she glanced down. "I really, really missed your penis."

"And he missed you too." The sentiment not needing to be faked. "But nowhere near as much as I missed you."

Having your super-hot rock star boyfriend—it still felt weird saying that—tell you he was going out with his band and meeting other women, did not fill me with joy. There was no spontaneous jump of excitement where I hoped he had a good time. But I understood. I mean, what was I going to do? Chain him to the bed and only let him out when he needed to play? As appealing as that was, I wasn't that crazy.

My other alternative would be to follow him. Embrace the crazy nagging self-doubt that yelled subconsciously in my head that he was going to find someone prettier, smarter and less neurotic. But then I'd forever be *that* girl. The one who rummaged through his pockets every time he went out without me. The one who planted their nose into the shirt he was wearing sniffing for other girl's perfume. The one who the minute he left on tour would be scouring the internet for pictures of him locked in someone's embrace. I refused to give in to my insecurities. New leaf, remember? And I was going to do something completely radical and trust him.

Besides, nothing I did or could do would keep Rusty from cheating if that's what he wanted. Not like opportunity was an issue so I was going to do what he'd been begging me to do since the day we'd met. Let go.

Look at me, free as a bird.

Completely not thinking about some groupie with their hands on my man.

Okay so I wasn't great at it, but I was trying.

So after kissing him goodbye and sending him off into the world of rock stardom, aka the recording studio, I called Renee and asked her to hang out. It had been a really long time since we'd spent some quality time together, and if anyone could get my mind off Rusty with other girls, she would. Nothing special, just two girls getting together and talking nonsense. The virtues of fisting were even debated. Here's a hint, not by me.

Renee was a special kind of snowflake and if nothing else she distracted me from kicking the furniture back at the house. Which would have been totally childish and unproductive. Not at all what I was doing before she picked me up and took me to her apartment.

And while it was good to be spending some quality time with my old BFF, Renee had important things she needed to do. Fisting may or may not have been involved and I sure as hell wasn't going to stick around to find out.

Which landed me back at Rusty's empty house.

Alone.

Ugh.

Well, at least that's where I was until Max called me from the bar.

I was just about to delve into another distraction that was

the World Wide Web, when a phone rang. The noise startled me, the archaic ring from a rotary phone piercing the air as I hunted for the source, finding it attached to the kitchen wall. I'd never even noticed it before and judging by the dust-covered mouthpiece, it had been a while since anyone had given it some attention.

But while the prehistoric communication device was fascinating, it didn't excite me anywhere near as much as Max's voice on the other end of the phone.

Rusty was just as miserable as I was and the ultimate solution was suggested. Me, go to the bar. I didn't argue.

"Slide in the back." Rusty held open the door with one hand while the other one remained tightly fixed around me.

My feet had barely touched the ground since leaving the club, our exit facilitated by a side door that spat us out into a back alley. His car parked in the darkness not too far away.

"You sure your friends won't mind you've disappeared? Weren't you supposed to be helping that Phil guy?" My body moved closer to his, my lips desperately seeking every inch of his exposed skin. "We can wait if you want." My breath held steady while I prayed he was just as desperate as I was.

"Yeah, babe. Waiting isn't going to happen. I don't really give a shit about anyone else, especially not Phil." His head tipped toward the empty back bench seat. "After missing you like crazy all day long, I finally have you with me. So you can see my concern for anything that doesn't involve removing your clothes right now, isn't high on my priority list."

"I like the way you think. You are so smart." My body stopped resisting as I climbed into the back. My butt sank into the leather as he followed closely behind, the door slamming behind him.

"What can I say, you inspire me. You should stick around if only for my benefit." He proved just how smart he was by putting his hands back on me.

"Shut up and kiss me."

Manners weren't something I was usually lacking. Please, thank you and of course I'm sorry, featured heavily in my dialogue but right now I wasn't in the mood to be polite. Rusty didn't seem to mind my lack of etiquette, putting his mouth exactly where I'd wanted it. On mine. He wasn't the kind of guy you needed to ask twice and the things he could do with that tongue were lethal.

Legs and arms filled the confined space, the seat not wide enough to accommodate the tangle of our bodies as we made out. As uncomfortable as it might have been there was no way I was going to stop, my back hitting the leather hard as Rusty reclined me back. The change in position gave us only slightly more room.

"Ali, please tell me you have a condom." His hand floated down between my legs. "Wasn't thinking I was going to need any tonight." His fingers slowly pushed up my skirt. "And not having sex with you isn't an option."

Ah. Shit.

Yeah.

That.

"Um . . ." My mental conjuring didn't help procure the condom we were lacking. "No. I didn't think that far ahead."

"Fuck." Rusty's hand stopped moving, the air in the car chilling by a few hundred degrees. "It's cool." He quickly got back on track, his hands getting back to work. "We'll make it work, I can do other stuff."

Birth control was something I had been taking religiously since I was sixteen. I never missed a pill, ever. I even took those placebo ones in the pack, just in case. You can never be too sure and as a product of an unwanted pregnancy, there was no way I would allow that to happen to me. But, even with my regimented routine ninety-nine percent guaranteeing I wouldn't be sporting a baby bump in nine months, I couldn't take the risk. My luck sucked severely, and I would be that one in a million statistic who would be rocking their bundle of joy. No way could I risk it.

"You have health screenings right?" My brain boggled over what I was about to say. The windows already fogged by the heavy breathing we both were doing. "For . . . diseases and stuff?" The heat in my skin rose as he stopped trying to pull down my panties and paid attention.

"Of course. Are you saying what I think you're saying?"

"I'm fairly sure you have no idea what I'm going to say." Considering I could barely believe it, I doubt he would even be close.

"Are you on birth control, Ali?"

"Yes, but it's not going to matter." My eyes widened as the breath I'd unconsciously been holding slowly pushed past my lips. "That's not where I want you to go."

"Whoa, what?" All further talk and/or removing of my panties stopped as Rusty sat back into the seat. "Are you suggesting—"

"That's exactly what I'm suggesting."

Rusty hadn't been shy about my curiosity of anal sex, an excitement we'd both seemed to share. Fingers had on more than one occasion found their way into my ass while we had sex, with the orgasms always being explosive. So while I hadn't explored the full capacity of my butt sex drawer, the poor butt plugs and anal beads sitting idly unused, my enthusiasm was still high.

"You think you're ready for that?" A wave of excitement flashed through his clear blue eyes. "Not sure the back seat of a car is the best place for your first time."

"You think you can get me wet enough?" My teeth played with my bottom lip, the thrill already surging through my body.

"That isn't even a question. You want to do this, let's go." He didn't give me time to respond as his mouth was once again on mine, the kiss so intense I was surprised the windows didn't blow out.

Maybe it was the kiss or his equally skilled hands but in no time my panties had disappeared. Gone. My skirt had also disappeared from my lower body; hiked up so far out of the way it was now doubling as a top. Its new purpose not bothering me in the slightest.

Not to waste this newly acquired access, Rusty's fingers soon found their mark, my body shivering the minute he touched my skin.

"Oh," I moaned as he pushed a finger inside of me, my back bowing off the seat.

"Um-hmm." Rusty grinned as he added another finger. "You still concerned about whether I can get you wet?"

In my head I answered, said something witty about his talented and agile fingers but words seemed to elude me as he added a thumb. The extra attention he paid to my clit making it difficult to remember my own name let alone his.

Lucky for me he wasn't looking for words as his lips stopped asking me questions and started kissing my neck, distracting me from the pinkie he'd now added to my ass. My body full, as he continued to give every single part of me as much of his fingers as they were willing to take.

"Rus-ty." My fingers sunk deep into his shoulders as every nerve ending in my body felt like it was going to explode. "I'm going to come." The disclaimer not really necessary given my legs were shaking with need and his fingers were absolutely coated by me.

"Not yet, sweetheart." He slowed down, his fingers taking their time to enter then almost painstakingly exit as he continued to finger my ass. "You're almost ready."

"I'm ready. Trust me. I'm ready." I begged, my body thrashing on the seat as the leather stuck to my butt. "Please, I can't hold on much longer."

It was maddening. Teetering so close to the edge, but just before going over he pulled me back. Each time I thought for sure I was going to explode.

"I'm going to need your help, baby." His hand slowed to a stop, while his other hand undid his belt. The rock-hard erection pressed against his jeans proved I wasn't the only one turned on.

"I need you in me." My fingers flew to his waistband in a flurry of unbuttoning and unzipping mayhem. My objection to just having regular sex no longer relevant. Ninety-nine percent sure sounded good enough to me.

"Just a second, babe." His hard-on hit his stomach as he pulled down his pants. "We're almost there." The fingers that had been in me traveled up and down his rock-hard length, stroking him.

Not willing to let him have all the fun, my hands reached down between my legs, coating my fingers before reaching out and touching his cock. The slide up and down both slippery and wet.

"You ready?" His cock circled my opening as I fought against the urge to push against him. "I want you to touch yourself, let me see you fingering that beautiful, sweet pussy."

"Yes." I moaned, my knees bending to accommodate him, desperate to be filled with him. "I'll touch myself, just fuck me."

"I love it when you say fuck." He smiled, gently lifting my legs up onto his shoulders, the roof of the car doing its best to hinder the situation.

"Finger yourself, baby. Make yourself feel good." The cock that had been threatening to enter me moved down the seam of my ass, stopping once it got to my entrance. "Take a breath, baby. Breath in and then breath out, real slow."

Breathing in and out shouldn't have been hard but as my mind see-sawed between frustration and euphoria I struggled. A ragged breath finally drawn in, before I slowly pushed it out and as I did, he pushed in. The pressure overwhelming me as I screamed out his name.

"That's it, Ali. Fuck you are so tight." He pushed in a little more, the pressure hovering somewhere between pain and pleasure.

"Oh, God." My body started to shake as he slid in deep, his hands locked around my waist as he continued to move. Small and controlled thrusts edged his length further into me.

"Relax, baby. Touch yourself. I need to feel you come while

my dick is in your ass." His face inches from mine as his body dominated the interior of the car. "Let me feel you."

It didn't take long, my body stretching to capacity as he pushed in all the way. The fingers that had been circling my clit dipped lower and entered me as I felt the overwhelming wave of pleasure crash over me in a rush. My body shook uncontrollably as I came apart beneath him.

"Yes, babe. Oh, God. That's it." His thrusts increased and then he too found his finish. His hot load filled my ass as I continued to convulse. Every single nerve ending hummed with static as the wave rolled over me again. My body boneless as my breath labored out of control.

"Wow." I panted, the pressure slowly receding as he pulled out his cock. "We need to do that again sometime."

"Fuck, Ali." Rusty's butt collapsed onto the seat beside me. "I didn't think sex with you could get any better, but wow. Yeah, that was fucking intense." He laughed as his hand rubbed up and down my naked leg.

"Aww, are you just saying that because we had anal?" My ass shuffled up the leather seat as I tried to give him more room.

"No, I'm saying that 'cause it's you." His hand stopped caressing my leg as his face became serious. "I'm in love with you."

The words just left his mouth as my brain went into free fall. *He didn't mean it, he was just caught up in the moment*, I rationalized as my heart desperately wanted to hear it again. The thought that he could be in love with someone who had so little to offer was crazy. I was so ordinary and he was so larger than life. We had nothing in common.

"Are you sure?" I stupidly asked, the words almost getting stuck in my throat.

"Yeah, actually I'm really sure." His face showed no hint of hesitation. "I'm in love with you. And not just because we had awesome sex." He lifted off the seat and moved closer to me. "Being in that bar tonight made me see what I'd been missing. You said when you met me that I don't give a shit about anything, and when it came to women, you were right on the money. I didn't care but that's 'cause I hadn't met someone worth caring about. I can't be that guy anymore. I love you, Alison."

If this was a dream then my subconscious was an asshole. A terrible horrible evil monster that I wanted no part of. But no matter how many times I blinked, the landscape didn't change. Same car, same guy and same weird and wonderful feeling that twisted in my lower gut. And other than the possibility that I was hallucinating—not sure if having a cock up my ass would cause that—then this was real. Those feelings were real. Those words he had said to me were real.

"You okay?" he asked, reminding me he hadn't heard my internal conversation. Oh, yeah. The guy had told me he loved me so I should probably respond or something.

"I love you too." The words flew out in a rush. "I love you so much." My arms reached out as I tried to hug him. Difficult given the tiny space of the back seat and my back pushed up against the door. We hadn't really thought this through.

"Well good, makes it easier." He gave me one of his panty-melting smiles. Just as well I was still missing mine. "Would have totally sucked if I'd been there on my own."

"So . . . what do we do now?" My eyes dipped down to the

messy back seat. My skirt still up above my waist instead of covering the parts of me that it should. The aftermath not nearly as spectacular as the moment had been.

"We're going to get cleaned up and go home. I need to hold you and then I'm going to need to make love to you properly. Nice and slow. Anal totally optional."

It didn't even seem like I'd asked him a question. Not one that really mattered anyway, like it was no big deal to ditch his friends and leave with me.

"What about them?" My head motioned to the window. The noisy, seedy bar's lights just barely visible. "Don't you want to go back in there?"

Not that I wanted to go back, but I wasn't expecting him to completely forget that it had been me who crashed the party either. My surprise arrival sabotaging his plans.

"Not tonight. They'll understand and I'd rather piss out razor blades than have to stop holding you right now."

For Rusty the decision was simple. He wanted to be with me so he was going to be with me. End of story. I had been the one who'd been resisting every step of the way. One day I was on my own, miserable and completely down on my luck and the next I was finding my way with a new tour guide. Showing me that it was ok to be out of control and unsure. He didn't even bat an eye at my crazy. All of which was completely acceptable to him, and what was even more shocking was that he—the hot guy I had once admired from afar—fell in love with me. With me. And oh my God, did I love him back.

"Take me home, Rusty."

"I love it when you see it my way."

Rusty

Life was pretty fucking sweet.

Like no shit. I felt like a superhero. Superman of course because we already established Batman had no sack.

In the space of a month my life had gone from pretty freaking awesome to goddamn spectacular. And I was riding that high all the way to the end.

The studio work was done. All of the tracks were set and ready for the airways. Even the cover didn't make me want to stab myself; it was exactly what we wanted. We even had a live gig all lined up which would hopefully not feature the live birth of my front woman's first child. And I had an awesome girlfriend.

Fucking outstanding. All of it.

And it was only going to get better.

I'd caught some heat from bailing from last night's Phil-tivities but the boys managed the shark-infested waters of Chasers just fine without me. We'd been satisfied that Phil's deep, dark secret was nothing more than his inability to be faithful, and while I thought it was bad form, it was none of my business. Phil even went home with someone, his obsession with hair-band ballads and spiraling into depression forgotten for the night. Even if it was only temporary, it was mission accomplished as far as I was concerned. Joey and Max hadn't been so thrilled the boom-chica-wah-wah went down on their couch, but at least they didn't have to listen to another ten hours of love songs and dedications. A win is a win.

Max calling Alison was beyond what I'd expected. Sure I had been a miserable son of a bitch who would rather have his dick slammed in a car door than sit in that fucking bar, but I was fully prepared to be a team player. Turns out, I wasn't the only one who was willing to make the sacrifice. Did I mention how fucking awesome my life was? Hells to the yeah.

"Dude, your stomach is doing that Alien thing again." My eyes stayed glued to Angie's stretched out T-shirt. A rogue arm or leg doing its best to find the ejection hatch. "Seriously, is that shit normal?"

"Yes, it's normal." Angie gave her belly a rub. "He or she just wants in on the band. Every time I play it's like a mosh pit in there."

"Hey, are you sure this gig is a good idea?" Max weighed in, his eyes also doing the stare routine on Angie's cargo hold. "I know we've joked about it but you cannot go into a labor on stage. I was watching TLC and yeah . . . I'm pretty sure the insurance will not cover the mess."

"It's my first baby, losers. It doesn't happen that way." She waved off our concern like the badass that she was. Had to hand it to her, she wasn't letting a little thing like being a life support system slow her down.

"Hi, everyone. I brought snacks. Anyone hungry?" Alison joined the party balancing two pizzas and a six-pack, even had a bottle of water tucked under her arm for Ange. My chest puffed out proud at the sight of her.

"Hey, babe. Let me help you with that." My feet were on the floor and walking toward her before she got much further. "You're awesome." The kiss she got was in lieu of wrapping my arms around her, which would totally be happening later.

"Rus, I am a little bit in love with your girlfriend right now, dude." Joey grabbed a longneck from my girl and gave her a shit-eating grin. "She got us pizza and beer. We didn't even ask for it."

"Well, thank you, Joey." Her cheeks pinked as she handed another bottle to Max, my bass player just as appreciative, shooting her a smile. "I thought you guys might be hungry, it's no big deal."

"Stand down, asshole. She's taken."

With the pizzas finally on the coffee table I was free to show my own personal brand of thanks. A lot more physical than the two she'd just received. And anyone who didn't dig the PDA could happily show themselves to the door.

"Thanks, Alison." Angie palmed the water that had been designated for her. "I could eat a horse." The lid of the pizza boxes was popped open and the savages dove in.

Oh, and another thing that I could add to my list of awesome. My best friend and my girlfriend were now completely kosher with each other. Angie had shelved her concerns and was on Team Alison with the rest of us. Another fucking win.

"So you guys nervous for tonight? It's been awhile since

you've been on a stage, huh?"

My girl had come a long way, from previously needing to get high just thinking about hanging out with the band to now being all cool, calm and collected while we ate pizza and conversed. To say I was proud of her was an understatement.

"I'm itching to play," Joey answered between chews, his slice of pepperoni getting demolished. "The stage is where we shine. Studios blow ass."

"Yeah, we're a better live band. Get a feel for the crowd and feed off the energy. Can't wait." Max was right on the money. We didn't trick up our sound so playing for a crowd was always going to be boss.

"And I am beyond excited you're going to get to see me play. Just be prepared to be wowed, woman. When it comes to guitar playing, I pretty much own that shit." Maybe I was arrogant but the chance to play our new stuff, with my girlfriend in the front row—no chance I was choking. I would be channeling my inner Jimmy Hendrix and setting fire to my axe.

"It will be a good time. Our last time playing together for a few months." Angie's belly on cue started rocking and rolling. The kid obviously agreed with the consensus.

"Wow, that's so cool." Alison got an eyeful of what we'd spent the morning watching. "Can I touch it?" She didn't even bother trying to extend a hand until she'd gotten the green light nod.

Watching Alison with her hand on Angie's belly was super surreal. One, there was a freaking human in there. A real life, living, breathing person that was going to come out and be part of this crazy awesome family. Two, for the first time ever—and I do mean ever—I could totally see myself doing that with a girl. Yep, I'm talking putting a ring on it, knocking her up and growing old in the rocking chair. All of it totally on the table if the chick sitting across from me would be my other half. Only way it was going to happen.

I was as surprised as anyone by the revelation, the marriage and kid thing not something I was counting on. I assumed it *might* happen later, but I sure as hell wasn't looking for it now. But I was smart enough to know that what we had was a once-in-a-lifetime deal, and I would sooner give up playing in the band and work a shitty nine-to-five job before I'd give up Alison. Planning a future, having babies—it was something that absolutely made me freaking happy beyond belief.

Maybe pregnancy was like the measles. You got exposed to that shit and before you knew it, you too were rocking a diaper bag. Honestly, no problems with it here.

"It's amazing that there is a tiny little version of you in there, all perfectly formed just waiting to be born." Alison echoed my thoughts as she pulled her hands away from Angie. "It really is a miracle."

Maybe we both were on the same train of thought, her eyes locking with mine and giving me a smile. That alone was enough to light a fire under my ass and start the baby-making right now.

"Knock, knock." Jason—the baby daddy—walked through the front doorway and into the room. "You guys done? I'm all for being supportive of the band but I need to take Angie home. And just for the record, I think playing a show tonight is crazy."

"Irwin, you should know better than to think we can tell Angie what to do." I gave the big guy a grin. Hell no. I liked my balls very much where they were, I wasn't about to tell our lead singer whether or not she could get on stage.

"We're done." Angie wrapped her arms around her dude as he helped her out of the chair, her struggle onto her feet a little more than when she'd arrived. Maybe Power Station Jase had a point.

"Hey, Angie. We can rain check tonight if you want? Honestly, the songs are solid, we can wait a little longer to give them airtime." As much as I wanted to play, I was willing to sideline it for the greater good.

"I'm fine, we're playing the gig." She shot down any further discussion, giving us all a tired wave and leaving with her knight in shining armor. She was adamant even if we weren't sold.

"So, Alison. You sing? We can always use the back up." Max broke the silence, the nice dude that he was making sure he didn't leave her out of the loop.

"Oh, no. I can't sing to save my life. Think about the worst noise on earth and then multiply it by a hundred. That sound —that horrible noise of death—is still better than I sing."

"No one is that bad." I threw my arms around my girl, glad I was finally able to give her the attention. "I bet you're awesome and just selling yourself short."

"Actually, I'm not. I'm really that bad. If there were any hope, I'd happily join the band. It's not like I'm doing much else." The playful mood of the conversation took a dive.

I gave exactly zero fucks about Alison not working. Zero. As far as I was concerned she could happily stay unemployed and be my head cheerleader. Certainly made shit easier for me in that we didn't have to deal with her nine-to-fiving. But, I knew deep down it ate at her—her not doing her own thing, not having her own cash. And if I had it in my power to make that girl happy, I was going to do it. Even if it meant I'd see her less.

"Hey, have you thought about working with a label? I know James and the boys were looking to expand, but given they are running it like an old-school ma and pa shop, it's been difficult to get staff."

Not sure why I didn't think of it before but Ali working with Power Station would be a good fucking move. For personal reasons—I make no apologies about being selfish—it would mean she'd be right there with me. We'd be in it together. But more importantly, it was something I knew she'd excel in. They needed someone trustworthy and organized and my girl was so anal she color coded Post-it notes.

"Work for the label? You mean for Power Station?" Her eyes got wide at the suggestion.

"Babe, I really hate that they impress you more than I do. As your boyfriend I'm going to have to insist you think I'm the bigger deal. Lie to me if you have to."

I was nowhere near offended to be honest, but I was hoping I'd be seeing that look of awe directed at me some time soon. Call me vain or conceited, I'd take it.

"You are a huge deal. Bigger than big. Massive." She turned on the enthusiasm, the boys laughing at her attempt at appeasing me.

"Laugh it up, bastards, but I'm a genius." It was really an amazing suggestion, adulation was definitely deserved.

"Well, you enjoy that." Max rose to his feet, picking up a

slice of pie for the road. "Joey and I are going to bail too. I'm hoping by now Phil's random chick has left so we can get some sleep. Oh and head's up, he's coming tonight. I fully expect he'll be a ballbuster, but he hasn't seen me play in years so couldn't really say no."

Joey followed Max's lead, the eye roll clueing me in that he wasn't thrilled about their couch tenant riding shotgun. Not that I blamed him, the guy was a massive drainer.

"Yep, see you tonight." I gave them both a chin tip as way of saying goodbye, my hands leaving Alison wasn't happening.

With our impromptu band meeting over and the guys heading out the door, my attention was fully on my earlier suggestion. The one that would see the two things I loved happily come together. The band, and the girl who pretty much owned me right now. As far as I could see, there were no negatives.

"You think they would seriously consider hiring me?" Ali asked, her train of thought obviously sharing the same redirection. "If nothing else the experience would be amazing."

"Well we can sit here and wonder or we can talk to the people in charge. All I know is, they need help. It's worth a shot, what have you got to lose?"

As far as guarantees, I couldn't give any. Me vouching for her would hopefully go a long way but as far as business was concerned, Power Station and their wives ran a pretty tight ship. But I also knew that nothing great ever came from playing it safe.

"True, it's not like I'm not already broke and without a job. Even if they say no, the interview process would be great experience."

Sitting in front of me was a different girl than the one I'd first met. The one who'd been screwed over by her piece of shit ex-boyfriend and life in general. And that was by far a greater achievement than any album or show I'd ever play.

"I'll make the call but whatever happens, know you are fucking awesome."

Working for a record label was not something I would have ever considered. With no piercings or tattoos, I wouldn't have thought I was cool enough. Turns out business was business, and law briefs could easily be swapped with record contracts and tour schedules. In fact, having an analytical background with a strong research drive was actually considered an asset. You heard me correctly, my skills were an asset. They hadn't even seen what I could do with a stationery drawer yet and Power Station's heavy hitters wanted to meet me. God, I hoped I didn't choke.

A very promising phone call landed me an interview next week with Ashlyn Evans ,their business manager. While I was slightly disappointed it was not with the band themselves, I was silently relieved I'd be able to get through the interview without hopefully saying something stupid. My mouth couldn't be trusted when I got nervous. Celebrations all round.

It just made the night even more special. Me, getting to see Rusty play for the very first time *and* knowing that pretty soon

I might be starting a challenging and exciting new career. Pinching myself was not out of the question.

You'd think after living in a city that had a population of over eight million people that I'd be used to crowds. The busy sidewalks and bustling streets should have totally desensitized me to the craziness. Yet, here I was in the middle of the sold-out club feeling like I was drowning.

A sea of endless bodies filled every square inch of space. Their fevered excitement reverberated off the walls as we pushed past. All of them there for one thing—Black Addiction.

It seemed that while I had been ignorant as to who they were, the greater people of New York didn't share the same affliction. And like it or not, my boyfriend was a celebrity.

"You can watch from here if you want." Rusty looked across the crowd as we waited at the area beside the stage. "It's pretty intense."

Intense was being conservative. Mayhem was more like it; I watched the insanity unfold as more people recognized him.

"If it gets too crazy just let security know and they'll let you backstage, unfortunately you won't be able see from back there but you'll still be able to hear." His concern poking through as the noise around us rose.

"You can go with the band. I'm fine, really I am." Or I would be, I wasn't about to fall into a heap when he needed my support. Especially when he'd given me so much.

"Are you sure, Ali? Jase is going to be here soon, I think some of the other guys. You want me to get someone to hang with you?" He was hesitant, concerned about me as always even when tonight should have been about him.

"Rusty. Go. I am fine. I would think that if Jase or anyone

else is around it would only make the crowd more frenzied so it's probably better they don't hang with me. Besides, they're tall and will just obscure my view not to mention their security getting in the way. I need to be able to see you clearly when you play, I want all my attention to be on you."

"That's my girl." My response earned me a very showy kiss, he didn't even care we were standing not far from the crowd. It was a really, really nice kiss too. I'm pretty sure the girls beside us gasped, their attention having not so discreetly been on my boyfriend's ass. Yep, that's right, ladies. He is all mine.

After letting the kissing go on a little longer—it would be totally crazy not to let the guy continue when he was so good at it—I convinced Rusty I would be completely okay by myself. His wave and smile disappearing behind the secure area where the rest of the band was no doubt gathered.

"Are you with the guitarist?" One of the girls screamed over the noise. Her T-shirt barely covering her breasts.

"Yeah, I am." I answered a little more smugly than I'd usually do. I couldn't help it. All in an effort to own it like I was trying to do. And if it made me feel good in the process, all the better.

"Wow. How did you land that? He's gorgeous," her friend piped in, her T-shirt only slightly longer.

"Oh I didn't land him, we're just using each other for sex." A voice I barely recognized as my own came barreling out of my mouth. My silent gratitude was offered to AMC for playing a rerun of *Pretty Woman* last night. The clichéd line better than one I could have come up with on my own.

And just like that they were stunned into silence. Who knew I had it in me? It was a pretty cool magic trick actually. I could totally be a badass.

Not sure why I said it, maybe it's because I was really done with being invisible.

I needed to not give a shit what they thought. Not even a little bit. Rusty and I were together and I was proud of it. Who cared? I was done looking for anyone's approval. Certainly not some stranger who was wearing a shirt that was three sizes too small.

Sadly, I didn't get to continue my fun, with any future movie lines being shelved as the lights dimmed on the shocked faces of my *new friends*. My smile widened in the darkness as I made out Rusty's silhouette on stage, my heart racing in the excitement. This was so cool.

The first note shot out of the speakers like an assault rifle, the guitar screamed as the drums and bass joined in, the crowd erupting as Angie started singing. Everyone around me raised their hands, jumping in unison to the beat as the first song played. Whatever I'd expected. They were better.

Flawless. The four of them played song after song with perfection, each dip and peak of the music, teasing more out of the crowd. It was exhilarating and my cheeks hurt from smiling so much but I was right there with them the whole time. Stunned at how good they were.

Sweat poured off Rusty, my eyes barely shifting from him the entire time. The spotlight showcased each subtle movement of his body as the curve of his tight black tee lovingly caressed every muscle. His fingers roamed the fret board with each chord progression, the innocent display so erotic it sent the two girls beside me into a screaming frenzy. Goose bumps covered my skin as I was drawn even further into the beat, the crowd and the noise around me receding as my vision tunneled on only one focal point. I completely got it. Totally understood why all those women were vying for his attention. The sensuality of his body commanded attention while seducing the audience.

As the last few chords rang out, there was no doubt what we were watching was the start of something huge. The band primed for even bigger stardom when the rest of the world heard what we had tonight. Their lives were about to change forever.

"Thank you, New York—Goodnight!" Angie pumped her fist in the air as the lights faded. The silhouettes of the band members barely visible as the stage plunged into darkness, the deafening applause roaring from every direction. The show was over.

I could barely speak. I'd screamed so much my throat hurt, being captivated like everyone else and singing back what lyrics I could. That enthusiasm he asked me to fake wasn't going to be necessary. It had been amazing, both him and the band and I had been right there with them. Breathing it in like oxygen.

A hand grabbed me from the dark, yanking me away from the stage and forcing me to turn around. The smile I'd been wearing for the past forty-five minutes was still plastered across my face, knowing it was going to be my guy. My proper appreciation finally being able to be shown for the mesmerizing performance I'd been treated too. He was so getting laid tonight. Sex, blowjobs, anal—whatever he wanted. I was going to go porno crazy on him the minute we got home. I totally understood the groupie thing now.

"Who the hell are you?" My smile slipped as it became evident it wasn't the sexy, amazing guitarist who had grabbed my arm and dragged me through the crowd but some other guy. A guy I didn't know.

"I want to talk to you. Don't freak out." The stranger's hand refused to let go as he looked me over with more interest than I'd like.

The man was older, maybe forty? His black hair graying at the sides. He might have been good looking once, his green eyes staring right into me as the deep lines of his face creased. He was strong too, his body looming over mine as his flexed arm refused to let me go. This was not good.

"Well I don't want to talk to you, asshole. Let me go." My fingers tried to pry myself away from his grip; the crowd completely ignoring what was going on.

"Stop trying to get away. I'm just trying to talk to you." The stranger continued edging me closer against the back wall.

My heartbeat thumped out of control in my chest as I started to realize how in trouble I was. Whoever he was, he was not walking away and Rusty was nowhere in sight. The excitement I had felt mere moments ago gave way to sheer terror as I wondered how the hell I was going to get away.

"I said NO!" I screamed with every bit of volume I had left, thrashing around as I refused to comply. If he wanted to hurt me, then I wasn't about to make it easy for him and I sure as hell wasn't going to go quietly.

"What the fuck? Phil, get your hands off her." Rusty appeared from the darkness; his face completely contorted by fury. "You let her go right now, or I'm going to put you in the ground." He didn't sound like he was kidding.

"This doesn't concern you, Rusty. Piss off." The guy—who'd been recently identified as Phil—refused to comply. I assumed him to be the same Phil who was Max's brother, but what he wanted with me was still a mystery.

"Like hell it doesn't concern me, you motherfucker." A swing aimed straight at Phil's jaw made contact with a crunch. "Get your hands off my girlfriend."

Rusty's punch forced Phil to let go, his hands releasing me as he grabbed at his face, the power of the blow making him step back. His eyes peeled back in shock that Rusty had hit him. No. Really. The guy looked surprised, like he couldn't believe that he'd taken a swing. Even though he'd been repeatedly asked to let me go, by Rusty and by me. Obviously he was dumb as well as scary. The confusion priceless as he looked between the two of us in a daze.

"You're dating her?" He spat out some blood just as Joey and Max arrived to catch the show. The offstage antics, the new attraction. The one I had unwittingly been dragged into.

"Phil! What are you doing?" Max pushed himself between his brother and Rusty. Not smart considering Rusty's fist was still clenched and ready to throw another punch. "Dude, what the hell is going on?" He looked to his friend for answers when his brother gave none.

"Your piece of shit brother grabbed Alison and was trying to hurt her." Rusty moved to my side, his body shielding me while he turned to Phil and yelled. "I swear if one fucking hair on her head has so much as a split end, I will end you."

The crowd that had been so uninterested while I was fighting off a would-be attacker had now started to gather, curious as to why the band they had seen on stage not so long ago was now in the middle of some kind of dispute.

"I wasn't trying to hurt her, asshole. I just wanted to talk to her," Phil spat back, the angry guitarist at my side not appeased by his assurances. Phil was clearly not bright, stupidly not showing fear despite Rusty's threats. *I* was worried what he was capable of and I was standing *behind* Rusty, seeing his body tense like it was itching for a fight. Standing in front of him? I'd have run as fast as I could in the opposite direction.

"And you?" He pointed his finger directly at me accusingly. "Do you know what you're getting into with him? He's a dog, Alison. Do you have any idea how many women he's been with?"

Why he cared was my first concern, with the second being why he felt he had to inform me of Rusty's past. I'd seen it with my own eyes, I knew he hadn't been a boy scout who went home early so he could go to church. My eyes were wide open as to who he was and what he'd done. Not to say it thrilled me that he'd probably slept with more women than I could imagine, but I couldn't be mad at him for something that happened *before* he'd met me. Since being together, he wasn't that guy anymore. I had no reason not to trust him, no reason to believe he would sleep around and cheat on me. It had been him who had been pushing for the relationship, why would he do that if all he wanted was someone else? No. He was mine, he loved me, and no crazy idiot was going to convince me otherwise.

"Phil, knock it off. This is not cool." Max shoved his brother, his anger starting to match that of my boyfriend.

"What the hell are you saying?" Rusty stared at him in

disbelief, turning to me to see if any of those words had stuck. "Alison, don't listen to him. He's obviously delusional."

"You're not good enough for her." Phil tore through the Max barrier and went straight after Rusty. "She's my daughter."

I'm not really sure what exactly happened next. Possibly a massive explosion causing the world to end, who knew? The noise disappeared as well, the yelling and the screaming completely evaporating into thin air as my brain tried to process what I'd just heard. I was this man's daughter. As in, the fictional character whose name was absent from my birth certificate was standing in front of me.

No.

None of it made sense.

My brain finally kicked back into reality. I watched security, with the help of Max and Joey, try to break up a hurricane of flying fists between the man I loved and some guy who apparently was responsible for my birth. And here I had thought the show on stage was explosive. Nothing like what was going on now.

"How are you my father?" The voice that hadn't been able to speak a few moments ago found its way out of my throat. My mother didn't even know who my father was and now *this* guy was volunteering? It made no sense.

My question had been enough to do what the security hadn't, both men stopping to face me as their fists stayed cocked, ready to strike. My need for an answer forcing me to go on. "How the hell are you my father? Answer me."

"Your mom and I were together a long time ago. We were both young. She got pregnant. I wasn't ready to be a dad so I left. I reached out to her a few years ago, she didn't want to tell me shit at first. She was still pissed, but finally she gave in. Took me three years before she finally emailed me a picture." His fist unclenched as he reached into his pocket and pulled out his phone—a photo of me lighting up the screen.

"Jesus Christ." Max grabbed the phone from Phil's hand, studying the likeness before looking back at me. "You had a kid? How the hell do you have a kid?" Obviously I hadn't been the only one in the dark, my dear dad forgetting to mention my existence to his own family.

"What are you saying? No. Shut up, you're lying," I scream- ed completely unconcerned about who was around and what they heard. None of this could be true. There was no way. Of all the people who could be my father, this man was not it. It just wasn't possible.

"Babe, listen to me." Rusty threw his arms around me. "I'm going to get you out of here, okay? Max is going to deal with his fucktard brother and we're going to leave." His lips hit my forehead as he pulled me in closer.

"Why is he saying that? Why?" My head shook as I tried to understand what would make someone play such a cruel and heartless joke. "Why?"

"Because it's true," the man who had sent my world crashing down around me answered. "I know that's not what you want to hear. But it's true. Call your mother. Ask her."

It was too much. The noise, the people, the staring. I had no idea which way was up, my head spinning so much I thought I was going to puke.

"Alison, let's go." Rusty made the decision for me as he slowly pulled me away. The crowd parted as we walked through. I passed the gallery of stares completely stunned.

Only able to remain on my feet because the strong arms wrapped around my waist were keeping me upright. Rusty refused to let me go until we'd exited the club.

It was in a daze that I got into his car, oblivious to what he was saying or what was happening. My mind checked out until we arrived back at his house. My body was carried up the steps and gently laid on his bed before I snapped out of my catatonic state.

Holy shit.

What the hell just happened?

"Ali, baby." Rusty shuffled on the bed beside me, his ever-present arms squeezing me closer. "It's going to be okay."

I'm not sure how he could make that promise; there was no way he could have known that. No way any of us could know how this was going to play out. My life was a series of catastrophes. One more epic than the last and it was definitely *not* okay.

"Do you think it's true? Do you think he is my dad?" It was crazy. Completely insane, but he had my picture. A picture I'd sent to my mother last Christmas when she'd gone through rehab again. Why would she give it to him?

"Honestly, I don't know. There's an eighteen-year age gap between Max and his brother . . . I mean the numbers match up. Phil went off the rails before Max was even born so, based on possibilities? It's entirely possible. If that is something you want to know, we will find out, but my only concern is you right now." His hand rubbed up and down my arm as he pressed his lips to the top of my head.

God, he was being so sweet.

I had completely ruined his big night. The preview of what

was about to come and the first time anyone other than the band had heard their new material. Instead of celebrating with his friends or having crazy, freaky groupie -like sex with me, he was dealing with the fall out that was my life. Yet again. It was completely unfair.

"I'm sorry," I whispered. My feelings were completely twisted into a mess of everything and nothing, my mind unable to focus. "Tonight was supposed to be about you, not about me."

"What have you got to be sorry for? None of this is your fault, do you get that? None of this." He bent his head so he could look me in the eyes. "This is one thing you will not own, this is not on you."

It was nice of him to say that, even if I didn't believe it. But, the writing was on the wall.

I was cursed.

Hindsight is always twenty-twenty. I wished I had asked more questions. Asked if Phil was indeed my father, how he could have walked out and forgotten about me for twenty-five years. How could he just choose now to wander back in, completely disregarding whether I'd want to know him or not. I wish I had asked why the hell he thought he had any right to even speak to me after deserting me. Leaving me to fend for myself with a mother who needed more care than I did.

But out of all those questions running around in my head, I asked none. My mouth and mind seized completely as I let some loser who at most was a sperm donor, completely disarm me. That's what I hated most of all. That I had believed I'd changed. That I believed I was strong, smart and able to take on the world. But I was none of those things. I was the same mess I always was. The same mess I guess I'd always be.

243

Twenty-One

Rusty

I **had no idea what the fuck I was doing. If I was making it** worse or if I was making it better, but all I knew was that I had to do something.

We'd been sky-freaking-high coming off stage. High fives and congrats being thrown thick and fast and all I wanted to do was get to where my girl was.

While Angie hadn't birthed her first born rocking out, she wasn't feeling great either. Enter baby daddy with a bunch of unspoken I-told-you-so's who got her out the door before Joey had finished making out with his bottle of Gatorade.

Joey and Max had no problem with me finding Ali before we continued to bask in the glory, my need to have her with me at desperate levels.

The stage had never felt that good. I guess I'd never had anything that amazing waiting for me after I stepped off it. It juiced me up enough to know that was how I wanted it to be from here on out. That she was as much a part of the *feeling good* as was the crowd. It was the ultimate in having my cake and eating it too. There wasn't a man alive who could tell me he was luckier.

So you can imagine my utter surprise when I pushed through the crowd to see Max's oxygen thief of a brother with his hands all over my girl. I'd just caught the tail end of her screaming no, more than enough confirmation that she wasn't digging the attention. Phil was my new public enemy number one.

But of course being an asshole wasn't enough for the man, he had to kick it up a notch and tell my girlfriend what a poor choice I was, topping it off with an oh-hey-I-am-your-father. That Vader reveal was not something any of us saw coming. Even the dude who had been bailing his ass out for the last ten or so years was just as clueless as the rest of us. Whether his claim was real or not, the guy had serious problems—my fist being one of them.

Now I'd never been much of a fighter, pointless in most cases. But seeing my girl look like she was about to pass out was enough of a motivation for me to get physical. Like a switch had been flicked, I was ready to WWE Phil into the middle of next week. Sadly, security and my band hadn't agreed.

Alison had passed out in my arms not long after getting home. Either from the exhaustion or the shock, it was no freaking wonder that she'd curled up on her side and gone nite-nite. Hopefully the sleep would give her some perspective, see the shitstorm raining down had nothing to do with her. Her apology of ruining *my night*, tearing me apart from the inside out.

It wasn't long after she was safely in dreamland that I'd got the message from Max. The dude's text was sent from my front fucking door where he stood, wondering if we could talk. I'd say conversation was definitely required.

"Please tell me that he is not with you?" I wrenched open my front door, my head swiveling, just hoping to catch a glimpse of the asshole. "If he's here, he's a dead man."

"Do you think I'd be stupid enough to bring him here after what he did?" Max walked through the doorway, his face fucking defeated. "If he were here, you wouldn't have to kill him, I'd be doing it myself."

"Take a seat." I gestured to the couch. "Got a hunch this is going to take a while." My ass hit the leather as he followed suit. My need to know what-the-fuck at an all-time high.

"Fuck, man. From everything I found out, what he's saying is true." His head fell back against the couch as he started to explain, the time between the club and my crib obviously used to gather intel. "He met Alison's mom when he was seventeen, knocked her up and bailed. Of course, he didn't bother sharing that with anyone figuring he was on the last straw with our folks. Not that it mattered, they threw his ass out a year later when he got arrested for DUI. Even *they* didn't know about Alison or her mom. All they did know was he started one fire after another and they were through enabling him." He balled his fists, hiking them up to his temple in frustration. "They'd seen what I hadn't. I'd always assumed he'd come good. He played me."

"There is no way any of us could have known it. Last time I checked you weren't fucking Nostradamus. What I don't get is why now? Twenty-five years he hasn't given a shit and now decides he needs a Father's Day card sitting on his mantle?" I wasn't even touching the fucking issue of what-were-the-chances-she-was-my-girlfriend. That small world crap, freaking me the hell out.

"Yeah, well I asked him that as well." Max rolled his head back, the conversation just as messed up on his end. "He ran into Melody Williams, Alison's mom, a few years back. He assumed she'd had an abortion or given the baby up when he left, neither of them in any condition to be parents. He was surprised when he found out she'd not only had the baby but kept her. His curiosity got the better of him so he pursued it. Seemed like she eventually was in a forgiving mood and started drip-feeding him info. The emails Nicole found spelt out that he'd parented and bailed on a child when he was eighteen, which is why she threw his ass out. And while we were worried he'd be getting friendly with a box cutter and a vein, he's been trying to track his kid with only the photo Alison's mom provided. He didn't make the connection that *his* Alison and *your* Alison were one in the same until the confrontation at the club."

"So him manhandling her in a club was his attempt to make up for lost birthdays? Five more minutes and we'd be sitting here talking about his funeral, not about his questionable birth control methods in his youth." Those weren't idle threats. I still wasn't convinced there was going to be any time in the near future where he was going to be safe in my presence. Best he keep away and not test the theory.

"Rus, trust me. I know. It took two of us to peel you off him. You and him in the same room is not happening." Max sat up like the penny finally dropped. "Fuuucckk. That means Alison is my niece."

"Dude, my head is going to explode right now. No offense but I wouldn't be expecting her to call you uncle anytime soon. Honestly, I don't know how any of this shit is going to pan out."

The extent of the damage was still unknown. It's not every day you find out the deadbeat who abandoned you, really is a fucking deadbeat. Not to mention the already existing condition which had been a shitty few months. If anyone were going to *Charlie Sheen* it, I'd say she had better reasons than most.

"You do whatever you have to. Goes without saying that if you need anything—just ask." His stare nailed me from across the room, the look he was wearing pretty serious.

Max and I were tight, and usually there'd be no doubt about him having my six. Problem was, the guy who was an issue shared the same last name.

"How's that going to play out with our conflict of interest?"

"He's my brother. I love him—that's not going to change—but there's no coming back from this. I'm done."

Everyone had their ceiling. The limit of shit they were willing to put up with and Max had obviously found his. I'd say he'd put up with more than most, his loser of a brother having to grow a pair and go it alone.

"Listen, dude. It's been a long ass night. I'm going to bail. My folks are freaking the fuck out and I have no idea where the hell Phil is." Max scrubbed his face as he got up to leave. Not like there was anywhere else we could go with the situation. Too many variables and all of them rested on the girl who was tucked up in my bed.

"Yeah, cool. Hey, thanks for stopping by and filling in the blanks." I held out my palm, his hand returning the shake.

Max paused before continuing to the door. "Sorry, I don't know much else. Keep me posted on how things go down."

I gave him a nod and he showed himself out, the evening well and truly a bust as I sat my ass back down on the couch. Sleep was going to be a while.

"Hey." Alison poked her head around the doorway, her eyes bloodshot from fatigue or tears—I wasn't good with either scenario.

"Come here, baby." I opened my arms as she walked over to me. Her body nestled into my lap. "Did we wake you?"

"I've been in and out." She yawned, her head resting on my shoulder. "I heard some of it."

While the last thing I wanted was to add to the misery she was already dealing with, I told her what I knew. The low down Max had given me wasn't detailed in any case, but better than the sketchy explanation she'd gotten from Phil. For the most part it sounded legit. The ages matched up and if her mom was throwing support behind it then I'd say it was probably true. Not what she wanted to hear, but the truth nonetheless.

"I need to call my mom, I need to know."

"You do whatever you need. I'm right here."

It wasn't my deal to tell her what to do. Whether or not she wanted to go digging up answers was always going to be her call and I would support her either way.

The phone call could have probably waited until the morning but she went ahead and made it anyway. The cell pressed so close to her face I was sure it was going to leave an imprint.

"Mom?" Her eyes met mine as soon as the call connected. "I

need you to tell me who my father is. The truth this time. I need to know."

There wasn't a lot I could do, so I held her hand and listened to the one-sided conversation. Her voice wavering between pained and anger.

"How could you have kept it from me? All these years you said you didn't know?" The rage kicked up in Ali's voice, her hand trying to free itself of my grip. My hold not relinquishing.

"Do you have any idea what you have put me through? Why would you do this? Why?"

Her mom confirmed that Phil was in fact her father and short of a paternity test, no more proof was going to be obtained. At least not tonight. Through all her rapid-fire questions, the only constant were my hands on my girl. My rock solid resolve that whatever happened, she'd do it with me by her side.

The call didn't end well, not that I expected anything better.

"Can you believe she knew this whole time? The whole time, Rusty. Her excuse for not telling me was she didn't want to hurt my feelings because he walked out on me." She paced, wearing a hole in the carpet.

"Like not knowing was so much better. Not to mention that he turns up back in her life after no contact, no child support, no anything and she just tells him everything about me. Like he has any rights." Her feet continued to move as her agitation rose.

"I don't want to hear how much she was in love with him and how she couldn't resist him now. What if he had wanted to hurt me, she just gave me up. Just like that." Her hands raked through her hair in frustration as she finally stopped. "She didn't even think about me. Not even for a second. Not to mention the lack of heads up that he'd come looking. She had deluded herself into thinking he wasn't going to do anything with the knowledge. Like that made any sense."

She needed to get it out and I was cool with being her sounding board, throwing the right amount of support and encouragement when she needed. It was sometime in the early hours of the morning when she finished her verbal assault on the two idiots who were her parents. We didn't even bother heading back to bed, just collapsed on the couch. Once again, zero fucks given as long as we were together.

For the second time that night she fell asleep in my arms, me following soon after. Regardless of what happened in the future, one thing was for sure. She wasn't getting rid of me. I was in this for the long haul.

•••

I had such a pain in the neck.

No, not the colossal fuck up that had happened last night but an actual pain in the neck. I stretched this way and that, trying to work out the massive knot that had formed at the base of my skull, but no dice. I needed a bottle of Advil at the very least.

My eyes dipped down to the beautiful girl who was sleeping peacefully on my chest. Her breathing had finally evened out and apart from the rise and fall of her amazing tits, she hadn't moved an inch.

Unfortunately we didn't get the opportunity to enjoy the solitude for much longer; my phone blaring obnoxiously from the side table took care of that.

"Shit." Alison jumped; her confused face took a quick look at the surroundings before she looked back at me. "Oh, hey." She gave me the first smile I'd seen in hours. It almost made me glad for the interruption.

"Hey." I brushed the side of her cheek as I grabbed my cell.

Whoever was calling me better have a good fucking reason. Mornings blew at the best of times but this particular morning, I wasn't in the mood to be sociable or polite.

"Talk to me." I didn't bother with a hello. The sooner the interruption was dealt with, the better.

"Rus." Angie's panicked-filled voice hit my ear. "I'm having the baby. Oh. My. God. That fucking hurts." She labored in between breaths. "So much fucking pain right now and these stupid drugs aren't working." More puffs of exaggerated breathing. "Get your ass down here."

Getting anything productive from Angie wasn't happening. Between a liberal amount of *fucks* and enough heavy breathing to put a sex line to shame, she gave up and handed the phone to a calmer Jason, who was able to say a little more than just expletives.

"She's in labor. We've been here most of the night." He stopped mid-sentence, bringing me up to speed no longer important. "You're doing great, sweetheart. Just keep breathing." The scream that came after not at all promising.

"Sounds like you got your hands full, buddy. I'll get there as soon as I can." The words left my mouth before I'd had a chance to think about what I'd just said.

Oh. Fuck.

A conundrum of epic proportions.

Angie had left early last night. Stepping straight off stage and out the door had meant she and Jase had completely missed the fireworks that happened later. Like a bad episode of a daytime soap, my girl now had family ties to our bass player—all helped along by his fucking brother who happened to be her father. Yeah, it didn't get any less crazy the more I said it.

And being that Angie or her big shot husband didn't have that very important nugget of information, she had no idea what we were dealing with i.e. Armageddon.

One look at the girl at the center of this mess and I knew I couldn't leave.

Even for Angie.

She would have to understand.

"On second thought Jase, I'm going to have to sit this one out."

"What?" I heard Angie scream as Jase relayed the message. "You need to be here when this baby is born, Rusty. You promised me."

"I know, and I'll be there but I need to take care of something first. You've got this Ange. You got the best guy for the job sitting right beside you."

I'd always be there for her. Always. But she had someone who was going to look out for her and Alison had no one. As hard as the choice was to make, I knew it was the right one.

"You can go." Alison glanced up at me under her lashes as I ended the call. "You don't have to stay here with me, I don't need a babysitter."

It was a half-hearted effort. One where she wasn't convinced I'd chosen her for something other than obligation.

My mental reasoning not having been vocalized.

"She's fine without me. It's been that way for a while now and it's time I saw that. But more importantly, I want to be here with you. I need to be *here* with you."

I had no doubt that if I walked out the door, she probably wouldn't be here when I got back. The shit would have festered so much in her head that the only thing that would have made sense was to leave. Hell, even I considered grabbing our passports and going to chill in Cabo until things settled. But shit had changed and we were going to face it together. It was about time I grew up and took a stand for something. Alison was better than any other reason I'd had.

"But—"

"But nothing." I lifted my fingers to her lips and silenced her, the panic playing peek-a-boo evident on her face. "I can see it in your eyes, babe. See those doubts, see you getting itchy feet like you want to run from this—and I get it. I have no idea what it feels like, but I understand it would be easier to leave the mess and go. But you are always going to come first for me."

"You have no idea what you are committing to." She shook her head, still not convinced I wasn't going to bail. "I don't have a normal life. Do you get that? I'm a disaster."

"Fuck normal, Alison. You are my world. As much as I hate to admit it, Phil was on the money about one thing. You can do better than me."

Those were words I didn't want to say. Not to myself and definitely not her but it was true. Having a piece of shit I had no respect for—the asshole who was also claiming to be her father—point it out didn't help but it didn't make it any more of a lie.

"What?" She coughed in disbelief. "It's me who doesn't deserve you."

"Let me finish. This isn't the I'm-not-good-enough speech and you need to find someone else." There would be a better chance of her and her parents sitting around a turkey at Thanksgiving dinner than me walking out the door. "I'm not a bad person and my life was pretty freaking sweet before you walked into it. The band was my life, the girls—well, they were just an added bonus. It's no secret I'd had more than my share."

"This isn't making me feel better." She shifted uncomfortably in her seat. Me and other women probably wasn't what she wanted to hear about, but it wasn't something I could deny either. There weren't many nights I wasn't with someone. Sometimes more than just one.

"I'm getting to the good part. Stay with me." I reached for her hand, needing her to be right there with me. "I'd assumed as long as I had my music and my friends, it was all I needed but I didn't realize how empty all that shit was unless you had someone to share it with. Coming off that stage and knowing you were there, I felt indestructible. Like I was bulletproof, Alison. You think any of those other girls gave me that? I'd been living in a vacuum, completely oblivious and now my eyes are open. You're not a disaster, you're a hurricane—exciting, unpredictable and keeping on turning no matter what life has thrown at you. You're still standing, and I've never been so happy to get caught up in the ride."

I hadn't meant to make her cry. Watching her eyes well up and making a tear trail down her cheek was like a punch in the face but I needed her to know I wasn't playing. Whatever forces threw us together; there was a bigger picture and both of us were better for it.

"I have no idea who I am. Literally, I have no clue." The second tear fell, my heart breaking in the process.

"You're you and that's all I want." I cupped her face in my hands desperate for her to see how much she meant to me. "Do you get that? You, as you are is enough for me."

"But it's not enough for me."

Those words sounded like a goodbye if ever I heard one. The pain just as raw as it had been last night.

"Then we'll do whatever it takes to make it enough, but me walking away isn't happening. I'm not losing you."

"Maybe I'm already lost."

I had been convinced it was a bad dream. That I would wake up and last night would be just a figment of my overactive and dramatic imagination. But it wasn't. It was real.

Both my parents had abandoned me. Sure, each of them in their own special way, but I hadn't been a priority in either of their lives. My mother only called when she needed legal advice, the only reason she didn't ask for money was because my grandparents were still subsidizing her. And my father decided he was going through some midlife crisis and . . . well I had no idea what he wanted with me. A connection? Just to know I existed? Someone to write as his emergency contact on his health insurance? *Neither* of them cared enough to ask what I'd needed and neither of them cared what their behavior had cost me.

But they hadn't been my biggest nightmare.

What tormented me the most through the night was that I had been living my life reactively. Every action a reflex of someone else's behavior and if I ever wanted the cycle to stop,

I had to. Stop that is.

I had my work cut out for me.

Waking up in Rusty's arms reinforced what I already knew. To be part of an *us*, I had to first be a *me*. And as much as it hurt to think about it, the only way that was going to happen was on my own.

It wasn't that I didn't love him, or doubted he loved me. Every single fiber of my being knew that he was the only man I'd ever love. I knew that walking away might mean I'd lose him forever, that I would risk losing a real shot at happiness but it was what I had to do all the same.

As much as I loved Rusty, I didn't love myself.

I could pretend I was a product of circumstance, like my insecurities were to blame but in the end if I was ever going to give myself completely to him I first needed to be whole.

It's what we both deserved.

And in the end if all I had was me, then I'd find a way to be okay with that.

I *would* be okay.

"Rusty, I need to go."

It wasn't a surprise when I finally said it out loud, I think we both knew it was coming but it didn't make it any easier to hear. I had never been happier than I had while I was with him. I'd learned a lot about myself and what I was capable of, but there was still more work to be done.

"Alison, don't leave. I'll give you all the space that you want. You have your own room and I will respect your boundaries. Whatever you want—I'll do. But you can't ask me to let you go. That's not something I can do."

I saw the pain in his eyes, how confused he was by me

wanting to leave. I died a little knowing that I was responsible for it, that this man who had given me more love, support and kindness than any other person I'd known, was hurting because of me.

"I love you." My heart ripped in two with those three words.

"I love you too. Don't do this." He wiped away the tears from my eyes that refused to stop falling.

"Please let me go, Rusty. I promise you, I'll come back. If you still want me after all of this, I'll come back." The words barely audible as I sobbed in his arms. Every second it got harder and harder to leave.

"I'll always want you." He pressed his lips to mine, kissing me between each sentence. "There isn't enough time or space that will change that. I'm always going to love you. Always."

I was supposed to walk out the door. Untwine my body from his, get off the couch, say goodbye and leave. It's what *needed* to happen but instead of my feet doing what they were supposed to, my hands and mouth took over.

I couldn't stop.

My fingers explored every inch of him, frantic to remember every single muscle by touch. He was pure oxygen and the more I inhaled the more I desperately wanted. I needed his kiss more than I needed my next breath.

He didn't stop either, his hands wrapping around me, bringing me closer as my body gave in. The T-shirt I'd been wearing somehow finding itself off me and onto the floor.

And because I didn't think it was fair to be the only one shirtless, I pulled his off too. Its removal earned me a grunt of approval as Rusty turned his attention to my bra. It didn't stand a chance.

Our fingers seemed to have minds of their own, clawing each other silently in a desperate need to get naked. Jeans—both his and mine—joined the pile discarded on the floor.

"Alison." He moaned as he ripped my panties from my body, their existence obviously offending him. "I love you. I need you." He breathed against my neck, my naked skin pressing against his as he pushed down his boxer shorts with a free hand. It felt like my skin was on fire.

It happened so quickly, my mind not registering what we were doing as his hard cock slid into me, my fingers digging into his shoulders as I gripped him. He filled me, the feeling overwhelming as he pushed deeper inside.

An involuntary gasp left my lips as he slowly dragged himself back out, my body mourning the loss. He didn't let the feeling last long, pushing back into me in another single, hard stroke. The slight sting of pain got me even wetter as he continued the sweet delicious torture. The same action repeated again and again until I was sure I would lose my mind.

I couldn't speak, my hips getting into the game as they met every single thrust of his with one of my own. My mind completely on autopilot as he bucked out of control above me, desperate for release.

"Rusty," I screamed as my body continued to rock against his, faster and harder—the need burning me alive from the inside out.

"I'm here, baby. I'm always going to be here." His lips covered me. My mouth, my neck—he left no part untouched as he grabbed my ass and held me still. "I'm here." He pulled out before one final thrust sent me spiraling over the edge, my body shaking as the orgasm took me.

"Yes, baby. Yes." He continued to pump, finding his own release; his hot load filling me as we both panted out of control. My body continued to shake as he teased the last wave of pleasure from it, his hands restless as they continued to move over my skin. It was almost too much, another orgasm taking me over the edge before he was finally done. My limbs like jelly as I collapsed on top of him.

Oh. Crap.

Having sex with Rusty had *not* been the plan. What should have happened was me walking out the door and saying goodbye, not ending up naked with Rusty's semi hard cock inside of me. It was a fail of epic proportions.

"Don't regret it," he whispered, as if reading my mind. "Don't ever regret a minute you spend with me."

"I'm so confused." My head nestled into the hollow of his neck, my brain trying to play catch up. "I was supposed to walk away."

"I'm never going to regret this, or you for that matter." He gently stroked my hair as I tried not to cry. "Even if you still leave me, I'll cherish every single time. It will hurt like hell, but there isn't a chance I would trade it. Any of it." He said without even a hint of hesitation in his voice.

"How can you say that? How can you not hate me right now for all this shit I am putting you through?" I hated it, how could he lay there telling me he was going to treasure the memories? I was dragging him through hell and he was going to cherish it? That didn't even make sense.

"Because you changed me, don't you see that? You've made me a better me than I could have ever been by myself and I'm thankful for that."

I'm not sure I would ever understand how any of the pain I was causing him could be a positive. Maybe it was something that was beyond my comprehension or maybe it just wasn't for me to *get,* but I hoped he would hold onto it. Hold on for the both of us.

• • •

"You can stay here as long as you like. The sofa bed is comfier than it looks." Renee pulled the bag from my hand as I walked through her doorway. "I'll even cook." She paused before adding, "Okay we both know that's a lie but I do great takeout. You're going to love it here."

It hadn't been easy walking out the door and leaving Rusty. I had almost changed my mind, plagued by the guilt of the breakup sex, but somewhere I found the courage to do what I knew had to be done.

He watched the entire time, not letting his eyes leave me for a second as I pulled my clothes from the closet and packed a bag. He didn't beg me to stay but he wouldn't leave either, staying silent as I left my keys on the coffee table, his eyes on me until I closed his front door.

I cried the minute I walked onto the street, not stopping until Renee came and got my pathetic butt from the front of my old apartment building. I had nowhere else to go.

"Thanks, I really appreciate this. I promise I'll pay you back for everything." I threw my arms around her, hoping the hug would help me not feel so empty. Sadly, it didn't.

"Pleeeeease. Like I would take your money." She screwed

her face up in mock disgust. "Your money is no good here. What you are going to do instead is find your happiness. That's all the payment I need."

She—like Rusty—was entirely too kind but I was too sad to argue so instead I accepted her kindness and hoped like hell I would live up to my side of the deal. Happiness didn't seem attainable. Not in the near future anyway.

While Renee didn't agree with my decision to leave—I was spared the name-calling or eye rolling—she didn't try and change my mind either. She just welcomed me into her home, which is probably where I should have gone the first time. Oh well, better late than never.

I meant what I said—I loved Rusty. I really did, but love didn't conquer all. My life was complicated enough and dragging him down with the sinking ship wouldn't be fair. If it were truly meant to be then he and I would eventually find our way back to each other. At least, that's what I hoped; the reality was entirely too depressing.

Renee gave me a few concerned looks but wisely didn't ask if I was okay—just like me feeling sorry for myself, it too had exceeded its limit. And with her usual brand of cheer and positivity, gave me a hug goodbye and headed out the door to work.

Work.

That was something else I needed to do.

It had been weeks since I had unceremoniously been let go, it was time I got busy either doing something that I loved or found something to do until I landed that dream job. Hell, at this point I'd do anything for the distraction, I wasn't too proud to go stack shelves at a store if that was all that I could get.

Staking shelves though wasn't in my future apparently with an early-morning phone call breaking through my mental life stock take.

"Hello," I answered benignly. The number was not one I recognized so I assumed it was just some telemarketer looking to sell me shit I couldn't afford and didn't need.

"Hello, is this Alison Williams?" The calm voice on the other end of the phone responded. "This is Ashlyn Evans, the business manager for Metamorphous Records."

Holy shit.

I had completely forgotten about my interview today. The one Rusty had helped me get when he floated my name past the powers that be at Power Station headquarters. My heart started beating wildly as I realized I had potentially blown the chance.

"Ashlyn, yes. It's me. I am so sorry." My mind scrambled for a plausible excuse. "I—I . . ." Nope, nothing. "I'm really sorry." Was what I finally agreed on, knowing that no matter what I said I was going to sound incompetent. Who would hire me for a position when I couldn't even remember to turn up for an interview? Bridges were burning, and I had no one else to blame but myself.

"Is everything okay?" she asked sympathetically. "Ordinarily I wouldn't have followed up on a missed interview, it's not like there aren't plenty of people in the city looking for work, but when we spoke last week I thought we sort of clicked. Are you sick? We could reschedule."

The chance to explain she was giving me was more than I deserved. Like she said, there were plenty of people who needed a job. I couldn't lie to her even if I wanted to. My chance at joining the team was probably toast but at the very least I was going down with my personal integrity intact.

"No, I'm not sick." I took a deep breath before continuing. "It's been a crazy twenty-four hours. I met a man claiming to be my father for the first time and that didn't go so well. Turns out he is also the brother of Max, the bass player for Black Addiction, small world huh? I also completely freaked out, broke up with my boyfriend and moved out. So . . . I guess you don't really need to interview me anymore. I mean, I know you were doing it as a favor to Rusty and seeing as we aren't together anymore . . ."

I really didn't want to go on. I hadn't meant to overshare so much but as soon as I started, I couldn't stop. It's not like I had anything more to lose so I thought what the hell. "Thanks for the opportunity, Ashlyn. I'm sorry I wasted your time."

I was ready for the well-thanks-for-the-explanation-we-don't-hire-crazy-people speech or the polite brush off. I didn't know Ashlyn well enough to know which one would be coming my way but was almost positive the phone call was ending in rejection. It was okay though, for the first time in a long time I wasn't completely devastated. Everything happens for a reason, right? Look at me with my positive spin. Maybe I was going to get through this mess after all.

"Hold up, you met your dad for the first time and you broke up with Rusty?" The disbelief evident in her voice. "Sounds like a pretty epic day if you ask me. I can't imagine what you must be going through. I'm sorry, Alison."

"It's okay, really. I'm pretty maxed out on emotions at the moment so I guess that's a positive." My mouth kept talking despite my brain telling it to shut the hell up. "Missing out on a chance to work with you sucks but at least I discovered a new industry I might be good at. I hadn't even thought of a music label so the new direction is really good. Trust me, that's progress considering up until recently I had no idea what I even wanted to do."

If I'd overshared before, I had no idea what my mouth was spewing now. I was almost certain my verbal spillage would garner no response, not unless you counted hanging up. No sane person would continue with this call, so I waited patiently for the goodbye or dead air.

Any minute now.

"So are you available Friday? I have an opening at three."

I must be hallucinating because she can't have said what I thought she just said. Maybe my brain had hit some self-preservation switch? Fooling me into hearing words that hadn't been spoken and saving me from the mortification. No one in their right mind could have listened to my tales of woe and *still* be offering me an interview. So one of the two had to be happening. I was either delusional or I had voices in my head. Both options confirming I was unwell.

"Um . . . you want to interview me?"

"Your qualifications haven't changed. I'm willing to over-look the missed interview based on extenuating circum-stances."

My mind was spinning. Was it out of sympathy or was she just being nice? I had been fully prepared for the rejection. Really. Truly. My peace made at the lost opportunity.

"But didn't you hear what I said? Doesn't that make you think I'm crazy? And now that I'm no longer with Rusty, you don't have to go through with this."

"Firstly, are you trying to talk me out of interviewing you?" She laughed before continuing. "*I'll* be the judge of whether or not you are suitable for the job. Secondly, Rusty handed me your resume, no promises were made. I wanted to meet you because you seemed like the right person for the job not because of who you were dating."

Floored. Absolutely floored.

"I can be there Friday at three. I won't be late." I stopped trying to fight it and welcomed my second chance. If this lady was crazy enough to give it, I was grabbing onto that lifeline with both hands.

"Fantastic. I will see you then." I heard the smile in her voice. "Oh, and Alison." She paused before going on. "It's okay that you're a mess. I don't know what it's like to suddenly meet a man claiming to be your father, but break ups are hard. I hope things work out for you and Rusty."

"Me too." I nodded my head even though she couldn't see it. "Me too."

Twenty-Three

Rusty

As much as I wanted to beg her to stay, I didn't. Instead I watched her get a few things, throw them into a bag and leave with what was left of my heart.

Nothing had hurt more.

I'd lived my life up until this point completely insulated from heartache, not because of some grand plan, but because I'd never fallen as hard for anyone, as I had for her. Alison was a game changer, and now I wasn't sure if I'd ever feel anything other than rage and hurt consuming me.

It was probably that train of thought that saw me trash my favorite red Stratocaster, the body exploding as I smashed it against my bedroom floor but even with Big Red's demise, Alison leaving was still the bigger blow.

By some miracle I was able to get my shit together enough to get myself to the hospital just in time for Jase to announce an eight-pound-nine-ounce baby boy had made his arrival. While I had completely missed the birth, Angie was so blissed-out on either amazing painkillers or motherhood that she was no longer angry at me. Just as well, not sure I could deal with her disappointment as well as my own shit.

"He's perfect." I looked at the swaddled bundle she was cradling in her arms, the little dude's eyes scrunched up oblivious to the world.

"I know," she answered, her smile not having left her face since I was allowed in to see her. "So we going to talk about the fact you look like shit? I may have just had a baby but I'm not fucking blind."

"Angie, give him a break." Jase shook his head, trying to go to bat for me.

"Thanks, dude, but you should know better than to argue with her. She isn't going to let up so we might as well get it out in the open. The two of you missed some fireworks last night and all of it ended with Alison leaving."

"What the fuck?" Angie said a little louder than she probably wanted to, junior stirring in her arms.

"Sweetheart, you are really going to have to downgrade the swearing." Jase took the baby from her, mini Jase settling with the change-over. "Sorry to hear that Rus, let us know if there is anything we can do." He gave me a chin tip being that his hands were occupied. The offer was kind even though there was jack anyone could do. Unless they could somehow convince Alison that she could sort out whatever she needed to sort with me by her side. Considering I had been unable to convince her, I wasn't sure it was a possibility.

"How could she just leave? What the hell happened?"

Unlike Jase, Angie wasn't content with my condensed version of events. I guess we'd been through so much together and she knew me enough to know there was more to the story.

Not that I was entirely comfortable with it but there was no point hiding it. Max and Joey had witnessed half of the showdown last night. It wouldn't take her long to connect the dots and work out it was more than a coincidence that Alison discovered Phil was her old man and then bailed.

"She's confused. A lot of shit went down." I pulled up a chair and started to recount the whole story. How I'd come off stage to see Phil's hands on her and almost lost my shit. Then the son of a bitch dropped the bomb that twenty-five years ago, he'd shacked up with Alison's mom, both of them neglecting to tell Alison. It didn't take a brain surgeon to work out what happened next. Even Jase blew out an under his breath "Oh fuck" with Angie letting it fly with a few more colorful choice words.

"Fucking Phil is her dad? Max's brother? How is that even possible?" She asked exactly what was rattling around in my head the minute I'd found out.

"Because babe, you don't have to be that smart to put your dick into someone and make a baby." I blew out in frustration, not thinking about what I was saying. "Oh shit, guys. I didn't mean it that way." My eyes glanced between the two of them, totally realizing how much of a dick I was being. The fact they themselves just had a baby completely overlooked by my throwaway line. It seemed saying the right thing wasn't in my repertoire today. Too busy being a miserable bastard.

"We know you didn't mean it that way." Angie let me off the hook and gave me a smile. "Phil made a human. The guy can barely make a sandwich."

"Yep." As much as I would have loved for the story to end there it unfortunately didn't. So I went on to fill in the gaps as to why I was now without the only girl I'd ever loved and rocking a bullshit mood. It didn't get any better hearing it out loud. My heart just ached a little having to confront that this shit was real. Me needing to sit on the sidelines and hope she found her way back to me.

"I'm so sorry, Rusty." Angie gave me a look I didn't like seeing. It was bad enough I was miserable I didn't want to drag her down with me. Especially not when she should be fucking ecstatic.

"Don't even go there, babe. You need to concentrate on you and yours. I'm all good. I could bounce out a window and land on my feet, whatever happens will be for the best. Besides, I'm going to be caught up making sure you don't make my new nephew soft to worry about any of that."

Sure what I was spouting was total BS but that's all she needed to hear. I'd deal, if it meant I'd go back to keeping things casual with ladies, then that's what would happen. No fucking way would I want something with anyone else. Right now I'm not even sure my dick would be interested in another girl, let alone my heart.

"Please know we're here for you, okay." Angie gave me a tight smile that clued me in she wasn't buying it. Honestly, I knew she probably wouldn't but at least she wasn't going to be a bitch about it and ride me.

"So what are you calling the little dude? Rusty is a good name, just putting it out there." I decided the conversation had strayed long enough from the reason we were all sitting around a hospital room. For once in my life, I wasn't comfortable with the attention.

"We haven't decided yet." Angie shrugged, shooting Jase

some weird non-verbal dialogue with her eyes.

"We'd decided." Jase grinned filling in the blanks. "But Angie changed her mind. We've narrowed it down to Declan or Zack. I'm cool with either but *someone* is having a hard time deciding." Naming the *someone* wasn't required as the raised eyebrow and loaded look were of enough a hint.

"It's important." Angie qualified, obviously needing to weigh in. "Our baby is going to be stuck with it for the rest of his life. We can't just throw out a name and hope for the best. Talk to Gwyneth Paltrow's kids in ten years, see how enthused *Apple* is about her parents' need for originality."

As much as I would have loved to continue the great baby name debate—it meant there was less time to think about my reality—I figured I should give them their space. It was time for me to bail and find a new way to distract myself. One that involved less people hopefully. It was on that note that I said my goodbyes, gave my yet-to-be-named nephew a kiss on the forehead and headed out the door. The sooner I tried to move on with my life, the better.

•••

I was a lying sack of shit.

All that talk about me trying to move on with my life was complete bullshit. It had been three days since she'd left and every single time I walked back into my apartment it would take me approximately twenty minutes before I'd cave. My body lost its battle of will with my head and I'd walk my ass into the room she used to sleep in and sit on the floor. Because that made sense, prolong the agony a little more—dig the knife in a little deeper.

Misery was the only word for it. My days and nights empty as I flicked into autopilot. The band, the bar, nothing could get me out of my funk. Not even tinkering on my guitar could shake me from my mood, the anger and pain literally eating me from the inside out.

Max and Joey took turns stopping by which made shit even worse. The unspoken sympathy in their eyes not something I wanted to see. In the end I stopped answering the door.

Was I supposed to just let her go? Was I supposed to fight? Both had the potential to blow up in my face and, yet sitting around with my dick in my hand wasn't an answer either. All I knew was I couldn't just pretend we didn't share something fucking real, that she didn't mean anything. Even if it meant I didn't get to sleep with her again. Even if she wasn't ever going to be mine. I just needed to be in her life, even if it was only as a friend. Yeah, 'cause that was going to be easy. See what I mean?

Lying.

Sack.

Of.

Shit.

So sitting around feeling sorry for myself and not achieving much else could only go on so long. My limit exceeded, as my need for answers remained unanswered. Talking to Alison wasn't going to happen either. Well not in the foreseeable future; not that I was going to let that stop me from pushing forward. I didn't do well with sitting on my hands. Nope. Improvise, adapt and overcome. Like a motherfucking marine.

First thing I was going to do was find out what the dickwad

who was claiming to be her father's intentions were, because he had no chance of fucking messing with her head any more than he already did. That much I could guarantee.

I had no idea where I'd even look. Max had been tight-lipped about the piece of shit's whereabouts and I assumed he hadn't been dumb enough to stay with his baby bro. But given the shit he'd pulled in the past you never could tell. The fact he'd been mooching off his brother and totally denied he had a kid for so many years didn't speak volumes of his character. Total douchebag, so rather than drive around the five boroughs in the hopes of finding him, needle-in-a-haystack style, I figured I'd start with his brother and see if he had any answers.

"Hey." Max greeted me at the door, the look on his face not dissimilar to the one he'd been wearing each time he'd come to visit me. "How are you doing? Have you heard from her?" He winced knowing it probably wasn't going to be good news.

"Haven't heard jack. And considering she left me and that was the last time we spoke, I'd say my mood is fucking brilliant. I'm sure she's doing peachy though, I mean why wouldn't she? Things have turned out so fucking stellar so far, what's not to be happy about." So maybe I wasn't done being pissed about the situation. I alternated. Pissed and sad. Obviously pissed didn't make me cry like a pussy for the company so it was the better of the two.

"Have you tried to call her, dude? Maybe she just needed a day or two to get her head around it. It's not like you to throw in the towel." Max gestured to the living room as he closed the door behind us. Obviously dumbass wasn't around or I doubt I'd be so welcome. I had threatened his brother on more than one occasion so Max inviting me in when there was a potential for homicide, probably wouldn't have happened.

"You think that's what I'm doing?" I stared at him in disbelief, the anger bubbling inside me until I wasn't sure the drywall wasn't going to get intimate with my fist. "Trust me, I want nothing more than to see her or call her. You think it's easy for me to sit around waiting?" He had no idea what I went through every night, the mental debate that kept me up for hours wondering if I had made the right decision in letting her go. "It's not about me. It's not about what *I* want. Seriously, dude, how would you feel if the rug was pulled out from under your feet? That girl has been fucked over so many times by so many people who were supposed to care about her, the fact she hasn't gone completely *Quentin Tarantino* is a fucking miracle. Someone needs to put her first for a change and if she wants space then that's exactly what I'm going to give her." I knew it wasn't Max's fault; the poor guy was left to deal with the fallout just like the rest of us. Still I couldn't help myself from taking a cheap shot, it was my gift that I spread my misery. Everyone should get a piece.

"Fuck, man. I am so sorry. Tell me what I can do? We need to fix this. I'm already catching heat from my parents and I've had to pretty much beg them to stay away. I can't hold them off much longer, their view is they've already been denied twenty-five years knowing their grandkid, they are going to do whatever they can now."

However bad I thought it had been for Max, it wasn't even close to the level of suck his reality had turned out to be. I'd been so consumed with my own pity-party that any shit he'd been catching hadn't even registered. Not only was his asshat of a brother MIA, leaving a shitstorm behind him, but he had to play interference with his folks who wanted to step up to the plate and do right by their granddaughter. Which to say the least was fucking admirable and something Alison desperately needed. And on top of all of that, he had to deal with me and my issues. Just another reason not to feel good about myself. I could safely say I wasn't going to be winning friend of the year.

"She's going to need all the family she can get, but she's already spooked." I rubbed the back of my neck trying to figure out a fucking solution. "You know where Phil is? I'm not going to kill him but I want some answers."

I was serious about not killing him. Not yet at least. But if my fist happened to slip and hit his face while we were conversing then, what could I do? Shit happens. Black eyes too. I'd make sure he'd still be breathing when I left though. I wasn't about to break a promise.

"You on the level with me, man? Bailing you out of jail isn't on my to-do list today, neither is paying for a funeral, because we both know that shit will land on me too." Max narrowed his eyes, trying to get a feel for the situation. Not that I blamed him. He knew me pretty well and had never seen me that mad. He had no idea what I was capable of. Truth be known, neither did I.

"I swear, I just need to know what his intentions are. If he is even thinking about leveraging her for an advantage . . ." The words stuck in my throat as I tried to rein in my anger. "It's just best he knows that shit isn't an option. I also want to know why the fucking Houdini act. Wanting nothing to do with her and then reappearing in her life like a bad case of herpes. He doesn't get to do that shit, and if he plans on having any contact with her, it's completely on her terms. If she isn't up for it, your brother takes any expectations to the sidelines and sits on the bench."

Phil would be begging for death if he even thought about hurting Alison again. On that rule I wouldn't be bending, so best he heard it sooner than later. The I-didn't-know wasn't going to cut it as an excuse.

"He's crashing at some girl's house in Brooklyn. He called me yesterday asking me to bring his shit. That's about all I know." Max shoved his hands in his pockets, the strain of the situation wearing on his face.

"The stones on him." I don't know why I was surprised, clearly the man thought of no one but himself. "He asked you to bring his shit? He should be thanking his lucky stars it's not torched on the fucking lawn. You been over yet?" It was no secret that I was hoping that the answer was a negative. The two of us delivering the asshole's prized collection of *jerk-off monthly* sounded like the perfect way to spend what was left of an already shitty day. Besides, if I had a witness there was less chance I'd lose my cool. See, both of us would luck out.

"No, not yet." Max shifted uncomfortably in his seat. "Rus, I'm not sure this is a good idea." He shook his head, un-convinced.

"Well either we go together or I go by myself. Your choice but either way, I'm going."

"Fine, but we're taking Joey too. No way am I going to be able to handle your ass if you channel your inner Hulk again." Max finally relented.

The compromise was fair, better to have more hands on deck and while Joey wasn't the sharpest knife in the drawer he had some killer upper body strength. You never know when you were going to need reinforcements.

"Sounds like a plan. Get Joey and I'll go start the Camaro. The sooner we sort this shit, the better."

While I knew making the trek to Brooklyn wasn't going to get back the woman that I loved, at least it felt like I was doing something productive. It beat the hell out of sitting on my ass and waiting for shit to happen. Now I just had to make good on my promise. The asshole needed to stay breathing.

Pulling myself together over the last few days hadn't been easy. The temptation to throw on a pair of yoga pants and eat my way from one end of Renee's kitchen to the other was almost too great. But I resisted. If for no other reason than she had terrible snacks. Low fat ice cream and sugar-free chocolate? Why the hell even bother? It was like taking a toothbrush to a knife fight, pointless and ridiculously unsatisfying.

"Look at you showering without being prompted." Renee had looked up from her second cup of coffee. "You are a machine. I'm so proud of you."

"Hmm." My hands wrapped the towel around my still wet hair. "I don't know about the machine part but I'm not out for the count just yet. Maybe I'm just a glutton for punishment."

"Bullshit. You're one of the strongest women I know." Renee's personal brand of motivation shone through as she handed me a cup of coffee. "Have you called him?" The *him* she asked about was unspecified but we both knew who she meant.

"I can't," I said, my heart aching at just the thought of him. "Not until I'm stronger."

"You know that doesn't make sense, right, Ali? If he cares as much as you say he does, he's going to want to be there for you. Why won't you let him?"

I didn't want to have the conversation. It was the same one that swirled around in my head on an hourly basis. Did I do the right thing by leaving? Had I been overly dramatic? The truth was, I didn't know. I was winging the whole situation and for once, I trusted myself that I was doing the right thing.

"If all our relationship is built on is him being my hero then I know we won't last. I needed to see I can do this on my own. To work out what I want, what I need. I know it doesn't make sense—"

She cut me off before I was able to finish. "Ali, it makes perfect sense. Hopefully he's smart enough to wait around until you're ready."

"I don't expect him too. It's been days and I haven't even called him. Why would he be waiting for me?"

It had been days where I hadn't even sent so much as a text message; I wouldn't blame him if he'd given up. He had options, ones that didn't have so much baggage. It would make sense for him to move on. It was selfish of me to ask differently.

"Um. Because he loves you, silly? I'm sure the man is just as torn up as you are."

"Maybe." I didn't dare hope.

"You're interview isn't until three, why are you up so early?" Renee put her empty cup in the sink as she went through her last minute out-the-door routine. The alarm on her phone buzzed as a reminder that she needed to get to work.

"I'm meeting my mom."

Hearing the words out loud just confirmed what I already knew. If I was going to really stop running from my past, I was going to have to confront it. Let it go and realize that it didn't define me. As much as I wanted this to be achieved remotely, I knew it wasn't possible. The woman who birthed me unfortunately was one of the loose ends I needed to take care of. And I thought the job interview was going to be scary. Ha!

"Ooooooooo. You think that is a good idea?" Renee silenced the obnoxious beeping and tossed her phone into her bag. Her feet hadn't moved any closer to the door.

"Nope, but I'm doing it anyway." Or so was my new motto.

Don't know where I'm going? Who cares, going anyway.

Don't know if it's going to all end up in tears? Who cares, I'll pack tissues.

It was time, and I was done being a casualty of my life instead of a participant.

"If I haven't said it before I'm so proud of you. Shit!" Her eyes glanced at the clock on the wall. "I've got to run." Renee's prolonged goodbye came complete with a squeeze and a stern "call me if you need anything." And the door closed behind her.

● ● ●

"Hi, sweetie." My mother slid into the booth opposite me. I'd been waiting thirty minutes, not that being late was anything new for her. I guess I should be glad she showed up at all, her maternal bond nonexistent.

"Hi." My fingers twisted nervously under the table as I watched the woman I barely knew open the menu in front of me. "I'm glad you came. I know you're busy." My voice did little to hide my irritation.

"Is that sass I detect in your voice?" She didn't miss the sarcasm. "I'm not sure why you think it's okay to speak to your mother like that."

Right. My mother. There seemed to be some confusion as to what this term actually meant, a dictionary was something she'd obviously packed away with her nurturing side. Both of them collecting dust.

"I just thought we should talk. It's been awhile, and with everything that has happened . . . I mean. We should talk, right?" Talking was the *least* we should be doing given the latest developments.

"Look, Alison." The pretense of concern took little more than seconds to fracture. "If this is about your father, I really don't know what to tell you. It's easy for you to stand there and judge me, but I was young. I could have had an abortion but I didn't. You should be thanking me for that."

Wow.

And my reason for why our contact was limited to a few phone conversations a year became immediately evident. No wonder I had been a complete basket case. When someone asks you to thank them for your existence, it doesn't set you up for great things.

Not sure why it had taken me so long to realize, but I was nothing like my mother. It wasn't because I didn't get knocked up straight out of high school, or because I had a college education. No, the reason was because I wasn't a self-absorbed child living in an adult's body. I was far from perfect, but I had more compassion and ownership over my shortcomings in my little finger than the woman in front of me had in her whole body.

I didn't need to keep running away from my past. I had been a mile away this whole time.

My eyes were well and truly open. And for the first time ever I knew exactly what I needed to do. I didn't need her approval. Or anyone else's for that matter. I had survived in spite of her. In spite of all of it.

"Where are you going?" She grabbed at my arm as I stood up and tried to leave. "Why did you drag me all the way down here if you were just going to leave?"

Her annoyance had once been the badge of my shame, my desire to please her winning out over my own self-preservation. But as I watched her eyebrows knit in their usual disappointment, I didn't feel a thing. This wasn't up to me to fix.

"Because I thought for me to move forward, I needed resolution. I thought I needed to work this out." I shook off her hand as my heart thumped loudly in my chest. "But I now realized that I can move forward just by walking away. Thank you, mother. Thanks for not having the abortion."

I left her speechless as I walked away. A genuine smile slowly formed on my lips as my feet carried me further from the table and finally out the door. Rusty had once told me I'd deserved better. He was right and I owed it to both of us to make sure that's exactly what I got.

The encounter might have left me shattered a few months

ago but now I was energized. I felt stronger than I'd ever been, and ready for my second chance.

●●●

In some crazy act of God, I had been given another shot at the interview. And it couldn't have come at a better time. I was going in all guns blazing, ready to wow Ashlyn and whoever else was in that room. I needed this job. Not because my bank account was currently running on vapors and I was living on my best friend's couch, but because I was ready to succeed at something again. I was done playing it safe and I was ready to show that I still had some fight left in me. A job would be the first step of many. Steps I would be probably taking alone from here on out. Either way, I wasn't scared.

Ashlyn welcomed me into her plush minimalist office. Her office supplies neatly aligned and color coordinated. I immediately liked her. The importance of desk order was so often overlooked, so it was good to see someone hadn't abandoned the practice.

"So, Alison, we're going to do this a little differently." She sat down in her luxurious office chair behind her huge wooden desk. "I've read your resume thoroughly and it's pretty impressive. But what I want to hear about is what you aren't good at. Your weakness." Her fingers tented in front of her as she waited for my response.

Um. What?

Wasn't the point of an interview to sell your virtues, not advertise where you sucked? Surely this had to be a trick question, maybe it was to see if I crumbled under the pressure or would answer evasively? No one wanted to hear about all the stuff I couldn't do, least of all me. I had a whole resume of good stuff I could do. Why couldn't we talk about that?

"You want to know about my weakness?" I parroted the question in a stupid and obvious attempt at stalling. "I'm too organized . . ." A nervous laugh bubbled from my throat. Yep. Wasn't fooling any one.

"You know, I sucked at interviews." Ashlyn leaned back into her chair, a smile playing at the corners of her mouth. "I'd get so nervous I'd almost be sick. It's pretty intimidating to be on and try and impress someone in just a short time." A lock of her beautiful red hair dropped in front of her eyes.

Well wasn't that the truth. I think my sweat glands had multiplied from the time I'd walked in the door, and all of them were doing their best to make me look like I was having a shower from the inside out.

"So tell me what you can't do, because I'm looking for someone who can do more than just regurgitate their resume." She waited patiently while I mentally ticked off my list of flaws and deficiencies. Ordinarily I would have asked her how much time she had, citing a pretty extensive list. But today, there was none of that as I relaxed into the chair. She wasn't going to get a bumbling, unsure little girl. That's not who I was anymore.

"I'm not great with relinquishing control." The first cab off the rank flew out of my mouth with very little effort. "In fact it used to scare the hell out of me. I'm getting better at it though, Rusty . . ." The mention of his name had me stumble slightly. "Rusty, worked with me on pushing out of my comfort zone. I may not like it but I now know I can do it."

Her brow rose at my response, her eyes curiously studying

me. Perhaps she had wanted to ask more about my failed relationship, but she didn't. It was either professional courtesy or she decided it was none of her business but thankfully she completely ignored the mention of his name and my momentary lack of focus. If it wouldn't have been so inappropriate I would have reached across the desk and kissed her. The kindness in not asking what happened with Rusty, overwhelming me.

"Tell me how. Explain how it was a challenge and why you think you have a handle on it." She pushed a little further, not content with single sentence answer.

"I've been a paralegal for a long time. Not because I wanted to, but because it was convenient. That's how I've lived most of my life. I'm willing to take chances now. Try something new, even if it means uncharted territory."

"Sounds like a positive to me. What else do you struggle with?"

With each new suggestion of things I did badly, I had an equally implemented solution to suggest. Whether it was achieved through my own personal growth or Rusty's wax-on-wax-off method, I'd gained a heap of confidence. The weakness I'd once seen in myself had slowly melted away.

"I guess I'm not afraid anymore," I responded as to why I was looking for a career change. "Fear doesn't have to paralyze me. There will always be things I can't do but that doesn't negate what I know I can do exceptionally well. I'm organized, I'm thorough, and my attention to detail is acute. It doesn't matter if I'm filing legal briefs or dealing with recording contracts. The skill set is the same and I'm ready to challenge myself in a new industry."

Well look at that. I was not only no longer a doormat but I could stand tall and proud all on my own. And even though I knew I wasn't perfect, I knew I'd work it out. It was a modern day renaissance, and I was my own Sistine Chapel celling.

Ashlyn listened intently as I spoke. With my deficiencies laid bare before me, the follow-up questions didn't seem at all nerve-racking like they usually were. I was able to answer with no hesitation. I'd never been so relaxed in an interview and even if I didn't get the job, I'd be hitting the next interview out of the park.

"Well, I think I've seen all I needed to see." Ashlyn tapped the stack of papers in front of her on the desk before tossing them in the trash. "When can you start?"

"Now?" I laughed, wondering if that meant I had the job. I didn't want to assume but surely that was a good indication.

"How about we start you off on Monday?" She laughed, either impressed by my enthusiasm or the tragedy I had nothing better to do. "I'll email a contract for you to have a look at and we can discuss any issues Monday morning. I'll forward your salary details as well." Her smile slipped slightly. "There's just one last question I need to ask you."

"What is it?" I asked, eager to get out the door and celebrate.

"You know we represent Black Addiction and that includes Rusty Crawford. Your personal life is none of my business except when it will interfere with your work. You don't have a problem with that, do you?"

Of course, I knew Rusty and the band were represented by Metamorphous, which meant by virtue at some point I'd be working with him. I mean, I guessed I would be or at very least seeing him.

"We broke up but neither of us hate each other." At least I hoped we didn't. I could really only speak for myself seeing as I really hadn't asked, but I guess it was entirely plausible he wasn't my biggest fan. "It's fine, we can work together with no issues," I said for my benefit as much as hers.

"Great, then there should be no problems. We'll be launching their new album soon, lots of work that will need to be done." She rose to her feet and adjusted her jacket. Code for the interview is over and you can leave now.

"Thanks, I'm looking forward to it." I followed suit and lifted myself out of my chair, extending my hand to say goodbye. "I really appreciate this."

"Let's be clear about something, Alison. You got this job all by yourself. No one did you any favors. It was all you, so be proud of that."

I nodded as I made my way to the door scared that if I spoke I might burst into tears. I was proud. Proud that despite the odds, I wasn't out for the count. And with a wordless goodbye, I closed the door behind me and let out a slow and steady breath. I was slowly clawing my way back.

"That's fantastic!" Renee pulled me into her arms as I told her my good news. Not sure if her joy was over my newly acquired employment or the fact my days on her couch were numbered. "We should celebrate. Crap. Um. I have a date tonight. Can we rain check?" Her scattered thoughts verbalized themselves as words as her brows furrowed in concern.

"Yeah, of course we can rain check. I don't start until Monday so we have plenty of time." I smiled, a little disappointed that my night of celebrating would be spent solo. "It can wait until tomorrow."

"Great, now tell me about your mom. How did that go?" She winced, assuming that because I hadn't mentioned it, it probably hadn't gone well.

"You know what? It was fine." I toed off my high heels and tossed my purse onto the coffee table. "I got what I needed and that's all that matters." A long breath pushed out from my lips. It had been a really long and emotional day.

"Do you need me to cancel?" Renee's face lit up in panic. "I can, if you need me. Do you need me? I can stay." The words rushed out without a pause.

"No, I don't need you to stay. Go on your hot date. I'm done talking about my mother and we can celebrate my new job another time." I sunk into the armchair where I'd probably be spending most of my night.

"Alison. I can stay."

"Renee. I'm fine." I gave her my best smile. "Don't make me get up to push you out the door. My feet are killing me."

"I'm going to have my phone on the entire time. I don't even care if it's rude. If you need me, just message me." She nodded before looking at her aforementioned phone. "He's downstairs, I'd better go. Love ya. Message me." The tail end of her sentence hung in the air as she disappeared through the doorway.

Renee was my best friend but I really didn't want her sitting home holding my hand. She also sucked at when it came to *friend* behavior. It wasn't malicious; she just lacked that gene that most people had. It was part of the reason why we were such good friends in the first place. Neither of us needed to be with each other every single moment of the day and no one's feelings were hurt. It worked.

Not calling Rusty the minute I'd left Ashlyn's office had been my biggest challenge. I scrolled through my phone contacts at least fifty times and hovered over his name. Each time I'd stopped myself from hitting the call button.

As much as I wanted to speak to him, I felt I'd trapped us in a weird kind of limbo. It had been me who'd walked out and said I needed space. It wasn't fair for me to call just to spread my good news. It was selfish and one-sided. What if he didn't want to hear from me? What if he was with someone else? What if he wished me luck on the new job but then told me never to call him again?

Damn, this was hard.

So pushing aside my disappointment, I settled on getting into my pajamas and catching up on *Netflix*. It was a good plan. There were a million episodes of something awesome I was sure to be able to binge watch, something so in-depth and distracting all thoughts of Rusty would fade away. Okay, so maybe that was a bit optimistic. I'd aim instead not being consumed by thoughts of Rusty for one evening. There, that was a better plan.

My television-fueled marathon was interrupted about an hour or so in, an unknown number lighting up my phone screen. Ordinarily I'd have ignored it. Let it go to voicemail but given the last unknown number had resulted in not only a job but turned around my outlook, I decided I'd take a chance and answer it. Maybe I'd unsuspectingly won the lottery. My luck had definitely changed.

"Hello, Alison speaking." I introduced myself waiting for the confetti cannons and loud, whirly siren announcing I'd won ten million dollars. It was better than just throwing out a random hello. See, improvements all-round.

"Oh, hey. This is Jason, Angie's husband." The voice on the other end of the phone responded.

"Jason?" I pulled the phone away from my ear and looked around the room like he might suddenly appear. "Um . . . hey. What can I do for you?" I was able to ask when I returned the phone back to near my mouth.

"Don't really need anything; this is more just an announcement call." I heard the smile in his voice. "I hope you don't mind that I got your number from Rusty, I wanted you to know Angie had the baby."

"Oh my God. Thank you so much for calling me. No I don't mind about the number, and I definitely wanted to know." I tried not to squeal in excitement as my pulse raced as I waited for the information.

It had been a *really* intense few days. I had completely forgotten that just before I walked out the door and broken up with Rusty, Angie had called in labor. And unless she had been extremely unlucky, or had the gestation of an elephant, she would have had the baby by now. Rocking a new little son or daughter in her arms. It would have been totally unreasonable for Rusty to call and yet, I wished it had been him on the other end of the phone.

"Congratulations!" I squealed genuinely happy for them both, my mouth and my brain at odds as to what to ask next.

"We have a little boy. His name is Zack." Jason filled the silence, following up by telling me when he was born and how much he weighed. He neglected to mention if Rusty had been there, and how he was doing. Something that I was ashamed to admit, was what I was thinking about the whole time he was talking.

"That's amazing." I found myself saying. "Please give Angie my best wishes. I'm so happy for both of you."

"You can visit if you want. I'm sure Angie would love to see you and our little guy is pretty cute. Takes after his mother." Jason laughed. With two gorgeous parents, the kid was not going to be short of good-looking genes.

"Um . . . so . . . Rusty and I aren't really together anymore." I bit my lip wondering what the protocol was. After all these were his friends, I had merely been a guest in their little circle so I assumed he would handle the news of our breakup. I guess our split was still relatively new, and he hadn't gotten around to telling them. It's not something you happily advertise— *guess what, I'm no longer dating.* There should be some kind of service to handle it. That was a million dollar idea in the making.

"Yeah, I heard. Doesn't mean you aren't welcome to visit."

Oh, so he did know. Which begged the question why we were having the conversation? Angie and I were friendly but we were hardly besties. Maybe it was a test? Ashlyn employing Angie and Jase to get involved to see if I was over all the Rusty stuff? I guess in a weird way, Jason and the rest of his band were kind of my boss. Was it too much of a conspiracy theory? And was it strange if I went to see my ex-boyfriend's best friend's baby? Damn, there were too many rules.

"Angie and Zack were discharged so we're back home. You should stop by." Jase made it clear that it was more than just a subtle invitation.

"Umm. I don't know." My internal argument continued, my decision not even close to being made.

"Okay, so let me re-phrase that. You *need* to stop by."

It was no longer a subtle hint. My presence, for whatever reason, was required. God, I hoped this didn't suck.

• • •

Sleeping on Renee's couch sucked ass. One rogue spring had seen fit to poke me right between the ribs. I was sure I'd be rocking some pretty nasty bruising, and my neck could no longer do a full one-eighty swivel. My range of movement was significantly less since waking up with my head hanging off the armrest.

The minute I got my first paycheck, I was getting an apartment. I didn't even care if it was a roach-infested closet in the shittiest part of town. As long as it was mine and I had my own bed that would be enough for me.

Renee had predictably not come home. When she received no 9-1-1 messages from me, her hot date had progressed into hot sex. Her night spent elsewhere. She'd texted around midnight to let me know not to wait up, a sigh of relief was breathed that the sexy time was happening somewhere else. Sure, I was more positive and less depressed, my mood a hundred times better than it had been. But even so, I didn't want to wake up seeing some random man's penis greeting me hello. Such a killjoy, I know.

I procrastinated for most of the morning. Yesterday's debate on whether or not to follow through and go see Angie raged on. My decision fluctuated wildly depending on the hour. In the end, I decided I would go. Babies were a good equalizer; everyone would be too caught up with the new addition to worry about the awkward. At least that was what I'd hoped.

"Hi." I tried to wave as Jason opened the door, the big teddy bear in my arms hampering my effort. "How's Angie doing?" My eyes darted around the room to see if there was anyone else around as Jase led me through to the living room. And by anyone I meant Rusty.

"I'm doing fine," she answered, sitting up alert on the couch, a little bundle swaddled in her arms with the tiniest tuft of black hair poking out the top. "It's nice of you to stop by, I asked Jason to call."

Sooooooo this wasn't just a social call. I was being sandbagged. Nice touch using the baby as a decoy, I didn't even suspect it. At least Rusty wasn't here, I could deal with the third-degree from Angie.

"Angie, I know what you are trying to do." I handed off the teddy bear to Jase as I sat down beside her. "But it's really between the two of us." I was proud of myself. Look at me being assertive.

"I'm not trying to do anything. I just wanted to talk to you." She tried her best to look coy. She failed miserably.

"Is Rusty going to be here, is that why you asked me to come?" I imagined this is where their well-meaning efforts to get us back together would have them tell us both to turn up at the same time. Like a happy accident we would both know was orchestrated. Predictable and I should have seen it a mile away.

"Nope I can guarantee Rusty isn't going to be walking through the door. Not today anyway." Angie seemed pretty certain in that, her lack of smile as also concerning.

"Why, where is he?" I looked around despite being told he wasn't here.

"At home." She glanced over at Jase who shook his head. Whatever she was about to say, he wasn't on board with the whole plan. "He spent yesterday in lock-up with Phil. Funny how the two of them ended up with a whole lot of bruises. Can you believe they *both* fell down the stairs? Even more interesting is that the house they were in didn't have any stairs. It's just crazy wouldn't you say?"

"They were fighting?" My eyes peeled back in horror as my heart started to beat wildly out of control.

"I didn't say that." She shook her head. "Neither did they, which is why the police let them both go this morning." The raised eyebrow told me she hadn't bought it. The police might not have been able to hold them if neither made a statement but no one was fooled.

"I need to see him. Is he okay?" It leapt from my mouth before I had a chance to stop it. Not sure I would have stopped it even if I could have. It didn't take much to work out why Rusty and Phil ended up in a fight. The common denominator—me.

"Yeah, I thought you might. From what Max said he has a black eye and some bruised ribs but it's nothing like the condition Phil is in." Angie sighed. "Look, I don't know what you are going through. It's got to be a total mind fuck. But Rusty—he's one of the good guys, and regardless of whether or not you are together he's going to be on your side."

"I know."

Ironically I didn't get to see much of the baby or stay. The conversation with the new parents also ground to a halt, my body did a quick one-eighty and made for the door fairly soon after. My feet barely touched the ground as I hailed a cab and hightailed it to Rusty's house, the place that I had been living at up until recently.

My pulse raced as the cab weaved through traffic, the thickness of the air making it harder to breathe, having nothing to do with the outside temperature. My mind was a muddle over what I was going to say, but even with the words not formulating in my head I knew I had to go see him. And if there was ever a moment in my life I was going to do something without question, this was going to be that time.

297

Twenty-Six
Rusty

I hadn't killed him. The intention was that I went to wherever Phil was hiding out, and just talk. Try and get a feel for why he felt the sudden need to connect with the kid he deserted. His answer didn't make me feel warm and fuzzy.

"What is he doing here?" He pointed his finger accusingly as I walked into the room beside Max.

"Just wanted to clear up any misunderstandings." My shoulders rolled with pent up tension. Talking hadn't been the only thing on my mind.

"I'm not trying to mess with her head, I just want to try and get to know her. I didn't even know I had a kid until recently." He tried to explain, like his ignorance somehow made it better.

The fucking useless bastard had assumed that after he did a see-ya-later on Alison's mom she would have done the same to her unborn child. Something I'd already been clued up via Max's earlier inquisition. It had been a chance meeting approximately three years ago that saw the previous two lovebirds reconnect, Alison's mom and Max's brother sharing more buried history than Tutankhamen.

"I was young, I wasn't ready for a kid. But I'm ready now, I want to be her dad." Phil continued, figuring he'd give parenting a go.

"Not too difficult now when there isn't a lot left to do, the harder stuff of actually raising the kid happening years ago while you weren't around." I wasn't cutting him any slack. *"Whatever happens from here on out is her call, it's not about you and your delicate sensibilities about being a dad. She says jump, you say how fucking high. We clear?"* My nerves wound tighter with each passing second.

"You're one to talk. You've gone from one pussy to the next. What qualifies you from thinking you know what's best for my daughter?" The dumbass unhelpfully added.

Just calling Alison his daughter was enough of a reason to hit him, as far as I was concerned he hadn't earned that right just yet. Providing the additional X Chromosome didn't qualify. Yeah, that didn't go over too easy either.

"Listen Phil, I don't give a fuck what you tell yourself to help you sleep at night—you made a choice. She didn't get a say. So regardless of your believed entitlement, you stand the hell down. As for me, I know how to keep my dick in my pants. Evident is the fact that I—unlike you—don't have a kid I abandoned."

He didn't agree.

Seemed like it was a bone of contention neither of us was willing to cave on. Which is how we ended up letting our fists continue the conversation. Max, Joey and Phil's latest lay, wisely watching on without interference. The brawl only came to a conclusion when both of us were rocking matching metal cuffs, having also earned a bonus free ride in a squad car.

My conscience was clear even if my face was sporting a black eye.

"Fuck." My right fist sunk into a bucket of ice water, the chill burning against my raw skin. The first-aid in the big house had been as lacking as their hospitality. I was in no hurry to go back.

"Rusty!" The door I failed to lock flew open, rocking against the jamb as the knob hit the wood. The girl I hadn't counted on seeing anytime soon, filling the space where the door had been.

"Alison?" I asked, not a hundred percent sure the left hook to my cheek hadn't messed around with my vision.

"Holy shit." She rushed in, her knees sinking to the floor as she knelt beside me and my faithful bucket. "What did you do?"

"It looks worse than it is." The fingers that had been getting numb courtesy of the chilled submerge, retracted from their ice bath to touch her face. "I can't believe you're here."

"I hate that you're hurt." Her eyes followed close along the path of her hands, surveying my face. Her fingertips brushed slowly against my purpling skin. Any beauty pageants were going to have to wait a while, the added bonus of no gigs booked in the near future, another win.

"My face is fine." Especially now with any pain I'd felt before ghosting with her appearance. Better than the four Advil I'd knocked back two hours ago that was for damn sure.

"I know you were fighting with Phil and it was because of me. You can't do that, Rusty. You can't fight over me." She lowered her forehead against mine, her breath slow as it pushed out against her lips.

"Babe, you're the *only* thing worth fighting over."

The last thing I wanted to do was add pressure to an already abundant load. I had promised her space, and come hell or fucking high water, I was going to give her that. But it was really—really—hard to look into those beautiful hazel eyes and pretend that it wasn't killing me every minute we weren't together.

"Do you hate me? I know I'm being selfish right now." Her eyes closed slowly as her arms wrapped around my chest, her breathing picking up tempo.

"I don't think there is a thing you could do that would make me hate you." I gave up resisting the urge to hold her and pulled her into my lap. "I might not like it, but I understand."

"I got the job. With the record label. I wanted to tell you so badly but I didn't know if calling you would be the right thing."

"I'm glad you got the job, babe. You're going to do awesome." The hand that had been throbbing like a motherfucker half an hour ago felt miraculously cured as it stroked her hair. "But you need to understand something. There aren't any rules for what we're doing. We're writing our own path. You want to call me, you call. You want to see me, then you come see me. No matter what happens in the future between us, I'm always going to want you in my life."

"Okay," she whispered, her head nodding against my chest.

"Good, I'm glad we cleared that up. So tell me more about the job." My need for her to keep talking at an all-time high. Meant there was less chance of her leaving, even if I knew eventually she still would.

"I start Monday, I'm getting my own office." Her voice hitched in a moment of excitement. "I think I'm going to really like it. I have some great ideas on how to streamline sales reporting."

"That's great."

"Can I ask you what happened with Phil?" Her head pulled away from my chest, those beautiful eyes of hers knocking me on my ass if I wasn't already sitting down.

"Of course you can ask me." It wasn't much of a secret. The police report meant our *chat* was public record, even if their account of events was slightly altered. "I just wanted to be sure he understood that regardless of his feelings, he was going to have to let you pick the speed. We had a difference of opinion." More like his beliefs didn't align with Alison's best interest.

"I'm still not sure how I feel about it. I don't know if I want to see him."

"And that's perfectly fine. You don't want to see him; you don't have to see him. He isn't even going to breathe in your direction without your permission." Not unless he wanted a repeat of what went down yesterday. And given he was in worse shape than I was when we parted ways, I didn't think he'd be volunteering anytime soon.

"What about you?" she asked curiously, the hesitation inching its way back into her voice.

"What about me?" I sure as hell didn't have any plans to see the asshole. The less we saw each of other, probably the better.

"You said that if I wanted to see you, that I should see you. But what if you want to see me, are you going to see me?"

"Don't worry about what I need right now." My arms stayed wrapped around her, absorbing every second she'd let me hold her. "I'm a big boy, I can handle it."

"What if I made a mistake, Rusty?" Her voice dipped so low

I wasn't sure I'd heard her right.

Every single muscle in my body tensed as a million different scenarios ran through my head. I had no idea what she was going to say. If this was where she confessed to going off the deep end and fucked around, it was going to take a hell of a lot of restraint. Not saying she didn't have every entitlement to do so, we weren't together. But fuck me, I wasn't sure I wanted to hear it. God I hoped she didn't run back to that piece of shit ex-boyfriend. Anyone but him.

"What kind of mistake?" My fingers stopped their restless strum against her back as I pulled her away from my chest.

Whatever she needed to say, I'd deal with it. Because it couldn't be harder than losing her had been.

"A really stupid mistake." She shook her head, gaining some of the confidence she'd lost. "What if I was so confused about what was happening that I pushed away the only thing that has ever made sense?"

My heart started to beat so fast I wasn't sure the bastard wasn't trying to rip a hole in my chest and power walk out the door. The sliver of hope she'd thrown my way all that I needed to go all in.

"Then I'd say, I need you and I want you back."

Complete no brainer. I threw my thanks up to whatever thought process got her to that point as I hoped all talk of us going our separate ways was done. It had been a miserable few days and I wasn't looking to repeat them. Not if there was a chance we could work our way back to each other.

"I think I can still work out who I am, without being alone but I want it to be different this time. I want to date you."

"I'd love to date you." My lips found their mark on the top of her head as I whispered internal halleluiahs. "You going to move back in?"

"It's probably better if I don't." A small smile teased at the corners of her mouth. "I'll probably end up sneaking into your room at night, kind of defeats the purpose."

"That really wouldn't be a problem for me, just so you know." Not a lie. Zero problems with her in my house or in my bed. It was preferable, actually. But whatever she decided was going to be completely cool with me.

"This time we need to go slow."

• • •

There was very little that could happen today that could tear the smile from my face. While my girl wasn't tucked up beside me when I rolled over in bed this morning, the let's-not-be-together bullshit was finally over.

If she wanted slow; I was going to give her rush-hour in the Lincoln Tunnel. That baby was going to be wound back to a crawl until she was ready to pick up the pace. As for dating, I was all about that too, happy to work my way through the bases while juggling some popcorn and a movie.

"You sure about this?" My hand hesitated on the door. I hadn't ruled out turning back and taking her somewhere else. Seemed like a much better idea than what was about to go down.

"I'll have to see them sometime, right? Better now than across a boardroom table. Besides, I'll have you with me. I'm going to be completely fine."

My plan had been to take a long drive somewhere and catch

a quiet dinner. Stick a toe in before jumping back in the deep end. Made sense considering the last time we went from hello-nice-to-meet-you to want-to-live-in-my-spare room. But that didn't seem on par with Alison's line of thinking. Our *quiet night* vetoed in favor of heading to the bar.

"You amaze me, you know that. If at any time you want to bail, just let me know. I've got zero concerns about being polite tonight." My inner caveman stuck his head out to have a look. I wasn't even going to make apologies for being so protective, I was embracing it for all it was worth.

"I'm good." Her hand did what mine hadn't and pushed open the door, the noise of the bar spilling out into the street. "We need to celebrate my new job."

Arguing wasn't going to happen. And rather than stand outside with my tongue on the floor completely blown-away by her, I decided to join her on the other side of the threshold. The siren's call of beer an added bonus.

"Wow! Fuck! You're back together?" Joey not so subtly announced our arrival, his eyes doing a ping-pong between us.

"Yeah, we're back together." My hand found its way around her waist, the PG-13 touching deemed acceptable first date behavior.

"Hey, Alison." Max totally ignored me as he mirrored the same wide-eyed expression Joey had been wearing. "It's good to see you." His additional what-the-fuck not spoken.

"Thanks, Max. It's good to see you too." The confidence she'd shown at the door slipped slightly as she came face-to-face with her uh-hum . . . uncle.

The noise of the crowd did nothing to drown out the weird we were experiencing. The unspoken acknowledgement of the crazy, louder than the AC/DC that was streaming out of the speakers.

"Well we're going to need a shitload of drinks." My solution was thrown into the ring. The edge needed to be knocked off pretty damn quick if the night wasn't going to end up a total bust. "So how about everyone gets a beer and we'll take it from there."

"Sounds good." Max nodded, the protocol for reuniting with his long-lost family not really discussed before we'd arrived. Mental note. Probably should have called ahead.

"On it!" Joey tapped the bar, the lack of alcohol something he could remedy. The icy-cold long necks found their way into his hands with little more than a wink and a smile.

"By the way." The beers were quickly distributed, mine finding its place in my hand. "We're celebrating. Alison got the job with Ashlyn, you're looking at the newest addition to Metamorphous." I raised the beer in a mock toast. "Kicking ass and taking names."

"Congrats."

"Sweet. That's awesome."

The chorus of congratulations flowed from Max and Joey, their happiness genuine as we celebrated with a drink.

"Thanks." Alison smiled, her body un-tensing slowly. "I'm really excited. It's going to be a challenge." I didn't believe it was only the job she was talking about. The new situation she'd found herself in also contributing to the *challenge*.

"So I guess we're related." Alison glanced up at Max, meeting the awkward head on.

"Yep. Looks like we are." Max shot me a non-verbal apology before continuing. His speech probably having been rehearsed a few hundred times before getting the opportunity. "I just want you to know that I honestly had no idea. My parents didn't even know. They are dying to meet you by the way. Of course, only if that's something you want."

"Your parents want to meet me?" she asked, like the thought hadn't even crossed her mind.

"Well, yeah. You're their grandchild; of course they want to meet you. My mom had two boys so . . . let's just say she's been pretty hard to contain the last few days." He gave her a shy smile.

"I think I'd like that." The words came out slowly, looking at me for reassurance. "I don't have a lot of family. My mom's parents moved to Florida after I was accepted into college, so I don't get to see them much. God, am I the only one whose head is spinning right now?"

"Nope, I'm still trying to wrap my head around the fact I have a niece." Max laughed, some of the tension easing out voice. "Lucky Rusty is a decent guy or I'd probably have to kick his ass. "

"You mean you'd *try* to kick my ass," I corrected, the need for said ass-kicking not necessary given I'd rather cut off my own arm than hurt Alison. "And it's kinda crazy you're related to one of my best friends. I mean, what were the chances? That's like some epic it's-a-small-world-after-all shit."

"You know, guys, this could actually be a lot worse. I say we completely lucked out in this scenario," Joey added, the dumbass having stayed silent during the whole exchange looking pretty smug as he finally weighed in.

"Oh yeah? How do you figure?" I prepared myself for the genius that we were about to behold. I was also prepared for disappointment. Joey meant well, but he wasn't the brightest Crayola in the box.

"Well, think of it this way." He nodded to her and then to me. "If Alison had made out with Max at the bar instead of *you*, it would be a totally different story. That's a talk show visit, right there." He laughed, thoroughly enjoying himself. "On the other hand, I'm totally safe too. My brothers and sisters don't have any adult children running around, so I don't have to take a blood test every time I date. Something Max is probably going to have to look into."

"Thanks, asshole." Max flipped him off. If he was offended, he wasn't showing it.

"I'm going to need another drink on that thought alone." Alison's eyes got wide as she took a swallow of her beer. "I guess it really could have been worse."

"Rest assured, sweetheart, you don't need to worry about *that* anymore." I pulled her into my side a little closer, my hand inadvertently brushing against her ass. So maybe I needed a refresher course on first date etiquette, but there wasn't a chance in hell she was going to need to worry about dating relatives any time soon. I'd let her walk away from me once, she wasn't getting a second chance to do it again.

A few more drinks and any residual weird had well and truly been eradicated. Max and Joey were doing their usual routine and trading barbs while my attention stayed on the girl who was working her way through her third beer. Her hands getting more touchy-feely a direct correlation to the rise in her blood alcohol level.

"I should get you home," I whispered into her ear, not really digging the responsible me that was doing the talking, but knowing it's the one that needed to be representing.

"Probably." She wrapped her hands around my neck making it harder for me to not kiss her. "It's been a really long day."

"Yeah, it has. We can do something tomorrow if you like." My mind reminded me that it wasn't my home that I'd be taking her too. "Come on, babe. Let me get you home."

"See ya, guys." Joey waved from the bar, me trying to wrangle Ali and get her home catching his attention.

"You need a hand?" Max lowered the beer from his lips, showcasing the grin that was now visible.

"I'm fine, Uncle Max." Alison giggled, obviously a little drunker than we'd anticipated.

"Fuck. I don't think I'm ever going to get used to hearing that." He laughed as he shook his head. "Let's just stick to Max, huh Ali?"

"Agreed." Her eyes struggled to stay open. "Take me home, Rus."

A wave of a hand was all the guys got, with my arms preoccupied with getting my girl back to the car.

Her hot breath on my neck as I buckled her into the passenger seat was driving me crazy, as was being so close to her body and not being able to touch her. My dick instantly got hard as the seatbelt stretched across her tits.

Fuck. My mind tried to focus on something else as I closed the car door and walked around to the driver's side. The action of buckling up repeated on my side. Her eyes locked on me the whole time.

It would have been easy to take her back to my place and take her to bed. Whether or not we had sex or not really didn't bother me. I wanted that body of hers beside me, with my arms wrapped around it. Pity, that hadn't been our new plan. I hadn't even kissed her yet, my mouth hungry to taste her again.

"Rusty." My name like a fucking prayer on her lips, she mumbled as I pulled into traffic. Her head rolled to the side as her eyelids pulled a lights-out, the rock of the car lulling her off to sleep. Her perfect tits rose and fell with each breath, the view getting caught in my peripheral making the crotch of my jeans get tighter, my dick so hard it could cut glass. The drive back to her friend's apartment was almost unbearable, every mile the bane of my existence as I hit every single red light.

I pulled into park and cut the engine of the Camaro. The ride and the excuse for having her in my car was over, as I slid my hand over and released her seatbelt.

"Are you going to kiss me?" Her eyes slid open to half-mast, a lazy smile making her look even more adorable.

"Wasn't sure if you kiss on first dates?" My lips went heat-seeking missile on her mouth as I gave up the fight. We'd kissed on our first, first date so the precedent had been set and I wasn't about to turn down a taste of those sweet lips if she was offering them.

The resistance wasn't there as her mouth opened allowing my tongue to explore, my hand reaching across and pulling her head closer. The heat of our breath fogged up the windshield as my tongue invaded her mouth. The moan that escaped between her lips served to encourage me further as every second we were apart was erased by that one kiss.

"You brought me to Renee's?" Her eyes did a quick survey of the landscape when she finally pulled her lips away from mine. The disappointment in her voice similar to the one I had rattling around in my head.

"We're doing slow, remember?" My forehead pressed to hers, the urge to throw the whole *going slow* idea out the window, fucking overwhelming. "We can wait, Alison. I've waited this long. What's a little longer?" Pity my dick didn't agree. The asshole screamed between my legs to shut the fuck up but there was no way I was messing it up. No way.

"Okay." She sleepily agreed, the day and booze taking its toll as she nodded her head. "We can wait."

Three dates.

Three separate occasions where Rusty had picked me up, we'd had dinner or gone to the bar *but* not had sex.

Me and my bright ideas, sucked.

We'd patiently waited. The tension between us palpable, as each time we denied what we both wanted. The anticipation hopefully would make it worth the wait.

He was harder to resist this time.

I knew exactly *what* I was missing.

While my libido hadn't agreed, it had definitely been for the best. Our heavy make out sessions at the end of those three spectacular dates, the highlights. But I wanted more.

I needed more.

"So where we heading tonight?" Rusty had asked, his hand threading through my hair as he kissed me. The last few dates had also *started* with make out sessions as well. It was a running theme. One that I thoroughly enjoyed.

"Your place." I grabbed at his T-shirt, not even trying to

hide what had been on my mind. The desperation I felt echoed through his primal growl as he kissed me.

"Whatever you want." His teeth played with my bottom lip. "My house it is."

It was the second day at my new job and while my body was still assimilating to the return to corporate attire, I had already fallen in love with my new role. The purpose and excitement of working in the entertainment industry made me giddy. The steep learning curve was no longer feared as I attacked each task with a renewed sense of purpose. But that's not what I was thinking about as Rusty held me in his arms.

"Take me to bed, Rusty."

I'd waited long enough.

The lack of argument was almost as commendable as the speed that he got us to his house. The car almost flew to our destination, the blurred view from the passenger side window only stopping once we'd reached his front door.

"God, I missed you." He pulled me closer, his lips restless as they moved over my skin. "I love you, Alison. I love you, so much." The front door slammed behind us as my hands got busy on him.

"I love you, too," I mumbled in between kisses. "So much. I need you. So much." Each word painfully dragged from my lips as I struggled to stop kissing him.

"I want you, baby. I want you tonight. In my bed. With me. The whole night." His sentence was interrupted as his lips and mouth reacquainted itself with my body. His hands ready to unbutton the front of my shirt.

"Yes, yes," I agreed as I slipped off my jacket.

Completely unrestrained, our bodies undressed each other.

Fingers fumbled blindly for buttons or zippers, each layer being peeled from our bodies heightening an already dangerous level of arousal. The bed he'd been so desperate to get me to, forgotten as we stripped off in the living room. Our clothes like fallen soldiers littered the floor as we collapsed onto the couch, our hands and mouths unstoppable as they roamed over naked skin.

"You're already so wet." His hands reached down in between my legs, the sweep of his thumb over my clit threatening to make me come with just one touch.

"Yes, it's been too long. I need you inside of me." I shamelessly begged as my hand reached for his cock. His hard length jerked the minute I made contact with his skin, the slow stroke up and down teasing the moan right from his throat.

"Not nearly as badly as I need to be inside of you." His mouth covered my nipple, the graze of teeth sending a slight sting of pain rocketing through my system. It wasn't going to take very long. Not at this rate.

No more words were spoken. The weight of his hard on pressing against my thigh as he shuffled into position, my body overwhelmed by every touch and caress.

"Ah," I cried out, his cock sliding into me in one slick movement. The lack of foreplay not a problem as my ready body welcomed him. His slide into me delicious as I bit down on his shoulder to stop myself from screaming. "Yes." The ragged breath escaped my mouth as tingles of every awoken cell echoed through my body. The feeling intensified as he withdrew and thrust back in again. The fullness of him almost too much to bear.

"Yes." The word muffled against his skin as he entered me

again, my fingers gripping his back so tightly I was sure he would be wearing bruises tomorrow.

"That's it, baby." He picked up speed, each dip and thrust of his hips bringing me closer and closer to climax. The rope-like muscles of his arms supporting him as his hips continued to pump, unrelenting. "I can feel you, Ali. Feel how close you are."

A war of will waged internally as I wished for the feeling to go on forever, my body begging for the release. Each drag of his cock sent me teetering closer to the edge. Every part of me enjoying the madness as his talented mouth sucked at my throat, his hard-on pummeling into me with no reprieve.

It was dizzying.

The sensation of a million lightening bugs licking my skin wasn't even close to what I was feeling as my body shattered under him. The crest of my orgasm overtaking me in a rush as the ripples of pleasure carried away any sanity I had left.

"Yes. Yes." He splintered above me as his own release came soon after mine. The sensation sent me a new wave of euphoria. The speed and intensity of it all, making my body shake.

"Are you okay?" His hand rubbed against my goose-pimpled skin, the aftershocks making my limbs boneless as I shivered in his arms.

"Yeah, it was—" I was unable to finish the sentence as my lips sought his out. The need for talking less than the need for his touch. I was a goner. There was no way I was leaving him. Not tonight. Not ever.

"Amazing?" Rusty finished, the grin on his face evidence enough he felt the same way.

"Yes. Amazing." I nodded like an idiot. The English language proved too difficult for me to use as nods and smiles became my preferred method of communication. The grin across my lips was unable to be contained as my eyes followed over each curve and dip of his amazing body, the ink that covered him enhancing an already impressive canvas.

God, he was hot.

Scorching.

Incredible.

Beautiful.

And all mine.

"So . . ." Rusty laughed, our sweaty bodies still intertwined. "I'm going to need to do that again. This time a lot slower. And I'm going to need to make you come a lot more too." His drop-dead gorgeous smile threatening to disintegrate the panties I was no longer wearing.

"You can do that as often and as much as you like. I think it should be an everyday thing." My fingertips trailed lazily against the curve of his muscles. "I'm not going anywhere."

His eyes shifted, the clear blue pools focusing on me as he read between the lines, my not so subtle hint that I was done with us being apart. "Are you moving back in with me?" He announced each word slow, letting each one settle before moving on to the next. Their purpose deliberate as he tried to confirm what I had been telepathically trying to tell him.

"Are you asking me?"

The last time we'd had the "move-in" conversation, we'd been on the street. Ironic because his offer meant that the *street* was not where I would end up, the ink on my eviction notice still not dry. I had no idea what would've possessed the crazy man to ask a stranger to share his house, but it felt like such a long way from where we were now.

In his arms.

Like this.

"Move in with me, Alison. Stay with me." His words were no longer a question as he focused on me, his intentions a hundred percent clear. There was no confusion as to whether or not he meant his bed as well this time, the hunger burning in his eyes confirming that's exactly where I would be spending most of my time. "I love you."

"I love you, too." The words flew out of my mouth with no hesitation. It was a reflex I was happy to have. "Yes, I'll move in."

I had imagined the moment differently. I'd expected that when it finally happened there would be some lead up. A candle lit dinner where he gazed into my eyes and told me he wanted to wake up with me every morning. But this . . . this was so much more perfect than any scenario I could have imagined. It was exactly where I wanted to be, with exactly the right person I wanted to be with.

• • •

Moving in with Rusty didn't miraculously solve all my issues. I didn't suddenly wake up a different person, free of the craziness my life had been all those years. Ha. How I wished that it could easily be erased. But it was one million times better than it had ever been. I was even less neurotic, not losing my cool every time life threw a little bump in the road. I was a work-in-progress in the truest sense but I was no longer working solo. That didn't mean I hadn't been strong enough to brave it alone, it meant I was smart enough to know I didn't have to. Besides, the company I was keeping these days was pretty freaking amazing.

"You sure you want to do this? We can stop at any time." Rusty's eyes clouded in concern. The hesitation not something he was trying to hide. "Absolutely no pressure, okay. This is completely your deal."

"I know." I swallowed, the decision already inching toward the bad-idea range. But curiosity is a funny thing, and like it or not, I couldn't just pretend some guy hadn't suddenly announced he'd contributed to my DNA. I had to at least meet him. If only to be sure that I hadn't dreamt the whole thing.

My fingers drummed restlessly on the table as we sat waiting. It had been completely my idea to ask Max and Phil to meet us at a local coffee shop. Rusty had given me the are-you-sure at least a dozen times, his protective concern still taking some getting used to.

"Do you know how amazing you are?" Rusty's thumb brushed over the top of my knuckles. "Like in rock star terms you're making me look bad."

God, I didn't ever think I was going to get used to that smile. The way his lips would curve and light up his whole face. The same kind that made me wonder if my clothes weren't going to spontaneously combust.

"I couldn't make you look bad if I tried." I playfully knocked his shoulder with my own. "But thank you." I was getting better at taking compliments, even if hearing them still surprised me.

"Hey." Max tipped his chin hello. Phil—I wasn't calling him dad—standing nervously beside him. "We cool to sit down?"

Max's eyes dipped to the empty chair opposite us, Phil's gaze not moving from Rusty.

I didn't blame him. The last time the two of them had been in same room he'd received a broken nose and three cracked ribs so sitting down and grabbing a latte probably wasn't his idea of a good time. But he was here so I guess that counted for something.

"Of course." I nodded. "Take a seat."

Max took a seat, Phil following close beside him. Their silence deafening as they stared at me, waiting for me to make the first move. Obviously both of them had received a pre-meeting briefing from Rusty. I shouldn't have been surprised. He'd been telling me the whole time the ball was entirely in my court, it wasn't just chance that had put the ball there in the first place.

"So Phil." How do I even start this conversation? "You probably know a lot more about me than I do about you."

"I actually don't know that much." He shrugged slowly. "Your mom only drip fed me info. Took me awhile before she sent me your photo. We had a lot of back and forth before she came around."

Well, thank God for small mercies. Still the fact she'd given the guy any information was still concerning, especially when she hadn't bothered to ask my permission first.

"So why now? I guess I'm just curious as to why you were looking in the first place." There were other questions I wanted to ask too, starting with how could you walk away from your child, but I shelved those for later. I wasn't sure I'd like his answer.

"Honestly Alison, I'm not really sure what to say." He shook his head not offering very much to the conversation. "Your mom and I were really young. I didn't think she'd had the baby."

"*Me*, you weren't sure if she had me." Anger bubbled inside me that he was still talking about the baby as it were a hypothetical. Like the product of their relationship wasn't sitting across from him twenty-five years later as an adult.

Max and Rusty exchanged a weird wordless exchange but didn't contribute anything. Not an easy task for my boyfriend given his vocal objection to Phil the first time we'd met. His white-knuckled grip on the table was proof of how much of a struggle it was for him. But he remained tight-lipped all the same.

"Yes, you, of course. Look, your mom was a lot of fun. She was beautiful. We had a lot of good times together," he added, his reminiscing making him smile.

Max cleared his throat in what I assumed was to caution him in what he might say next about my mother.

"But we were crazy kids and we had no business being parents. I didn't even know about you until three years ago and then I wasn't sure if I should try and find you."

From everything Rusty had said, my father was an idiot. Which meant he must have been my mother's soul mate. It was the only reason I could come up with as to why of all the men she'd been with, she chose this one to procreate with.

"So you found me. I'm not sure what you were looking for."

"I wasn't really sure either. I guess I just wanted to know my daughter. I mean there was a kid out there that was mine."

"You mean me, you wanted to know *me*." It was frustrating more than anything else that I felt we were talking about me in the third person. This mythical person who had somehow disrupted two lives. It had all been inconvenient.

"Yes, you. I mean I wanted to know you."

"Is there something you want to ask me?" Not sure why I paid him the courtesy, I guess secretly I was waiting to see if he'd redeem himself. If he would ask me if I'd had a good life or even better, ask me what I wanted out of all of this.

"Not really, I was just sort of hoping to get to know each other. I'm your dad, don't you want to get to know me?"

It's funny. There had always been a small part of me that knew that my father wasn't going to turn out to be some fairytale prince. While other girls may have had the fantasy that a sudden and tragic case of amnesia had been the reason why their daddy had disappeared, I knew better. The reality was staring me straight in the face. This part of my life probably wasn't going to get a happy ending and I was okay with that. After all, you can't mourn the loss of something you never had in the first place.

"To be honest, Phil. I'm not sure I do."

"What do you mean?" He looked at me genuinely confused before his attention turned to his brother, like Max would have some secret knowledge as to what was going on in my head. "Did you say something to her?" His accusing tone directly squarely at Rusty.

"You might want to remember why you're here, Phil." Rusty's hand reached for me and gave it a little squeeze. "And if you took half a second to listen to what *you* are saying, you would see nothing *I* could ever tell Alison would be half as bad as what's coming out of your mouth."

"What?" Phil turned his attention to me. "I don't

understand?"

Phil had wrongly assumed that because we shared genetic material that I would have immediately welcomed him into my life.

He was mistaken.

He was a stranger, someone who knew nothing about me other than a few details he'd learned from someone else who knew little about me—my mother. The fact that they were my parents was unfortunate. For me and for them. But I think I deserved the right to be a little bit selfish. The people who were going to be in my life had earned their place. No one was owed, and I wasn't allowing them in out of obligation.

"I'm not saying never but right now, I really like where my life is heading. A big part of that has me evaluating what's important in my life."

It might have been the first time I'd said it out loud but it had been a long time coming. Something that Rusty had been trying to show me since our first night together. That it was okay to choose who deserved to be in my life and who didn't.

"So am I supposed to wait around until you make up your mind?" He wasn't able to hide the agitation, our meeting not going according to his plan.

"Seriously, bro? Did you really just ask her that?" Max broke his self-imposed vow of silence. His interjection saved Rusty from one of his own. Neither was really needed. I had this.

"No. You aren't supposed to wait around. Not unless that's something that you really want." Time would tell if he would be part of my life, it certainly wasn't a decision I'd make in a week, or maybe even a month. "Thanks for coming to meet me though. Maybe we can try it again sometime in the future." Or maybe not. Either way, it would be for the right reasons.

"We can go now." It wasn't my attempt to be dramatic but I didn't think it was fair to waste any more of anyone's time. It might not have been what Phil wanted but it was a start and time would tell if he had what it took to stick around.

"Yeah, we sure can." Rusty stood up not needing to be asked twice. "Max, you need anything before we bail?"

"Nope, all good here." Max rose from his chair, tipping his chin to his brother that he should do the same. "I'll see you both soon."

"Thanks, Max." I didn't need to fake the smile. "See you, Phil."

We didn't wait for them to leave, getting to our feet and saying our final goodbyes.

"You good?" Rusty asked me when we finally got back to his car.

"Yep, I am."

For me, the meeting hadn't been about resolution. It was totally fine for things to be left open ended. If it was meant to be, it would be. Life didn't always have to be tied up neatly in a big fancy bow. Rusty had helped me see that. Happiness was the most important thing. If you had that, then everything else would fall into place.

Screw the safety net.

It was more fun without it.

I was free.

But more importantly I was happy.

Epilogue
Rusty

"**C'mon. Why is this thing taking so long?**" Alison's muffled voice floated from the bathroom door. The wood doing its best to keep whatever was going on in there a secret, while her inability to keep quiet was doing the exact opposite.

"Hey, babe. You okay in there?" I tapped against the barrier between us wondering if she was taking another excursion into experimentation without me. "Something you need?" I was more than happy to volunteer my services. Whatever was required had my undivided and full attention.

"Yep, everything is good. Just go back to doing whatever it is that you were doing," she called back unconvincingly. Her tone—like the situation—way off.

"Ali, you want to open the door, babe?" My feet stayed exactly where they were, her request of me to leave not getting any airtime.

"Not right now." The words lacking the confidence she'd been rocking the last few weeks. Whatever secret bathroom business was going down, it wasn't good.

"So let me rephrase the question. What are you doing in there?"

"Stuff."

"You want to be more specific?"

The conversation could have gone on longer. My need to know why she was holed-up in the bathroom was of paramount importance. I had nowhere else I needed to be either which meant I had all kinds of time, something she soon realized when I heard her footsteps moving closer to the door.

A chorus of expletives and rustling of papers stalled her initially, but finally the metallic click at the door signaled the lock had been disengaged.

"Oh, fuck it." She huffed as she shuffled back into the bathroom. Her face devoid of color as she sat on the closed lid of the toilet. Her knees pulled close up to her chest as she wrapped her arms around them, her eyes floating between me and the bathroom counter. Her own little science experiment going on around the sink.

"What the hell is this?" The neatly lined sticks pretty fucking obvious they were pregnancy tests so my question was more rhetorical. "You're pregnant?" My eyes following the lines of maybe ten separate tests as pink or blue lines started to appear. The magnitude of what I was seeing stuck between holy-shit and what-the-fuck.

"We'll know in another minute. Don't look at them yet. They aren't ready." She breathed out a slow and steady breath. "I might be."

"Babe, are you okay? Have you been sick? Why didn't you tell me?" Despite my own mind feeling like it was about to explode—was I really about to become a dad?—I was more concerned about her. That fact she might have a baby on board and she hadn't shared the information.

Had I missed something? Because I was under the assumption that whatever happened in the future, it was going to be a partnership.

"Because there was no need for both of us to be freaking out. I'm late and I'm never late. Even though I'm on the pill, it's not a hundred percent guaranteed." She shrugged, letting her feet fall to the floor. "I figured I'd do the test and see what happened. Of course you need an engineering degree for some of these things." She laughed nervously, not able to hide the fact she was freaking the fuck out. "How do they expect you to raise a kid when you can't even pee on the damn stick?"

"Look at me." My knees sunk to the floor in front of her as my hands cupped her face. "We're together now. No matter what that stick says, nothing is going to change that. You don't have to do any of it alone, and freak outs are much better shared. If you're going to be pacing nervously wondering if we've got a bun in the oven, then I want to be part of it. In fact I insist I be part of it. My skills wearing a hole in the carpet are legendary, I want it all, Alison. The good stuff and the scary stuff too. You get me?"

"God, you're going to make me cry. I am so fucking knocked up." Tears started to form at the corner of her eyes as she raised her hands to cover them. My need to hug her took over as I wrapped my arms around her.

"So if you're knocked up, we have a baby. We'll do it right. Kid will have the coolest parents alive."

Kids weren't something we'd figured would be happening

right now, but if life threw that curve ball at us, it wasn't something I'd dodge. Alison was it for me, and while there was no ring on her finger, I knew she was going to be my forever. Besides, I wasn't so much of a planner to begin with so the baby carriage coming sooner than later wasn't a big deal. As far as I was concerned it had been in the cards, who was I to mess with the timing. Universe obviously knew better than I did.

"You would be okay with it? Really?" Her hands lowered allowing me to mop up some of her tears with my thumb. Her beautiful hazel eyes wide with genuine wonder. Yep. I was a totally goner. No way in hell I'd ever leave this girl. Like it or not, she was stuck with me and I wasn't apologizing.

"I'd be more than just okay. I love you, Alison. I'm here for the long haul, marriage, babies—all of it. Whatever the schedule is, I'm down."

If I didn't think she would have assumed asking her to marry me was a knee-jerk reaction I would have asked her right then, no hesitation on my part. Absolutely zero. This girl had me literally down on my knees and I was thankful for all of it, but I was fairly sure I could pull off something a little better than a bathroom proposal. When I did pop the question it would be something she wasn't going to forget in a hurry. I'd go all out and she would have no choice but to say yes.

"I love you too." She leaned forward and rewarded me with a kiss, "I think we can look now. It's been long enough."

"We'll look together."

"Okay."

A few more tears were wiped from her eyes before I pulled her into my arms. I took the opportunity to give her some more reassurance, my mouth doing most of the reassuring as my lips found hers. The kiss lasting a second or two longer than it needed to but I wanted to be good and sure she was convinced. I liked to think I was thorough, and I never gave up an opportunity to kiss that sweet mouth of hers.

The smile that had been lacking when I first walked into the room was now firmly in place as she picked up to look at the first stick. Its fate no longer controlling ours.

"It's negative." Her eyes widened in genuine surprise, her hands reaching down and grabbing one of its neighbors. "This one too."

"Looks like it was a false alarm." The remaining line of baby-indicating wands also showed the no-dice reading on their windows. "We're not having a baby after all."

"Well . . . it looks like we dodged a bullet on that one, huh? What a relief." Her tone didn't match the *awesome* her words were trying to spell out.

"Is maybe a little part of you disappointed?"

"No . . . Yes . . . I don't know." She shrugged. "It's really not a good time and I was praying that I wasn't." She took a long breath before continuing. "But part of me, obviously the crazy part, really wants to have your baby. Insanity right?"

"Nope, makes perfect sense because there's no one else I'd want to have a baby with other than you." I pulled her into my arms, my lips kissing the top of her head. "It will happen for us, babe. It's obviously just not our time yet."

"So what do we do now?" She mumbled against my chest, the tiny vibrations freaking magic.

"We practice. A lot. And often." I laughed, loving the feel of her body against mine. "And you let me love you in the only way I know how. In case you didn't get the memo, that's pretty intense. It's not for the faint hearted. I hope you can handle it."

"Yeah, I can handle it. I've got some of my own crazy, intense love to give."

There was shit in this world we'd have no control over. And no doubt with an album scheduled for release and a tour on the horizon, things would get messy. Ups and downs were bound to happen. I welcomed all of it. Not because I was an arrogant asshole who thought it was plain sailing from here on out, but because I knew whatever life tossed our way, it would be worth it to have this amazing woman by my side.

I wasn't living the dream.

The dream was living in me.

"Hey rock star, you want to go practice?" Alison's smile hinted that the chaste hug we had going on could use an upgrade.

"Lead the way, babe. You've yet to see my best moves."

To keep up to date with all T Gephart's

news,

appearances
and releases,

please subscribe to her mailing list at

http://eepurl.com/bws5Av

Acknowledgements

The biggest thanks will always go to my amazing family—Gep, Jenna, Liam and Woodley. They were there every step of the way, and I couldn't imagine doing this without them.

Thanks to my circle of trust. Everyone has earned their place, no one is there out of obligation and I love you all. PS. You're stuck with me for life.

Special thanks to my beta team who were reading ninjas on tight turn arounds so I could get this book done. Maz and Danielle, a million thanks still isn't enough.

Thank you to the authors who have now become friends. Can I say I love you without freaking you out? Too late, I'll always freak you out. Lili Saint Germain, JB Hartnett, Skyla Mardi, CJ Duggan, Lilliana Andersen, Rachael Brookes, JD Nixon, Natasha Preston, Kirsty Mosely, Ker Dukey, LA Casey, Jill Patten, Tillie Cole, Andie Long, Abbi Glines, Chantal Fernando, Christina Hobbs and Lauren Billings, Penelope Louleas, Jay Crownover, Kim Karr, SC Stephens, Joanna Wylde and Kylie Scott—you rock my world.

Hang Le. Lord have mercy. There is no one else I trust with my covers and branding. You are a genius who knows exactly what will work and nail it each and every time. You have my eternal thanks and adoration. You and your vision are brilliant as is the work that you produce. Seriously, don't ever leave me.

Thank you to the bloggers and blogs who have supported me. I was late to the game and every book more and more people are discovering me through your shares, likes and reviews. Every single one of you is appreciated, and I love you all.

Thanks to the T Gephart Entourage. Your enthusiasm and excitement is contagious. I love playing with you. Who needs a street team? Organized activities were never my forte and I like what we have going on a whole lot better.

Thanks to my Fictionally Yours, Melbourne team with special mention to Penny Rudge. Some things in life are meant to be, clearly we were meant to meet and make magic happen. #ThereAren'tEnoughHashTags.

Thank you to my editor, Nichole Strauss, from Perfectly Publishable. DUDE! (Shouty caps needed) I struck the lottery when I found you. I know I can (more frequent than not) be manic, and my MS sometimes looks like it has Touretts, but each and every time we work through it and all my worry is for nothing. You are a goddess.

Thank you to my proofreaders MK Harkins and Marie Mason. Your pick-ups save my ass.

Thanks to Max Henry from Max Effect for her boss formatting. My words have never looked so good. Talented beyond measure.

And last but not least, a massive thanks to all my readers. I still find it hard to believe anyone wants to read anything I write and it doesn't matter if it's one or a million people, every single one of you is important to me. No words are enough and I have nothing but love.

About the Author

T Gephart is an indie author from Melbourne, Australia. T's approach to life has been somewhat unconventional. Rather than going to University, she jumped on a plane to Los Angeles, USA in search of adventure. While this first trip left her somewhat underwhelmed and largely depleted of funds it fueled her appetite for travel and life experience.

With a rather eclectic resume, which reads more like the fiction she writes than an actual employment history, T struggled to find her niche in the world.

While on a subsequent trip the United States in 1999, T met and married her husband. Their whirlwind courtship and interesting impromptu convenience store wedding set the tone for their life together, which is anything but ordinary. They have lived in Louisiana, Guam and Australia and have traveled extensively throughout the US. T has two beautiful young children and one four legged child, Woodley, the wonder dog.

An avid reader, T became increasingly frustrated by the lack of strong female characters in the books she was reading. She wanted to read about a woman she could identify with, someone strong, independent and confident and who didn't lack femininity. Out of this need, she decided to pen her first book, A Twist of Fate. T set herself the challenge to write something that was interesting, compelling and yet easy enough to read that was still enjoyable. Pulling from her own past "colorful" experiences and the amazing personalities she has surrounded herself with, she had no shortage of inspiration. With a strong slant on erotic fiction, her core characters are empowered women who don't have to sacrifice their femininity. She enjoyed the process so much that when it was over she couldn't let it go.

T loves to travel, laugh and surround herself with colorful characters. This inevitably spills into her writing and makes for an interesting journey - she is well and truly enjoying the ride!

Based on her life experiences, T has plenty of material for her books and has a wealth of ideas to keep you all enthralled.

Website:

http://tgephart.com

Facebook:

www.facebook.com/tgephartauthor

Goodreads:

www.goodreads.com/author/show/7243737.T_Gephart

Twitter:

https://twitter.com/tinagephart

The Lexi Series

Lexi
A Twist of Fate
Twisted Views: Fate's Companion
A Leap of Faith
A Time for Hope

The Power Station Series

High Strung
Crash Ride
Back Stage

The Black Addiction Series

Slide
Sticks
Stand

www.ingramcontent.com/pod-product-compliance
Lightning Source LLC
Chambersburg PA
CBHW030659120726
47905CB00001B/277